About *Mind Over*

"A dynamic novel that takes readers on a roller-coaster ride of emotions that echo their own scream-inducing moments...all while reminding us that even when it seems the world is off-track, God is in the seat beside us, promising we'll be okay when the ride stops. Reserve space on your 'keepers' shelf for this one!"

    LOREE LOUGH, award-winning author of 83 books, including reader favorite *From Ashes to Honor* (#1 in the First Responders series)

"Lynda Lee Schab is a new, fresh addition to Christian fiction, combining her own distinctive author voice with humor and thought-provoking storytelling. I laughed right out loud in places and experienced the ministry of the Holy Spirit in others. I'm eager to see what's next from Lynda Lee Schab."

    SANDRA D. BRICKER, best-selling and award-winning author of *Always the Baker, Never the Bride*, the first in a four-book series

"A fast, fun read in the tradition of classic chick lit. Madison 'Madi' McCall lives in an ordinary world, yet dreams of being a fairy-tale princess. In her quest to find her inner princess, Madi faces her responsibilities and the stresses that crowd her life. Along the way she overcomes challenges, learns to accept God's grace, and grows her faith."

    MEGAN DIMARIA, author of *Searching for Spice* and *Out of Her Hands*

"With a smart, snappy style, Lynda Lee Schab delivers an entertaining tale. Be prepared for chuckles aplenty as Madi learns a hard-won lesson about trust."

    VIRGINIA SMITH, author of *Third Time's a Charm* and the Sister-to-Sister Series

"An engaging story of the proverbial ostrich with her head stuck in the sand. And who hasn't been there a time or two? With doses of humor, gentle insights, and an eclectic supporting cast, Schab had me rooting for heroine Madi to learn the truth that would ultimately set her free. A fast-paced, highly enjoyable story."

    JULIE CAROBINI, author of *Fade to Blue*

The *Madi* Series

Lynda Lee Schab

Mind Over Madi

Book One

When the matters of the heart
are all in the mind…

Madily in Love

Book Two

Sylvie and Gold

Book Three

MIND OVER

Madi

LYNDA LEE SCHAB

OAKTARA

Waterford, Virginia

Mind Over Madi

Published in the U.S. by:
OakTara Publishers
P.O. Box 8
Waterford, VA 20197
www.oaktara.com

Cover design by Yvonne Parks at www.pearcreative.ca
Cover images © www.shutterstock.com: close up of woman, Ipatov;
© thinkstockphotos.ca: istockphoto collection
Author photo © Cari Weber

Scripture taken from the HOLY BIBLE, NEW INTERNATIONAL VERSION®. NIV®. Copyright © 1973, 1978, 1984 by International Bible Society. Used by permission of Zondervan. All rights reserved.

ISBN: 978-1-60290-303-6

Mind Over Madi is a work of fiction. References to real people, events, establishments, organizations, or locales are intended only to provide a sense of authenticity and are used fictitiously. All other characters, incidents, and dialogue are drawn from the author's imagination.

Printed in the U.S.A.

TO MY MOM,
for always believing in me.

Acknowledgments

Several years and much sweat and tears went into writing this book. But, even more, lots of love and joy have been poured into these pages. I'm still in awe of God's goodness in getting *Mind Over Madi* into print. And there are many people He used to make it happen.

Thanks to my mom, my biggest cheerleader, encourager, and laughing buddy, who finds humor in the same silly things I do and provided much inspiration for *Mind Over Madi*. If it weren't for you, Mom, I'd have given up on this writing thing a long time ago.

To my dad, who so generously paid my way to my first ACFW conference in 2009, which played a direct role in this book's publication.

To my husband, Rob, and our kids, Zach and Lyndsey, for listening to me say "Not now, I'm writing" one too many times and loving me anyway.

To Susan Miura, world's best critique partner, who makes me a much better writer and spoils me with the coolest gifts ever.

And big thanks to my other priceless critique partners, who point out my missing commas, story inconsistencies, and typos. You all manage to balance the negatives with plenty of encouragement and smiley faces. A special thanks to Jenness Walker, Deb Harper, Leigh Delozier, Cathy West, Patricia Woodside, Val Comer, and Nicole O'Dell, who provided valuable feedback on *Mind Over Madi*.

To my two fabulous friends, Cari Weber and Diane Loew, who offer constant support and brag about me to everyone they meet. A little embarrassing maybe, but so flattering! And Cari, it's plain to see that you're an award-winning photographer. Taking photos of me that I actually like is a huge feat!

To FaithWriters.com, for jumpstarting my writing career. And a special shout-out to site administrator and dear friend, Deb Porter, who told me all along that *Mind Over Madi* would be published one day. You are appreciated more than you'll ever know.

To Terry Burns, my Texan agent, for working so hard on my behalf.

To Ramona Tucker, my awesome editor, for falling in love with Madi and taking a chance on me!

And, finally, thank you, God, for opening more doors for me than I deserve and allowing this small-town girl to realize her big-time dream.

*When the matters of the heart
are all in the mind...*

1

Anger is a manifestation of a deeper issue...
and that, for me, is based on insecurity, self-esteem, and loneliness.
NAOMI CAMPBELL

I'm on the run. Unfortunately, not a very fast run. Heels have a way of slowing a woman down. Especially a woman who lives in tennis shoes, loafers, and flip-flops. Why, oh why, did I let Christina talk me into wearing my heels today? Christina is almost sixteen. She could probably hike the Grand Canyon in heels. Me? A couple hours in pumps and my calf muscles still ache three days later.

Not that I knew when I put them on this morning I'd be darting through the halls of church, fleeing from the likes of Claudia Boeve. Claudia is a hundred and ten pounds of tofu-eating energy who wants to convince me to join her Losing Means Winning Workshop. For the past couple months, she's been tossing around hints like the salads she eats daily for lunch. But, right now, I have no interest in joining her group. I am a Wendy's woman—hear me roar! Or Burger King, McDonalds, Taco Bell, or whatever fast-food chain I happen to crave at any given moment.

I duck behind a large potted plant to catch my breath. My heart is racing after the two-hundred-foot-dash from my pew to the atrium. I chalk up my breathlessness to the adrenaline—not too much fructose corn syrup—coursing through my veins.

Peering between leaves, I survey the throng of people still exiting the sanctuary. As soon as I catch a glimpse of Claudia, I'll hightail it in the opposite direction. My husband, Richard, has gone to pick up Emily, our nine-year-old, from her Sunday school class. He'll meet me and our fifteen-year-old twins—Christina and Max—at the car.

A tall, willowy blonde stands in front of the bookstore, chatting with one of the associate pastors. The blonde is Sarah Price, a friendly acquaintance who happens to be a clinical psychologist. Catching sight of her reminds me that I've been meaning to set up an appointment. Not that seeing a shrink is something I'm dying to do, but I need professional advice, due to some, um, issues I've been dealing with lately. Okay, not really lately. More like for thirty years. I only just realized it might do me good to talk to someone. Better late than never.

Affixing an invisible sticky note to my brain to call Sarah's office first thing in the morning, I intently search the faces in the crowd for Claudia. Someone grabs my arm and twirls me around, causing me to lose my balance. I crash to the floor, butt first.

The only thing worse than falling in public is falling while wearing a skirt.

I lock my legs together and struggle to my feet. My friend Sylvie does her best to help me up while trying to maintain a straight face.

"So not funny, Sylv."

"Sorry. You're usually not so...unbalanced."

"Yeah, well, blame Christina. She made me wear high heels today."

Sylvie looks at my feet and raises a perfectly tweezed eyebrow. "I would hardly call those heels. They're wedges. Now these," she points a toe, "are heels."

And so they are. At least four inches. Which explains why today Sylvie is almost my height of five-foot-eight.

"What are you doing hiding behind a potted plant, anyway?"

"I'm avoiding Claudia. She spotted me in church and wants to invite me to be a part of her stupid weight loss group."

"Joining might not be such a bad idea."

I fold my arms across my chest. "Thanks, Sylv. Why don't you come right out and call me Orca?"

She sighs. "I'm not saying you're fat. It's merely the whole health thing, you know? It would be good to learn more healthy eating habits."

"I do eat healthy."

Sylvie grabs the big black purse from my shoulder, as only a best friend would do. Unzipping it, she pulls out a bag of chocolate-covered candies and a bulky napkin that holds the other half of the cinnamon roll I grabbed for breakfast. "Care to change your statement?"

"So I didn't have time to make an egg-white omelet this morning, Miss Calorie Police." I snatch back my purse and shove the food inside.

Sylvie holds up a French-manicured hand. "Okay. I'm done now. Are we still on for coffee Thursday? Because there's something I need to talk to you about."

Her words are washed away in a wave of jealousy as, over Sylvie's shoulder, I catch a glimpse of Richard. He stands by the coat rack, chatting with a woman whose back is to me. She wears a clingy off-white dress that shows off her, uh, assets more than should be legally allowed in public. Even though I can't see her face, I know who she is. There's no mistaking that gorgeous head of long, thick, auburn hair or the sleazy—er, figure-hugging—dress. Seriously, there is only one person I know who would ever wear something so...provocative to church.

Fawn Witchburn.

I can't help but notice men's reactions as they walk past Fawn and Richard. The guys try with all their might to avert their eyes but can't help sneaking a peek when they think their wives or girlfriends aren't looking. What the men don't realize is that the women detect Fawn even before they do. The looks the women give her aren't quite so appreciative. I watch as a few of the ladies blatantly veer their husbands off in the other direction.

And there is Rich, trapped in her treacherous web.

Although, for someone who's trapped, he doesn't seem to mind. He grins like a goofy schoolboy.

I scowl like a jealous wife.

"Earth to Madi. Did you hear what I said? Are we still on for Thursday?"

"Mmm."

Sylvie glances over her shoulder and then moves to block my view. She looks me in the eye. "They're only talking."

I sidestep her blockade. Rich says something, and Fawn throws her head back and laughs.

"Talking, hmm?" My heartbeat picks up speed again, but this time it definitely has nothing to do with running. Unless you count the running Fawn's hand is doing down my husband's arm. The touch only lasts a second, but it makes me want to hurl one of Sylvie's stilettos at Fawn's back.

"Come on, Mads. Richard is her daughter's teacher. They're probably talking about Lexi."

Speaking of daughters, my two approach Rich from behind. When they're a couple feet away, Fawn sharply turns away from them. I suppress a gasp at her cleavage, which would put any Playboy centerfold to shame.

Fawn sashays off as nearby men pretend they're brushing something from their shoulder while stealing one last look at her behind.

Pigs.

Richard joins the pig party and watches for a second before turning his attention toward our daughters.

"Are you okay? You look like you swallowed a bag of Emily's Sour Skittles." Sylvie frowns, tiny lines appearing on her forehead.

"I'm fine. Now that the witch has flown off on her broomstick, I guess it's safe to go out. I'll see you Thursday." I brush past Sylvie and emerge from behind the plant.

"I'm working tomorrow. Call my cell if you need to talk," Sylvie says from behind me.

I lift a hand in response.

Emily smiles a toothy grin when she sees me. "You look so pretty today, Mommy."

"I picked it out," Christina brags.

"She does look great, doesn't she? I love a woman in a dress." Rich drapes an arm around my shoulder.

"I'm wearing a skirt."

"Skirt, dress, same thing to me." Rich laughs it off but my back tenses. For some reason the compliment—and smile—seem phony. How can he say I look great in my knee-length denim skirt after ogling Fawn mere moments ago? There's no comparison. Does the fact that he said "dress" mean he is still thinking about her?

I give myself a mental slap. I know all about how wrong it is to make comparisons. This is what I mean about issues. Definitely time to call Dr. Sarah Price.

I spot Claudia coming out of the bookstore. She waves in my direction, too perky for a normal human, and I kick myself for not rushing Rich and the kids out of there when I had the chance. Then a plus-sized woman in a navy suit passes by me, and I realize the wave was meant for her. The woman gives a tight smile but can't disguise the irritation on her face. Guess Claudia's been trying to rope her into joining her group, too. I wince as I feel her pain, while at the same time I'm relieved it's her and not me.

I definitely will not be joining Claudia's group. Seeing Fawn talking to my husband has made me understand there are times when sugar is not only a craving, it's the difference between sanity and a mental breakdown. And right now, fat and sane trumps healthy and locked up in a loony bin.

Bring on the chocolate!

Adolescence is a period of rapid changes.
Between the ages of 12 and 17, for example,
a parent ages as much as 20 years.
AUTHOR UNKNOWN

Tuesdays are errand days. It's now three o'clock, and I'm happy to report every errand for today has been crossed off my list: bank to pay the mortgage; dry cleaners to drop off the cranberry-stained suit Rich wore to my cousin's wedding two weeks ago; gas station to fill up my Dodge minivan; church to drop off a bag of groceries for the food pantry; orthodontist to pick up Max's retainer.

I debated even going out at all this morning because the forecast called for freezing temperatures with blowing and drifting snow. But by noon, all was still calm and it was obvious the weather man got it wrong. Again.

Welcome to South Haven, Michigan.

Now, as I make my way inside from the garage, I have to say it feels good to be home. The wind has picked up, and we may get that snow after all.

Charlie greets me at the door. I often wonder if our sable Burmese cat is, in fact, a dog that rolled around in too much fur and grew a long, skinny tail. Charlie has many more dog tendencies than cat, such as greeting me at the door, tail wagging. Hey, at least there's always someone happy to see me, even if it's only because I'm the source of freeze-dried fish treats. Yum. Almost enough to make me go rushing to Long John Silver's for dinner.

"You'll have to wait a minute for your treat, Charlie." I try to remove my boots without stepping on him as he prances underfoot. In a whirlwind of action, my boot catches his backside. While most cats would emit a hiss or at least an angry meow, Charlie leaps away, turns, and simply glares at me through big green eyes. This is the only way Charlie can express his displeasure because he doesn't have a voice at all—hence the name, in honor of Charlie Chaplin, the great silent movie actor.

My youngest daughter, Emily, once heard me use the phrase, "Cat got your tongue?" and is convinced another cat did, indeed, steal Charlie's tongue. Even though Charlie has no trouble lapping up milk like it's his last drink before his nine lives are used up and he's sent to that mouse-infested kitty heaven in the sky.

The light blinks on the answering machine. I toss the stack of mail I retrieved on the way in onto the counter and tap the "play" button before putting Charlie out of his misery and treating him to a reward of fish breath. Makes me want to brush my teeth just thinking about it.

"Yes, Madison, this is Sue from Cedars Plastics. I'm calling to inform you that the part-time office position you applied for last week has been filled. Thanks for your interest. And good luck."

Click.

Rats. Another one to scratch off the list. That makes, what, three so far this month? This one held such promise, too. The interview went well, the people seemed nice, hours were good.

Six months ago, after much thought and prayer, I decided to re-enter the work force. We could use the extra income and, although I love being a stay-at-home mom, for the last couple of years I've felt the need to do something more with my life. Not that raising children isn't *doing* something, but I want to make more of a contribution to society.

Okay, that's not exactly true. We do fine on Rich's salary and the desire to give back to the community by joining the work force isn't burning a hole in my heart.

The real reason I'm job hunting is that I'm dying to get out of the house!

There. I said it. I am bored, bored, bored. Making cookies, cleaning the house, volunteering at church…there was a time when that was enough for me. But I want more from life. As I approach forty, I'm reevaluating my life and what I've accomplished so far. Raising three great kids may seem like a lot. Correction: it *is* a lot. I love my kids like crazy, but who says I can't love them while I work? I need to do something for *me*.

My attention shifts as the machine plays the next message. A familiar voice slices into my kitchen. "Hey, Mads, it's me. I need your help. I can't decide—auburn passion or platinum? I know my hair won't fall out if I color it twice in one week, so I guess if I don't like the red, I can go with platinum. The girls cast their votes, but I want the opinion of my very best friend. So call me back, 'kay? It's a matter of life and death."

I half-smile. Everything is a matter of life and death to Sylvie. The girls at the spa where she works are constantly polling each other on important decisions like: Which garish color of nail polish should Karina slather on her three-inch acrylics? What should Rhonda name her new Toy Poodle? Or, how should Brandi style her hair for her date with a Hell's Angel?

I glance at the clock, sure that by this time Sylvie has made her agonizing decision and is now a Reba McEntire look-alike. Or perhaps a Marilyn Monroe.

The familiar sound of the bus's robust engine and squealing brakes informs me school's out. Thirty seconds later, the door slams and Emily loudly makes her way inside. She kicks off her snow boots and drops her jacket and purple glittery backpack to the floor. I clear my throat. She glances at me, picks them up, and hangs them on the appropriate hooks next to the door.

"Hey, you." I pull her into a hug. "Have a good day?"

She exhales dramatically. "It was okay."

"Do you want to talk about it?"

She purses her lips and cocks her head. "No." She plops down on the kitchen chair and hunches her shoulders in typical nine-year-old sulking style.

I ruffle her hair, then pull out a chair for myself. "Hmm...Ginny Thompson stole your lunch money again?"

"No."

"Um...Tommy Jones didn't say hi back?"

Em flushes slightly at my mention of the boy she has a crush on. "Nooo."

"You walked out of the bathroom with a string of toilet paper trailing from your shoe?"

"Mom!" Emily giggles. "How embarrassing!"

I count off on my fingers. "If your lunch money wasn't stolen, and Tommy said hi, and you made it out of the bathroom with clean shoes, it couldn't have been that bad."

"It's just...Jessica picked Dana as her reading partner instead of me."

"Ah. And you feel bad because Jessica is your best friend."

"Duh," she says, reciting one of Christina's favorite words. It even comes complete with an eye roll. Lately it seems Emily is turning into her older sister before my very eyes.

"Well, sometimes even best friends need a break from each other, sweetie. It doesn't mean she likes you any less. I'm sure she'll choose you next time."

"I bet Sylvie would *always* pick you for a reading partner."

I suppress a laugh. "Sylvie has other friends besides me, Em."

"Like who?"

"Well, there's...uh, Carmen from church. And Deborah, her neighbor."

Emily sits back in her chair and folds her arms across her chest. "And you expect me to believe she'd pick one of them over you? I don't think so, Mom."

It's confirmed. My nine-year-old has transformed into a teenager in ten minutes flat. I shudder. One hormonal daughter is bad enough.

"So are you going to be okay?"

She shrugs. "I just won't pick her next time. Then she'll see how it feels."

I open my mouth to lecture her about how paybacks are wrong, but the door slams again, and Christina, the *real* hormonal teenager, storms in. Emily takes this opportunity to jump up and sprint for her room before I can stop her.

I turn my attention toward my older daughter. Christina kicks off her fashion boots. She wouldn't be caught dead wearing clunky snow boots—or a jacket, for that matter—to school. She'd rather risk frostbite and maintain her cool image. She tosses her bright orange backpack on the counter, knocking over a vase of flowers.

"Hey!" I scrunch my eyebrows together.

She stomps over to the vase, sets it upright, then proceeds to exit the kitchen.

"Excuse me—there's water all over the counter."

Christina whips around and huffs back to the kitchen. She unrolls way more paper towels than necessary and rams the wad into the spill.

"Is there a problem?" My voice carries an edge. I cross my arms over my chest and wait for an explanation.

"I'm bloated, okay? I have cramps and my head is killing me. I think I need a doctor's appointment." She hesitates a beat. "Brittany said if you go on birth control pills, you have lighter periods."

I gape at my daughter. "Are you serious? I know you didn't imply that you want to go on birth control pills."

Christina gives me her best disgusted look. "Forget it. I should've known better than to try to talk to you about it. Sweep it under the rug as usual and pretend I never brought it up." She brushes past me.

I grab her arm. "You *didn't* try talking to me about it. You blurted it out of nowhere. This is definitely an issue we need to discuss."

She pulls her arm out of my grasp. "You know what? I don't want to talk about it. I'll just have to deal with being anemic for the rest of my life and cramps that measure a twelve on the pain meter. I'll be in my room bleeding to death." She grabs her stomach and hunches over as she heads off toward her room.

"This conversation is not over, Christina. And there's Midol in the medicine cabinet!"

The backdoor slams and Christina's twin brother, Max, walks in, whistling the tune to "God bless America." He traipses into the kitchen without removing his shoes. I wince at the dirty water marks he's leaving on the floor. Not that my floor is clean, mind you. Now that I think about it, maybe I'll grab the mop and smear the water around to save me from having to fill up the bucket. It could work.

"Hi, honey. How was your day?"

Max shrugs and grunts. At least one of my kids is acting normal today. Turning his almost six-foot frame in the direction of the fridge, he grabs the orange juice off the shelf and guzzles it right out of the carton. Any other day I would comment on his disgusting behavior or at least smack him on the back of the head to punish him with a nose full of liquid. Today I don't have the energy.

Instead, I join him in front of the fridge, flinching as my socked foot lands in a puddle of muddy water. I open the freezer, pull out a package of Edy's Dibs and, junkie-like, start popping them into my mouth until it's stuffed to capacity. Max stares at me like I'm psychotic, then saunters off.

Since my now chipmunk-cheeks prevent me from reminding my son to remove his shoes before stepping onto the carpet, I am thankful—and surprised—that he does for once. Dirty vinyl is one thing. Mud-stained carpet is a whole other matter.

Oooh. Brain freeze. Clutching my head with one hand, I shove the carton back in the freezer with the other. Then I mentally retrieve the sticky note I filed away in my mind at church on Sunday about calling Sarah Price.

Nothing like a mouth overflowing with ice cream and chocolate to make a woman question her sanity.

Five minutes later, I'm speaking with the receptionist of the Reflections Counseling Center.

"You're in luck." Her tone is so cheery I feel like I've won the lotto. "A couple minutes ago, I received a cancellation with Dr. Price for tomorrow afternoon. Will that work for you?"

As I hang up the phone, I'm thinking that maybe the sudden opening didn't have to do with luck at all.

3

Hunger, love, pain, and fear are some of those inner forces
Which rule the individual's instinct for self-preservation.
ALBERT EINSTEIN

It's just the kids and me for dinner.

Twice a year, the schools have two days of parent-teacher conferences and it is day number two, so Rich won't be home for a couple more hours. Thoughts pop up, uninvited, of Fawn Witchburn sitting across the desk from my husband in a blouse unbuttoned to her naval. She's wearing one of her famous micro-skirts, spidery legs crossed, putting on her best sultry face, complete with Botoxed, dark-stained lips. Every time I see Fawn, she's wearing the same blazing brown lipstick, at least thirty shades deeper than the Passion Pale I prefer.

Thinking about Fawn makes me grumpy. I try to think happy thoughts, but my mind is not cooperating.

I eye the casserole I took out of the oven a minute ago. A crispy, black ring is visible atop the bubbling and horrid-looking concoction. Cooking has never been my forte, but I was cold and wanted an excuse to turn on the oven. I grab the casserole dish with two blue floral print potholders and tip it upside down over the trash can. Potatoes and hamburger ooze in between a milk carton and the wad of paper towels I retrieved from the floor earlier from Christina's bad throw.

"Good riddance." I desperately hope the steamy liquid will not seep through any unseen holes in the trash bag and leave a stinky, sloppy mess for me to clean up later. Then I do what I always do in a dinner emergency: Call Vino's.

While I wait for the pizza to be delivered, I remember that this morning Emily complained of having no clean jeans. I unenthusiastically saunter into the laundry room. My shoulders droop as I stare at Mount Washmore, and I consider running outside to grab the ladder. I attack the pile, pluck out all of the denim, and start checking pockets.

My kids are well-aware that I have a pocket rule. Whatever I find is mine. If they can't take the time to check before throwing their pants in the hamper, I have full rights to their pocket trash. When the kids were younger I would find all sorts of useless things: rubber bands, paper clips, candy wrappers, pennies, marbles. These days it's rare to find anything except a lone quarter here and there. That's why I'm surprised when I dig my hand in one of Max's jeans pockets and pull out a pink sheet of paper folded into a heart. Because of the pocket rule, I feel absolutely no guilt upon opening it. I read:

Dear Max,
  She thinks you're hot, too. Go for it!
Amy

My first thought: *Who is She?*
Second thought: *My son, hot? Shudder...*
And the third: *How could Amy do this to me?*

I tell Max all the time how much I like Amy. She is cute, bubbly, and a regular churchgoer who clearly loves the Lord, not to mention wears a Promise Ring, given to her by her parents when she turned fifteen. Vowing not to have sex until she's married places her at the top of my list for acceptable dates for Max. In fact, in my book, this makes Amy perfect daughter-in-law material. Not that I am encouraging my son to start looking for a wife before he finishes high school....

The note indicates Max might be interested in someone else, and I am a bit offended for my little Amy, almost like Max is betraying her. But the note is from Amy, and she doesn't sound offended at all. In fact, she is the one encouraging Max to "go for it!"

I wonder whether or not I should bring this up to Max. But there is something weird about talking to my son about a girl who thinks he's hot. I tuck it in my shirt pocket, in case I get the urge to pursue it.

Rich's shirt sleeve waves to me from the hamper. I pull it out and start to toss it into the basket of light-colored clothing, when something catches my eye. There's a smudge on the collar.

Upon closer inspection and a quick sniff, I realize the smudge is lipstick. Dark brown.

My pulse quickens. Coincidence? Me thinks probably not.

I shake the shirt loose from my fingers like it's a rattlesnake.

The phone and the doorbell ring simultaneously, and I don't know whether to be irritated or relieved. I holler to Emily to answer the phone while I go collect the pizza from the pimply delivery boy who looks all of thirteen.

"Mom? Sylvie's on the phone." We do a switcheroo, as Emily swaps me the phone for the pizza. She skips off to the kitchen, seemingly over her earlier bad mood. Guess it transferred to me. Of course, my current irritable state might have something to do with finding lipstick on my husband's collar.

"Hey, Sylv."

"Thanks for calling me back," she quips.

"Sorry. It's been a little...crazy around here." If there's one thing I'm an expert in besides indulging in sweets, it's hiding my emotions. I waste no time falling into the "everything's peachy" mode.

"Yeah, yeah, excuses, excuses. I guess I forgive you, but only because I love my hair! You've got to see it. I look exactly like—"

"Wait, let me guess. Lucy Ricardo?"

Sylvie laughs. "Um...no. But you've got the color right."

"Carol Burnett?"

"Forget comedy. Think class."

"Hmm. Wilma Flintstone? I've always thought of her as classy."

"Very funny. No, the next time you see me, you will do a double take. It'll be like you're looking at Nicole Kidman. You know, back when she was a full-fledged redhead."

I snort.

"What's so funny?"

"Sylvie, you're five-foot-three. Forget the fact that you have olive skin and brown eyes—not quite Nic's milky white complexion and baby blues."

"Topaz. Not brown."

"Same thing."

"Not really." She sighs heavily into the phone. "Leave it to you to ruin my moment."

"Sorry. I can't wait to see the new 'do. I'm sure it looks fabulous."

"So, anyway, here's the real reason I called—besides wanting to brag about the fact that I'm Nicole's clone...have you checked your mail today?"

I glance at the pile of mail I tossed on the counter earlier. "No. Why?"

"Look through it and call me back."

My interest is piqued. "Okay..."

I hang up and turn my attention toward Emily and Max, who are munching away on the pizza, arguing about whether mushrooms are a vegetable.

"Where's Christina?"

"She's in her room. She doesn't feel good," Emily says.

"I don't feel so good either." Max drops the remains of a pizza slice onto his plate and sits back in his chair.

"You shouldn't have wolfed down three pieces in, like, four minutes, then." Emily swats him in the gut, causing him to groan.

A sudden desire to hug my less-than-perfect kids wells up. I approach Max and Emily, embracing them from behind in a group-therapy sort of hug.

"Did someone die or something?" Max asks.

"No. Do I need a reason to give my kids a hug?"

"Whatever." Max sticks a piece of cheese on his chin. "So what did you do at school today, Em?" he asks, straight-faced, cheese string dangling from his face to his plate.

Emily giggles and pops a glob of cheese onto her nose.

With intense affection, I watch them banter for a moment before tossing two napkins on the table. "Be sure to clean up after yourselves."

To my kids, "Clean up after yourselves" means transferring their plates from the table to the counter. I would call them back to the kitchen, but I welcome the mundane chore of wiping the table and doing the dishes. My hands immersed in a sink full of bubbles, I try to think of ways to bring up the lipstick to Rich. I even try to pray about it, but again, my mind refuses to cooperate. It keeps reverting back to the fight between Mom and Dad that I witnessed when I was only ten....

"You're not sorry, Ron. You're just sorry you got caught!" Mother's voice is high-pitched and louder than usual.

"Maxine, it was a mistake. It won't happen again."

I crouch behind the big brown recliner and hug my knees to my chest, as I listen for the first time in my life to my father cry. I don't want to watch, but the potted plant next to the chair isn't plush enough to keep me from peering between the leaves to witness the scene in full.

"You're right it won't happen again. Because you're out of here. I want you gone by morning, do you hear me?"

"Maxine, think about the kids."

Mother's laugh is laced with contempt. "I'm sure that's what you were thinking about when you were having sex with her, right? The kids? Don't talk to me about the kids. You *did this to them. Not me!"*

Dad lashes back. "Maybe if you were there for me more, I wouldn't have to—"

"Get out!" Mom shoves him in the chest, and he staggers backwards....

I don't remember what happened after that. All I remember is waking up to my mother and father sitting at the breakfast table, eating scrambled eggs in silence. I had never experienced silence so deafening....

By the time I hear the garage door opening about twenty minutes later, I haven't come up with a plan as to how to confront my husband. I have no other choice than to wing it.

Behind me, Rich lumbers in, removes his boots, and sets his briefcase on the counter. I don't dare turn around.

"Hi." He comes up behind me and kisses my cheek.

My shoulders tense.

"What's wrong with you? Are you PMS-ing or something?"

I whip around, sending a few bubbles flying through the air. "Why do you automatically assume I'm PMS-ing when I'm in a bad mood? Not everything is related to hormones, you know."

"Okay...sorry." He stares at me as though I'm a bright yellow caution banner.

I narrow my eyes. "So how did conferences go?"

He shrugs. "I have a good class this year. I didn't have any major problems to discuss with the parents. That was nice for a change."

"What about Lexi Witchburn?" I look him in the eye. The eyes give everything away and will tell me immediately whether he's lying.

"Lexi?" He turns away and opens the fridge. "She's got some emotional issues, but overall, she's a good kid. Why?"

"Did you meet with her mother?"

"Yeah. Her appointment was yesterday." He removes a can of soda and pops open the tab.

"What did you talk about?"

Rich frowns, glances at me, then shifts his gaze toward the coffee maker. "Where are you going with this, Madi?"

I cross my arms and try to take deep breaths without being obvious. A full minute passes before I walk over to the laundry room, retrieve the shirt, and throw it into his chest.

He makes a face. "What's this?"

"That's what I'd like to know. It's your shirt. The one you wore to school yesterday. Only you forgot the club soda. Or maybe you weren't aware that club soda removes lipstick stains. Make a note of it."

He glances at the smudge and his shoulders fall. "Madi..."

"I think it would be best if you moved out for a while."

Irritation flashes across his face. "Move out? Over this? You don't even want an explanation?"

Willing myself to remain calm, I say, "There's no way to explain it away, is there? It's certainly Fawn's color. It's definitely on your collar. Which means she had to get pretty darn close to you to leave it there. And, frankly, the thought of it makes me sick. If you're going to cheat, Rich, couldn't you have chosen someone a little more...classy?"

Rich's brown eyes bore into mine. "You're unbelievable. I know what your dad did to your mom, and I get that you've been burned yourself in the past. I've tried to be understanding and patient with you throughout your jealous phases and insecurities. I've listened to your ridiculous accusations and have offered to go with you to counseling. I've reassured you a thousand times. But I don't think I can do this anymore."

The lump in my throat makes it impossible to swallow. I don't want to cry, but tears threaten, and I blink several times to hold them off. I lift my head a little higher. "So go, then."

"Are you serious? You really want me to leave?" Rich hesitates, as if waiting for me to beg him to stay.

"You didn't deny it."

"Deny what? That this is Fawn Witchburn's lipstick? No, I didn't deny it, Madi. I am tired of denying it. I'm sick of defending myself. You obviously haven't believed me the last thousand times I've told you I love you—and only you. That I always have been—and always will be—faithful to you. How many times do I have to say that for you to believe it's true?" He raises, then drops, his hands in exasperation.

I want to believe him. I do. My heart wants to trust. But my mind refuses.

"Just go," I whisper around the lump, which has grown to softball-size in the last two minutes. This time, it's I who avoids eye contact. Instead, I focus on the gold knob on the utensil drawer.

Peripherally, I see Rich shake his head before he walks away. Thirty minutes later, I'm still in the same position, arms folded, leaning against the kitchen counter. He reappears, lugging a couple of suitcases and a black duffel bag.

"I'll be at Ray's. Tell the kids I'll call them tomorrow."

As soon as the door closes, my ducts open and the tears I've been holding back are unleashed.

♛
4

You cannot escape the responsibility
Of tomorrow by evading it today.
ABRAHAM LINCOLN

"Your dad's an idiot, Madi Lee."
I want to say, "Don't talk about Daddy that way!" But I keep my thoughts to myself.
"After all I've done for him." She shakes her head. "Idiot."
"Is he coming home?" My tone is hopeful, but my heart knows better.
"You think I'd take him back?" She emits a sardonic laugh. "I wouldn't even consider it." She gives me a hard look. "Men are pigs, Madi Lee. Don't ever forget that. It doesn't matter how much you do for them, or how much sex you give them, eventually, they'll get bored and toss you aside like a pair of dirty socks."
"Will I still see him?" My eyes fill with tears that spill over onto my cheeks.
"Why would you even want to?" The look Mom gives me does not reflect sympathy, which makes me long to retract the question.
"Because he's my daddy!" I want to scream. But I don't. I shrug.
"The courts will say he has the right to visitation," Mom says. "But I'm going to make it miserable for him."
And I don't have one doubt that she will.
That night, I cry myself to sleep. As I do on many nights after that....
I'm numb. For the last hour, I've been sitting in the dark living room, alone with my thoughts and the bits of fingernails I've gnawed off. A quick run of the hand vac will definitely be in order.

What am I going to do?

Thinking things through isn't exactly my strong suit. Consumed by my distress, rationality has taken a back seat. Not that I regret confronting my husband, but now that he's gone, panic has set in.

But the hurt I feel at his betrayal justifies my decision. Being made a fool of is something I will not accept. So it's better to go through the pain and hardship of divorce than go on living with someone who can't uphold the vows he made to me eighteen years ago. No matter how sorry he says he is.

Not that he's apologized. He hasn't even admitted to any wrongdoing. Then, again, he didn't deny it, either.

Anyway, I refuse to be humiliated even further by letting him stay. That would be like saying what he did is okay. And it is so not okay.

The kids are unusually—and mercifully—quiet, which buys me time to collect my thoughts and pull myself together before facing them. Richard should have been a magician. He came and went without any of the kids spotting him. Figures they'd each be holed up in their bedrooms during the time he was home. Totally not fair leaving me to do the dirty work of bearing the news.

I suppose I could lie. Not give them the whole truth in order to bide some time until Rich and I can tell them together. But our kids are smarter than that. They'll know something is up and demand answers. Might as well come out with it.

Rubbing my eyes, I inhale deeply, uncurl my legs from under me and make my way to the kitchen. Charlie trails me and witnesses me sneaking a couple of Edy's Dibs from the freezer. I bribe him into not telling on me with another freeze-dried fish treat.

"Mommy, I'm tired." Emily's voice from the hallway startles me.

She *must* be tired. It's one of the only times she calls me Mommy anymore. I swallow the last of my Dibs. "It *is* past your bedtime, isn't it?"

Some mom I am, letting my current emotional state affect my mothering duties, which usually include tucking my kids into bed at night.

"Where's Daddy?"

"Let's go get you ready for bed."

I usher Emily to her room, where she modestly asks me to turn my back while she changes into her pajamas. I comply, although I can't help thinking how it wasn't that long ago when she ran around naked with no inhibitions. My baby is growing up.

After a quick trip to the bathroom to brush her teeth, she crawls into bed, pulling the lime and turquoise comforter up to her neck. The bed sinks under my weight as I perch on the edge.

"When is Daddy coming home?" She repeats the question I've been trying to avoid answering.

"He's already been home, sweetheart. But he left again. You must have been in your room doing your homework or reading or something."

Emily's mouth makes a slight downturn and confusion spreads across her face. "Where did he go?"

I say a quick prayer for the right words. "Dad's staying with Uncle Ray for a few days."

"You had a fight?"

"Yep." I brush a chunk of bangs away from Em's eye.

"A bad one?" Her lip quivers.

"Mmm...kind of bad."

"Like last time?"

Emily's referring to two months ago, when Rich and I got into a doozy of an argument over the holidays. This past Christmas was the year for us to visit Rich's mom, Nancy, in Cleveland, but for the first time ever, my mom's entire family from across the country, including Kansas, California, and Washington decided to spend the holidays all together in Michigan. They organized a huge reunion with aunts, uncles, and cousins I hadn't seen in years. Mom didn't just ask us to stay in town for the holidays-slash-reunion, she demanded it. She argued that Nancy would certainly understand.

It's a rare occasion that I agree with my mother, but this was one of those times. I told Rich this was a special event that might not ever happen again in my lifetime. I even suggested we could visit his mother for the next two Christmases in a row. But he maintained his mother is seventy-five years old with no family living nearby. And because we see my mother more often than either of us will admit we even care to, and only get down to Ohio a couple times a year, Nancy should get her fair turn.

So Rich ended up going to visit his mother alone while the kids and I stayed in Michigan. What made it worse was that half of my cousins didn't even show up for the so-called reunion. I felt horrible about the whole thing and called both Nancy and Rich to practically beg forgiveness. I vowed to never take my mother's side again. To this day, I suspect she may have made up the whole family reunion thing to manipulate me to stay in town.

That's my mom.

Emily chews her bottom lip as she waits for an answer.

"Not like last time. This is different."

"Is Daddy mad at me?"

I pull her into a hug and smooth her hair. "No, sweetie. Dad and I both love you very much. This has nothing to do with you."

"Promise?" Her eyes are bloodshot, either from exhaustion or because she's holding back tears, or both.

"I pinky promise." I hold my fingers out in the air and wait until she hooks her tiny pinky with mine. "Mommies and daddies are silly sometimes."

"Why didn't he say good-bye?"

Because he's a jerk. "He said to tell you he'll call tomorrow." I smile my most reassuring smile.

I stay with Emily and play with her hair until her eyelids get too heavy to keep open any longer and she drifts off to sleep.

I know exactly how you feel, baby.

I tiptoe out of her room and make my way down the steps to Max's room. After months of begging, Rich and I heeded our teenaged son's plea to move his bedroom to the basement.

Light shines from under Max's door. I rap a couple times and nudge it open. He sits at his desk, working feverishly on something, scribbling words on a sheet of paper. His MP3 player is attached to his ears, making him oblivious to my presence. The music can be heard blaring from the tiny transmitter all the way across the room, and I wonder if there may be sign language classes in our future.

Sneaking up on him and scaring him to death doesn't seem like a sensible option, so I slide to the left, hoping he'll catch a glimpse of movement. My good intentions don't help. When Max catches sight of me, he starts so hard he scares the daylights out of me. I feel my face contorting like something you might see in a Jim Carrey movie. Max knocks over a glass of water. Fortunately it tumbles to the floor instead of all over his schoolwork. The earphones fly from his ears, along with the MP3 player, and land right in the middle of a pile of dirty clothes. I place a hand to my chest and feel it pound against my palm.

"At least I got that thing away from your ear before you go deaf," I tease.

Max doesn't answer. He is busy hiding the paper he was writing on. He slides his history book on top of it, acting nonchalant. Silly boy—he knows me better than to think I'd miss something like that.

"What are you working on?"

He hesitates a beat. "History. Test tomorrow."

"Hmmm. It's after ten. Do you think maybe you should hit the sack?"

"Yeah. I was done anyway. I'll ace it—as always." He flashes the large, lopsided grin I adore. He got his braces off a month ago, and I can't stop admiring his teeth—the overbite bucks he inherited from his dad now transformed into a perfect row of pearly whites.

"Don't forget your retainer."

Max rolls his eyes. "Yeah, yeah."

I step behind him, put my hands on his shoulders, and lean down to kiss his head, at the same time spying for clues of what he had been writing. The darned History book is too big. Frustration nips at my emotions. Some might call me nosy, but I prefer the term *curiosity-inclined*. Particularly in the goings-on in my kids' lives. And particularly the things they don't want me to know about. Visions of the note I discovered earlier in Max's jeans pocket dance through my head. Does he realize it's missing? I picture him tearing through the pile of laundry looking for the note, distraught over the fact that it isn't there, likely wondering where he dropped it or whether I have already plucked it out and added it to my growing collection of pocket trash paraphernalia.

Which, of course, I have.

Maybe he is writing a love note to the girl who thinks he's hot. Maybe it's a romantic poem.

Maybe I need to put my mind in park and stop all of the wondering. After ten, I tend to get a little loopy.

Max cranks his head back toward the ceiling and stares up my nose. "Good night, Mom." His tone is polite, but what he really means is, "Would you please leave?"

I take the hint and reluctantly give in to the realization that I may never know what Max was writing. "One more thing, honey. Your dad is staying with your uncle Ray for a few days." Or longer.

Max cocks his head. "Why?"

Making light of it usually works with my son. "Oh, you know. We had a disagreement, and we need a breather. He said he'll call you tomorrow."

The way his eyebrows are creased tells me he's in processing mode. After ten seconds or so, he shrugs. "Okay."

I expel a breath I didn't realize I was holding. "Okay, sweetie. See you in the morning."

"Night, Mom."

Thankful my son didn't ask a million questions, I make my way upstairs.

I poke my head into Christina's room. My daughter is curled up on her bed in a fetal position, mouth slightly open. It's tempting to run and grab the camera to prove to her once and for all that she does, indeed, drool, but I don't want to give Christina a reason to despise me. Or, should I say, *another* reason.

She has kicked the blanket in a heap around her ankles and I pull it up to her neck. "You'll feel better in the morning, Sleeping Beauty." I lean down and brush my lips across her hair. The apple-scented shampoo still lingers from her morning shower.

At the thought of princesses, I recall my sixth-grade play. I landed the part of Cinderella and my real-life boyfriend at the time, Dwayne Michaels, played Prince Charming. I'll never forget the wrap party when the whole cast celebrated at Pizza Palace. Dwayne ignored me the entire evening and spent every dime he had on game tokens for the wicked stepsister, Connie Williams.

Totally ruined my princess moment.

From then on, I decided three things:

1. Princes only exist in fairy tales.
2. Being a princess is way over-rated.
3. Food (especially pizza) provides excellent first aid for broken hearts.

At that thought, I head downstairs to finish off the two leftover slices of Vino's pepperoni deep dish pizza. Most likely it will leave me feeling frumpy and ashamed of my lack of willpower. But, right now, I hope it will offer the emotional ointment I need so desperately.

♛

5

Mark my words, Madi. All men are losers.
Even when you think you've found a winner,
it's only a matter of time before he breaks your heart.
MY MOTHER

All men cheat.

At least, that's what my mother's told me—a gazillion times. Okay, so Mom has valid reasons for her opinion. Let's look at the facts. My father cheated on her. The three men she's dated since she and my father divorced twenty-eight years ago cheated on her. And she's positive her married boss is having an affair with a cashier at the convenience store where she works.

"A much younger cashier," she keeps stressing.

And then, of course, there's all of the cheating going on in Genoa City, where most of Mom's favorite soap characters may not be young but are inherently restless.

So there you have it. She's been burned a thousand times, as have the women in Soap Opera Land. To my mother, that proves it. All men cheat. Period.

There have been phases in my marriage when I completely trusted my husband. And, during these times, I've argued that Richard is the faithful man that Mom believes does not exist. I've reminded her that he's a fourth-grade teacher and a youth leader at church. He's an involved parent and proves it by being in the front row of every one of Emily's dance recitals, Max's band concerts, and Christina's...well, Christina really doesn't have a thing. But if she did, he'd be there too.

I've admitted to Mom that, yes, Richard lacks a little in the romance department. He doesn't often bring me flowers or whisk me away on romantic vacations. Sometimes a couple weeks go by without an "I love you." But all in all, he's been a good husband, a good father.

But Mom always looked me in the eye and came back with, "He may not have cheated yet. But you wait, honey. He will."

I haven't wanted to believe it. But Mom is right. All men do cheat. Even fourth-grade teachers and church youth leaders. Even my husband. Maybe I knew it was only a matter of time.

So here I am, sitting at Mom's kitchen counter the day after Rich left. I watch her prepare a chicken dish for my brother, Zach, whom she babies way too much. So what if he's divorced and lives on his own? He's thirty-four years old, for crying out loud.

I'm probably just jealous, wishing someone would cater to me like that.

Mom dumps a can of cream of mushroom soup over the pan of chicken breasts and some of the soup splatters onto her own. This isn't surprising, since her double Ds get in the way quite often.

Stifling a yawn, I listen halfheartedly as she complains that she was asked to pick up an extra shift at the store. As she drones on about life's unfairness, I debate whether to come clean about the cheating thing and deal with the inevitable "I-told-you-so." It turns out I don't have a choice.

"He cheated, didn't he, Madi Lee?" Mom uses my middle name every time she's cranky or in pain from one ailment or another. Which pretty much means every time she talks to me at all.

"How would you know that?"

"It's in the eyes. The eyes give everything away."

I rub my eyes and wonder if mine are giving away my annoyance. That Mom guessed before I could tell her is downright maddening.

"So who was it? That second-grade teacher? The one who looks like a hooker?" She frowns. "What's her name…Karen, Carla…"

"Kirsten. And she's actually very nice, Mom." She's also a lesbian. But I'm not about to tell Mom. "And, no, she's not the one."

Mom grunts and waves a spoon at me. "I can't say I'm surprised. I warned you this would happen." She rattles out a long strip of tin foil and seals the top of the baking pan. I knew the "I-told-you-so" was coming, but it still irks me. Mom gives a knowing nod. "I understand how you feel honey—believe me."

Yeah, yeah. How could I not believe her? You hear something a gazillion times, you tend to start believing it.

"I don't want to talk about it." I'm not about to launch into a discussion with my man-bashing mother about the details of my husband's affair. And I especially won't reveal the name of the woman who stole him away. It's bad enough that Mom predicted this moment. She doesn't need to know that Richard was lured into temptation by the likes of Fawn Witchburn.

Mom puts down the empty soup can and comes around to my side of the counter. "I'm sorry, honey." She pulls me into a rare hug, squeezing my head to her chest. After about ten seconds, I'm gasping for air and struggle out of her embrace.

She loses her balance and stumbles backward, her mouth forming a small O before flattening into a thin straight line. She frowns but keeps quiet, which says more than a thousand words.

"Sorry, Mom, but I was suffocating in there." I wheeze. "I appreciate the comfort and everything, but next time can you wait until I stand up to give me a hug?"

"I've been considering a breast reduction, you know." She goes back to her chicken, popping the pan in the oven.

"I think you should do it." And that's the truth. Her shoulder and back pain has burdened her for far too long. The Grand Canyon has shallower crevasses than my mother's shoulders from the bra straps.

"Just be thankful you don't have this problem." She glances at my chest and retreats into silence.

Ouch! Comments like this are so typical of my mother. I love her with all my heart, and I know she loves me, but our personalities don't mesh. I compare hers to a scouring pad—coarse and abrasive. I'm more like a sponge—absorbing everything, and taking a hard squeeze to get anything out. But squeeze too hard and you may get soaked. Verbally, that is. I've got a pretty tight rein on expressing my emotions, but I've been known to mimic Mom's harsh tendencies, proving that no matter how hard I fight it, small flashes of my mother appear in me from time to time.

Lord, help us all.

I glance at my watch. "I should go, Mom. I have an appointment."

"What appointment?"

"Oh, it's just…uh…a doctor's appointment. No big deal."

She narrows her eyes. "You're not pregnant, are you?"

If it weren't such a dumb question, or if I was in a better mood, I might laugh. "Yeah, right. That's not possible anymore, remember? Richard got, you know, the snip."

"That doesn't mean anything. Eleanor's daughter got pregnant with twins after her husband was fixed. It happens more often than you think. Of course, if Richard has been cheating, you two probably haven't had much sex lately. Well, *you* haven't, anyway."

My heart stings. Will I ever get used to Mom's bluntness?

She goes on. "It's a good thing, though. It will be hard enough raising three kids on your own. How on earth would you handle a baby?" She grunts.

"I'm leaving now." I grab my purse and jacket off the barstool, give Mom a quick pat on the back, and make a beeline for the door. When I am almost to my car, I hear my mother shout, "I told you so!"

She never can resist getting in the last word.

The Reflections Counseling Center waiting room is crowded. There is one empty seat available between a man who resembles Charles Manson and a woman absorbed in picking the lint balls off her sweater and piling them up on the glass end table beside her chair.

The woman adds another chunk of lint to her pile. The man eyes me and smiles, displaying a gap where his two front teeth should be. He pats the seat next to him.

A chubby girl in a brown parka barrels past me and squeezes into the chair. The man's smile disappears, and he grabs a nearby magazine. Somehow, I doubt he'll get a lot out of *Cosmo*.

With no empty seats left, I lean against the wall.

So I let my mother believe my appointment is with my family doctor. It's not a lie, exactly—I *am* seeing a doctor. Just not of the physical variety. If I'd told Mom that my appointment was with a psychologist, she would have bombarded me with all kinds of advice, since she's been to more counselors, psychologists, and psychiatrists than the number of years I've been alive.

Which is exactly why I have no interest in her advice. So many counselors, so little change.

Then again, one has to *want* to change in order for counseling to work. And my mother seems quite happy to be unhappy. I'm sure all of those psychiatrists she's seen over the years aren't complaining, either. People like her keep them in business.

I, on the other hand, *do* want to change. At least, I want to be changed, if not do the work required to get there. But at least now my jealousy thing is sort of validated. Rich never denied that he cheated, which says more than if he'd have come right out and admitted it. To me, this says I'm not the only one with major issues.

"Madison." The receptionist and patient retriever smiles at me from the doorway.

Pushing myself off the wall, I am peripherally aware that Charles Manson is watching my every move over the pages of his *Cosmo* magazine. So aware that I don't see the *Newsweek* on the floor and I step on it, my foot sliding forward while my body reels backwards.

Not a good combination.

I land on my back and, before I can catch my breath, I am staring up at Charles himself. He offers a grubby hand. I take it—because what else can I do?—and am hoisted to my feet. All eyes are on me except for the lint-picking girl, who is still focused on her sweater.

"You can thank me later," Charles whispers with a wink.

He is still holding my hand. I recoil and yank it away.

"Are you all right?" The receptionist asks as I step past her into the back hall.

I laugh it off. "I'm fine, although I'm not so sure about my ego."

Once inside Sarah's office, I sink into a comfortable brown recliner. I am digging through my purse for hand sanitizer when Sarah enters.

Sarah Price could be described as classy and chic. Tall and willowy, her blonde hair is swept up in a messy bun. She wears tailored black trousers and a peach tank, topped with a soft beige sweater coat that hangs casually to her knees.

Now I wished I'd dressed up a little instead of simply grabbing the first thing I saw in my closet—a not-so-chic red jogging suit I got on clearance at JC Penney's.

Sarah smiles and rolls out her desk chair so she's sitting on an angle about three feet away. She crosses her long legs and swings a pointy-toed snakeskin boot with a three-inch heel.

"Great boots," I say.

"Thanks. DKNY. Got them on eBay for a steal."

Her idea of a steal is probably more than my last month's heat bill.

"Thanks for squeezing me in. I called at the last minute and didn't expect to get an appointment so soon."

"Must be a God-thing because I had a cancellation only fifteen minutes before you called. So…" She reaches over and picks up a pair of rose-framed glasses from her desk and slides them on. "It's good to see you, Madi." Smiling, she waves a pencil in the air. "Not that I'm glad you need to be here or anything. What's going on?"

I take a deep breath. "Things have been a little, um, rocky."

"Meaning…"

"My marriage, mostly." I swallow a lump in my throat. "I've wanted to set up an appointment with you for a while now. Some, uh, personal issues from my past have been affecting my marriage. But I think I waited too long. Yesterday, Rich moved out. He's staying with his brother right now." Which is a topic for a whole other session. Ray is a cross between Shia LaBeouf and Jude Law. He's got a killer smile and an ego to go along with it. He and Rich may be brothers, but they are at opposite ends of the spectrum when it comes to personalities. The fact that Rich decided to stay with him came as a shock to me, especially because they aren't that close. Then again, nothing about Rich's behavior shocks me anymore.

"What happened?" She takes out her notebook, poised to write.

"He cheated on me."

"And you know this because…"

"Because he came home from a school conference with a chocolate lipstick stain on his shirt."

She stares at me. "And…"

Okay, one of Sarah's tendencies is becoming clear. She trails off, leaving me to finish her sentences. I hope it doesn't get annoying.

"And the mother of one of his students wears that same color lipstick."

Sarah frowns. "Did you ask him about it?"

"Sort of."

"Sort of?"

"I've tried to convince myself otherwise, but for a while now, I've suspected he's been cheating. The lipstick was the icing on the cake. The *chocolate* icing." I nod solemnly.

Sarah scribbles something on her notepad. "Tell me about your childhood."

Wait a minute. Weren't we talking about my husband? "What do you want to know?"

"You said you intended to come in even before your husband left because of some issues you want to deal with."

"That's true."

"So let's back up so I can get a clear picture of who Madi is. What was your childhood like? Was it happy? Did your parents have a good marriage?"

I can't help emitting a bitter laugh. "Hardly."

Sarah sits there silently, and I realize she's waiting for me to elaborate.

"My dad had zillions of affairs," I explain. "My mom let him get away with it for a while, but finally she had enough and sent him packing. Or, I should say, she sent his clothes flying out the second-story window while he ran around with a garbage bag and desperately tried to retrieve them before all the neighbors started leaving for work in the morning."

"And you witnessed this?"

"I couldn't *not* witness it. Mom doesn't exactly do things quietly."

"How old were you?"

"Twelve."

Sarah scribbles something on her notepad. "Do you remember how you felt then?"

"I don't remember."

"What *do* you recall about that time?"

"I remember thinking what a jerk my dad was. But I also knew my mom was pretty difficult to live with."

"Were you angry at your mother for telling him to leave?"

I consider this a moment. "I don't think so. Maybe. I don't know. I don't remember being mad at my dad, though. I remember thinking that some men simply seem destined to cheat."

She cocks her head. "Do you really believe that?"

"I said *seem*."

"How did you find out about your dad's affairs?"

"Do we have to talk about this? Can't we talk about what I'm going to do now that I'm on my own with three kids?"

Sarah writes something else in her notebook. "We can talk about whatever you want."

Of course we can. I'm paying *her.*

I take a deep breath and expel it toward the window. I watch a mother chase after her toddler who has taken off running toward a snow bank. Seems like a million years ago since my kids were that little.

"I'm mad at God." There. I said it. I thought I would feel better saying it out loud. But I don't. In fact, I feel worse.

"Everyone gets mad at God sometimes, Madi. It's nothing to feel ashamed of. The key is to be honest about your feelings and work through them. But the longer you hold on to that anger…"

"Yeah, yeah. I'm giving a foothold to the devil. Tell me something I don't know."

She presses the pencil eraser against her chin. "Hmmm. How about, 'God loves you'?"

"Pfft. I know God loves me."

She puts the pen to her lip. "Are you sure about that?"

"Of course I'm sure. Jesus loves me, this I know. I've been singing that song since I was five."

"You'd be surprised at the number of women I see who don't truly grasp that truth. And how we regard our earthly dads has a lot to do with how we relate to our heavenly Father." She hesitates a beat. "For instance, if a woman had an abusive father—either physically or verbally—chances are, she considers God an angry disciplinarian and has a hard time thinking of Him as tender and loving."

"My father wasn't abusive."

"No, but he chose another woman—or women—over your mother. Over you. As a young girl, you may have associated this with lack of love toward you and your mom. Transferring that doubt of lovability over to God is a natural tendency. You may not feel like you were mad at your dad back then, but anger is the easiest emotion to suppress. And it comes out in a myriad of ways. Does that make sense?"

No... "I guess so."

"What you need to realize, Madi, is that you are a princess. Whether you feel like one or not, God sees you as royalty." She pauses again. Obviously I don't seem convinced, because she continues. "I like to think of it this way. Eve was the very last thing God created on earth. Therefore, the woman is the crown of creation, so to speak. A princess."

I recall the memory I had last night about playing Cinderella in the school play. Interesting that Sarah would mention princesses. It's as if she'd been peeking in on my reminiscence.

Okay, too much deep thinking for one day. I swallow and look away, trying to come up with a way to shove this under the rug. Charles Manson's face flashes across my mind.

I rub my hands on my jeans. "So...you don't happen to have any hand sanitizer, do you?"

6

Maturity is knowing
when to be immature.
RANDALL HALL, GUITARIST FOR LYNYRD SKYNRD

My favorite princess is Snow White. But right now I feel like one of her dwarves. I am Grumpy.

As I exit Fred's Market, three bags hang over my arms. Two are plastic (read: let-the-whole-world-see) and contain healthy items, such as carrots, lettuce, bananas, and two Weight Watchers frozen entrées. The other bag is paper, which conceals one carton of Edy's Dibs—Rocky Road with Chocolaty Almond Coating.

My mom's earlier mention of chocolate reminded me I am all out of my secret indulgence. Well, not really secret. Not to my family, anyway. They know of my crazed addiction to these little delectable, bite-sized treasures. Dibs are like bonbons, only better. Just as fattening, I'm sure. But you know, sometimes I simply have to ignore the nutritional value information plastered on the package of every food item. Sometimes I have to indulge. Especially after a visit with my mother. And today, a visit with my mom, followed by an appointment with my new shrink, certainly justifies my need for Dibs.

But the whole world doesn't have to know about it. I slouch out like an alcoholic, my addiction hidden within the brown paper bag. Can you blame me? What if I run into Claudia Boeve? She would be apt to go into her normal guilt-ridden spiel about health risks and man's evil plot to process-food the world into oblivion. Not to mention she'd have even more reason to convince me to join her weight loss workshop.

Whatever.

Okay, so the truth is, I know I can go overboard sometimes. I may be only ten pounds overweight, but that doesn't mean I don't struggle with gluttony. However, preaching to me about it only sends me running to the kitchen.

Back to my juggling act. I am managing these bags while digging through my gigantic purse for my car keys. It doesn't help that it's 20 degrees outside, and my fingers are as cold and stiff as popsicles. And judging by the color they're quickly turning, I'd say grape popsicles, at that. Makes me regret not hunting for my gloves, which are somewhere in my van—probably under the seat hanging out with the Burger King wrappers and used Kleenex.

I give myself a mental kick for not remembering to pull out my keys when I put away my debit card. It's one of those things I always think of the second I step into the parking lot. I seriously think God should have created women with three arms. That's something I'll be talking to Him about when I make it to the other side. That is, if I make it at all. The way things are between me and God at the moment makes me wonder.

Aha! Success! The keys jingle noisily in my hand as I pull them from my purse without dropping a bag. Ringling Bros., here I come! I pick up the pace. My goal is to get home a few minutes ahead of the kids so I can crack into the Dibs. I point the remote toward my van and pop the hatch. As I reach out to pull it up, a black leather-gloved hand appears out of nowhere and touches my arm.

I scream.

Not just loudly, mind you. Killer-on-the-loose loudly. All three bags thud to the ground and the lettuce head rolls out of the plastic bag and into the snow. So much for my juggling act.

When I realize who the hand belongs to, relief and dismay collide. It is no mugger at all, but my husband, who is crouched over, bear-like, chasing after the leafy green ball now making its way under the van. I snatch up the brown bag like any good addict and hold it to my chest. The coldness from the snow caked to the sides eases the contractions of my heart. Or maybe it's the smell of the chocolate.

"Are you okay, ma'am?" A middle-aged, portly man scurries to my rescue. His brown and white jacket strains against his belly and a couple of stains decorate the front pocket. Looks like they came from the same dark shiny food item that clings to his left cheek.

"I'm fine, thank you. It's only my h-hus-husband." I choke out the word. "He startled me, is all."

"Are you sure?" The man frowns, intently searching my face, perhaps for some clue that I'm being coerced into lying, maybe even have a knife pressed against my back. He then narrows his marble-sized eyes at Richard, who stands next to me holding out the wet head of lettuce.

Rich steps in front of me, holds up his left hand, and flashes his wedding band. "It's okay. Like she said, we're married. See?" The annoyance in his voice rings clear.

I grab the lettuce and toss it like a softball into the back of my van. I turn back and smile at this stranger, whose willingness to come to my aid is refreshing. "It's okay. Really. But thanks for your concern."

The man shoots Richard one more suspicious glare and ambles away, shaking his head.

I whip around. "What do you think you're doing? You scared me to death! Are you stalking me? And why aren't you at work?"

"I took some vacation days, Madi. In fact, I asked for the rest of the week off, plus next week. Midwinter break is next Thursday and Friday, so it's the perfect time to take off. I want to get this worked out." He pushes his hands into his coat pockets.

As I take a moment to study my husband, I'm irritated at how great he looks. He's supposed to look haphazard, with wrinkled clothes from living out of a suitcase, chin stubble from being too distressed to shave, and eyes bloodshot from no sleep due to anguish over the fact that he's traumatized his family. What he's not supposed to be is well-dressed, clean-shaven, and so darned good-looking!

I'm suddenly feeling extra unattractive in my jogging suit. Although I can't feel my feet through my white Nikes, at least I didn't wear clunky snow boots that measure a ten on the frump-o-meter. But I still feel like a slob. Why didn't I take more time this morning to style my shoulder-length hair, which currently hangs lifeless against my face? Those stubborn gray roots must be a vision. Why didn't I break open the box of Nice 'n' Easy that's been sitting in the bathroom cupboard for the past week?

Meanwhile, Richard looks like he's stepped out of *GQ* magazine, with his sandblasted Levi's and L.L. Bean black leather jacket. The jacket I bought him for Christmas. The one that makes him look like he could be Orlando Bloom's older brother.

Swoon...

As drool threatens to pool at the corners of my mouth, I snap out of it. My husband will not manipulate me into forgiving him with his good looks. I turn my attention to the two plastic bags still on the ground. I pick them up and shove them into the van, then, more gently, prop the brown paper bag between them.

"I'm not in the mood to talk, Rich."

"It's not all about you, Madi."

"It's not about me at all, is it?" I raise my eyebrows and give him my best witchy expression.

Rich rolls his eyes. "I can see you haven't come to your senses yet."

"I don't have time for this."

"When do you predict you'll have time? To talk, I mean."

I ram my fists into my sides. "I don't know. I've never been cheated on before—at least, that I know of. I'll keep you posted, 'kay?"

He runs a gloved hand through his hair and stares off into the distance for a couple seconds. "I'm trying to be civil here, and you're being malicious."

"That's me—Malicious Madi."

"Just let me say one thing."

"Nope. No more talking." I close the rear hatch and make my way around the side of the van.

"Madi, please."

I stick my fingers in my ears. "La la la la la la la la la la la la..."

"C-mon, Madi, you're acting like one of my students." His voice is slightly muffled but I hear every word.

If I were the princess Sarah says I am, perhaps I would gracefully ignore his comment and exit quietly. But, because Grumpy is my persona, I turn and scowl. "I'll give you fourth-grade, Rich." Then I do something I haven't done in thirty years. I stick out my tongue and blow, spit flying.

I climb into the van, back out, and gun it. Richard stands there, shaking his head. So blowing raspberries at my husband may have been a little immature. But it sure made me feel a heck of a lot better.

When I round the corner of my street, I see the school bus parked at the end of the driveway. Drat. No time to sneak any Dibs before the kids get home. Guess I'll need to wait until they're all in bed tonight.

I watch Em hop down off the bus steps and trudge toward the house. By the time I pull in, she's scrounging through her backpack for her house key. She looks at me and waves.

"Good timing." I smile and climb out of the van, then pop the hatch to retrieve the bags from Fred's Market.

"Did you buy anything good?"

"Mmmm, there might be a Reese's Peanut Butter Cup in there."

Her eyes light up the mention of her favorite candy bar. Quickly inspecting the bags, she picks up the one with the candy inside and dashes into the house.

As I'm putting away the few groceries, Christina makes a dramatic entrance. She kicks off her boots, sending them slamming against the wall. Without a word, she proceeds to march past me like a soldier heading toward the front lines of the battlefield.

"Hi, honey."

She ignores me and continues through the kitchen.

"Christina." My voice is steady and firm.

She stops but doesn't turn around.

"I said hello."

"Hi." She says it with all the sweetness of an angry Rottweiler. "Is that it?"

"What's wrong?" *This time,* I want to add.

Her body twists abruptly and, as she looks at me, my heart swells. The pain on her face is heart-wrenching.

"Why did Dad leave?" Christina boldly meets my gaze, demanding an answer. I hadn't had time this morning before the kids left for school to tell Christina about her dad. Max or Emily had obviously beaten me to it.

"We're having some—"

She averts her eyes. "Forget it. Blake dumped me for Paige Hardaway, okay? Life sucks right now."

Now my heart isn't merely swelling, it's breaking. "I'm sorry, sweetie." I take a step forward and, in response, she takes one back.

"I want to be alone." She turns and practically sprints off toward her room.

My feet want to move, to run after her and pull her into an enormous hug and not let go until the pain subsides. But I don't. Because not only do I want to respect my daughter's request to give her some time alone, but because if I did chase her down, I'd probably say some things I'd regret later. Things about boys being pigs. Things my mother said to me about my father when I was younger that have stuck with me all these years. Possibly even things about Richard.

And I refuse to traumatize my daughter like my mom traumatized me. Won't do it.

I decide to give Christina ten minutes to herself before attempting any form of conversation. So I walk back to the counter and put the rest of the groceries away, wistfully regarding the Dibs as I transfer them to the freezer.

Besides my unhealthy eating, another bad habit I have is letting the mail pile up before going through it. As I look at the stack now, which doubled when I threw today's stack on top of it, I remember Sylvie's phone call yesterday requesting that I look through the mail and call her back. But, despite my growing curiosity, talking to Christina about her present heartache takes precedence.

Emily is engrossed in an episode of some new show on Nickelodeon, and Max isn't home from school yet, so I decide there's no time like the present.

I'm not sure if Christina is ignoring me or can't hear the knocking over Carrie Underwood's voice blaring from her CD player, but it requires three attempts before the volume is turned down and the door is opened.

Christina's beauty never fails to astound me. Her hair is pulled back in a ponytail. Several dark blond strands have escaped, and one or two stick to her cheek, probably held there by dried tears. She never uses a ton of makeup, but traces of mascara are visible under green eyes, now puffy and red. She wears an old baggy pair of red sweats and a black oversized Adidas T-shirt. Giant Daffy Duck slippers cover her feet, making them appear three sizes larger than her actual six and a half.

To me, Christina looks prettier at this moment than when she spends an hour in front of the mirror. At almost sixteen, she is growing into a woman, but right now she's a vulnerable little girl.

I wrap my arms around her. She lets me hold her for several seconds, then pulls away and shuffles over to the CD player, hits a button, and the song "Before He Cheats" starts again.

"You know, you're going to wear out that CD," I say.

She shrugs.

"Do you want to talk about it?"

Another shrug. She falls back onto her bed and stares at the ceiling. I notice a picture of Blake on her nightstand. Let me rephrase that: I notice two pictures. One of Blake's left side and one of his right, the ragged edges on each indicating it had been ripped in half. I glance over at the pink wastebasket in the corner and see other photographs shredded inside the can and the pieces scattered around the floor. Glancing back at the torn photo on her nightstand, I assume that even though she ripped it in two, she can't bring herself to throw her favorite one away.

Blake is dressed in jeans and a black sweatshirt, relaxing against a tree. The fall colors are brilliant. Yellow, red, and orange leaves cover the ground around his feet. It looks like he's flirting, his head tipped down a smidge, blue eyes taking in the photographer. A crooked smile displays straight white teeth, the result of three years of braces. I have to admit, he is a good-looking kid. They make—er, *made*—an attractive pair.

"That was a great picture, huh?" Christina asks, rolling on her side, eyes resting on the torn pieces.

"I remember when that was taken. You guys had just started going out."

"Yeah." Her breath catches. "Why did he have to go and be such a jerk!" She buries her face in her fuzzy purple throw pillow and lets out a muffled scream.

I sit down on the bed, pick up her legs, and lay them over my lap. "Any chance it was all a misunderstanding?"

"Sure, if you call me walking in on him kissing Paige Hardaway a misunderstanding." Her still-muffled voice is laced with resentment. "Not many ways to misunderstand that."

I cringe and pull the pillow away. "Well, 'jerk' is definitely the right word, isn't it? His loss, right?" I'm playing the cool and understanding mom, but defensive anger surges. She doesn't deserve this. Part of me wants to engage her in a male-bashing session. The insane side of my personality wants to blurt out that Christina isn't the only one recently stung by a cheating man. That her own father is no better than Blake.

But, as badly as I want to say it, the words won't come. Traumatizing my daughter by attacking her dad wouldn't be a good mom choice.

"Are you and Dad getting divorced?" Christina is nothing if not blunt.

"It's too early to talk about that. We're...going through some things."

"Guess it runs in the family. Grandma and Grandpa, Uncle Zach, now you and Dad..."

It's as though Christina had knocked me over the head with her CD player. "Nobody said anything about divorce, honey."

Christina lies there silently, opening her mouth as if she wants to say something but can't decide how. Then, abruptly, she swings her legs off my lap, stands up, and starts the CD over again.

"I wanna be alone now." Tears spring to her eyes.

I debate whether to push the issue. The birth control matter needs to be discussed, but bringing it up now might not be such a good idea. I put my hand on hers. "Okay, honey. But if you feel like talking—"

"I'll call Brittany." She avoids my gaze. I puzzle over her sudden coldness, but then I remember she is a fifteen-year-old hormone habitat.

I stand and kiss the top of her head. She pulls away like I might give her an infectious disease. With one last sympathetic glance, I walk out of her room, shutting the door behind me. Carrie's voice follows me down the hall.

The pile of mail is the metal, and I am the magnet. I grab the stack and thumb through: Water bill. Heat bill. Credit card solicitation. Latest issue of *Marriage Forever* magazine.

I pause and let my eyes linger on the cover. "How to affair-proof your marriage." Ha! I've read articles like this before. Have even followed some of the advice. Look where it got me. I sneer at the blissfully happy couple on the cover.

"Just you wait, honey," I say to the blond Barbie doll adoringly gazing at her Ken. "Someday that smile will be erased from your pretty little face. It could be six months or six years. But, eventually, Ken will take your heart and twist it...chop it up...break it into a million pieces. And no matter what you do to 'affair-proof' him, he will cheat—mark my words. They *all* do."

I gasp as I realize my grip on the magazine is crinkling the edges and turning my knuckles white. Oh, God. What am I doing? I'm taking out my anger on an inanimate object. I'm talking to the model on the cover of a magazine. I'm going insane in the middle of my kitchen. And, worst of all, I am turning into my mother!

I snap out of it and place the magazine on the counter as lovingly as I would a newborn baby. I pat the cover. "Sorry about that, sweetie. Hope it works out for you."

Resuming my mail sorting: ortho appointment reminder card for Christina (her braces come off this summer). Phone bill. And last, but not least, a plain white envelope with my name scrawled on the front, the lines angling slightly upward toward the postage stamp. The return address reads Anita Watkins. Hmmm. Doesn't ring a bell. Tearing the envelope, I pull out a formal sheet of letterhead with *Anita Watkins—Pampered Chef Consultant* centered in bold at the top. *What is this, Sylvie? You wanted to give me a heads up about a Pampered Chef invitation?* That is so like Sylvie.

I read:

Dear Madison,

Do you realize it has been twenty years since we've graduated from Lakeshore Heights High School? Wow! Where does the time go, right? You also may have noticed you did not receive an invitation to the twenty-year reunion. There's a good reason for that—we didn't have one! (LOL) Anyway, I thought it would be a brilliant idea to organize an intimate gathering of select classmates. Out of 120 students in our graduating class, you're one of only 25 invited! Lucky you! (grin)

We'd positively love for you to join us for dinner. (Unfortunately, the restaurant doesn't serve Pampered Chef dishes but contact me if you'd like to have a party, K?)

Be sure to bring along your old yearbook and lots of high school memories.

You are welcome to bring along your significant other (if you have one, of course—grin)

We are so looking forward to seeing you again! It has been way too long! Twenty years, to be exact!

Have a really, really, really cheerful day! (smile)

Sincerely,
Anita (Langerak) Watkins,
Pampered Chef Consultant
214-555-7937

PLACE: Reggie's Classy Diner on Waterway Court
DATE: Friday, February 9
TIME: 6:00 p.m.?
RSVP: No need! We have reserved the party room, which can accommodate 10-30 people. Oh—feel free, however, to RSVP if you would like more information about having a Pampered Chef party or discovering your dream job and becoming a consultant yourself!

Okay, the first thing that strikes me is that the letter contains an excessive number of exclamation points! And an overly perky tone. And way too many LOLs, (smile)s and (grin)s—it's a letter, not an e-mail, for crying out loud. Lastly—and most annoyingly, I might add—it includes several dozen too many Pampered Chef plugs.

Thus, because of these nauseating distinctions, I'm not surprised to discover Anita Langerak, now apparently Anita Watkins, is the woman behind the letter.

Anita was the typical perky-pants cheerleader, class president, and valedictorian. In high school, Sylvie and I dubbed her "Anita Chiquita," not only because of her banana-colored disposition but because of her...uh... banana-shaped honker. The summer before our junior year, Anita got a nose job, which eliminated the hook completely, but the name stuck. We considered changing her nickname to "Sunny" to simply describe her personality, but "Anita Chiquita" has a certain ring to it. Who cared if her banana nose had been squished to a normal shape? Once a banana nose, always a banana nose.

The fact that Anita Chiquita is a Pampered Chef consultant does not astound me in the least. I've been to enough home-based parties to know that it takes a Chiquita personality to succeed in that type of thing. Which is exactly why I lasted only six months after signing on with Tupperware. But hey, the products I earned as a Tupperware demonstrator have gone to great use. Heaps of leftovers (not to mention mold) have seen the insides of those containers.

Due to the fact that Sylvie gave me a heads-up about the letter, it's clear we have both been invited to this "intimate gathering." Although it's pretty humorous to see "intimate" and "Reggie's Classy Diner" used in the same sentence.

I'm a little baffled about why Anita Langerak would invite Sylvie and me at all. Anita had never been a great pal of ours. In fact, I don't think I ever had more than a two-minute conversation with her. Unless you count the time she grilled me mercilessly about my brother, with whom she was utterly infatuated throughout high school.

Wait a minute—could it be? Did she invite me because of Zach? My thoughts venture into the uncharted territory of my brother and Anita Langerak as a couple. I shake my head. I can't envision it because it is the most ridiculous thought I've ever had, next to the one about me wolfing down cartons of Dibs while wearing a size four. I'm all for Zach finally finding Mrs. Right. Lord knows he could use a good woman in his life. But Anita Langerak? No way.

But wait. I frown and glance again at the signature. Anita is obviously married. So what would she want with my brother?

Never mind. I don't want to know.

A Christina-sounding scream rings out from upstairs, releasing me from further icky thoughts of Anita and Zach. It's not a window-shattering scream, so I know there isn't a killer loose on the second floor of my house. Since I'm working on taming my freak-outs, I head toward the stairs in a swift but calm manner. I refrain from bounding up the stairs two at a time with fear gripping my heart.

By the time I reach my daughter's bedroom, however, I wish I had.

7

If you have never been hated by your child,
you have never been a parent.
BETTE DAVIS

I feel like Princess Mulan in the middle of a fierce battle.

Christina stands on her bed, Daffy Duck slippers looking oddly out of place, *Seventeen* magazine in her outstretched hand. The pose reminds me of a ninja preparing to strike. Her blue-green eyes are the size of two six-person hot tubs and almost as watery. "Where'd it go?"

Emily stands on a nearby chair. "Get it, Mommy! Get the spider! But don't kill it, okay? Put it in a jar and let it outside." Her lip quivers.

My heart quickens. *Arachnophobia* is my middle name. For a second, the temptation to hop up onto the chair with Emily is overpowering. Then I remember—I am the mom. I'm supposed to be brave enough to kill a spider with a single tissue instead of a roll of paper towels, a twenty-pound book, or an entire can of Raid.

But Emily is here. Only God knows how she can be deathly afraid of spiders and protective of them at the same time. The last time I squashed a spider in her presence, she cried about it for weeks.

"She can't let it outside, spider-hugging freakazoid," Christina snaps at Emily. "It's twenty degrees. It would die. But then again, it's going to die anyway!" Without taking her eyes off the floor, The Mouth, also known as my oldest daughter, throws a high-pitched, sarcastic comment my way: "Do you think you could get up here a little slower next time? Now it got away."

Which is exactly the reason I wish I had bounded up those stairs. The ugly little sucker might have been dead already. Then again, maybe not. Because of the arachnophobia thing.

At the risk of making light of my marital situation, I have to say that Richard would come in handy right about now. He is one of those courageous men who can squash a spider with his bare hand and not even go into a seizure-like shudder. Amazes me every time.

"Are you just going to stand there?" Christina whips her head in my direction and swipes at the imaginary spider on her shoulder.

What would Mulan do? She would march forward in pursuit of her enemy, that's what. I scan the floor, then take a step forward. This is good. I'm making progress, even though my heart is thump-thumping against my chest so loudly I can barely hear Christina whimpering.

Or maybe the whimpering is coming from me.

I find my voice. "Okay, this is ridiculous. We are a million times bigger than a little spider." My attempt at confidence falls flat. If I really meant it, I would be on my hands and knees, shaking blankets and peering inside the four pairs of shoes strewn under Christina's bed instead of standing here like a big, fat chicken. Imagine—scared of something probably as large as my fingertip. I might start clucking at any moment.

"It's not some tiny thing, Mom. It was big, black, and hairy. Very hairy," Emily states, hands planted on her hips. "But that still doesn't mean we should kill it. You're not going to kill it. Right, Mommy? Even if it's hairy?"

It's hard to believe it is a big, black, hairy spider. Not in Michigan, anyway. Our winter spiders tend to be brownish-white, almost translucent. Not hairy. And typically not large. Still…the thought is enough to hold my legs in place.

"Max!" Christina starts screaming for her brother.

"Christina, don't holler for Max. I can handle this."

"Uh, Mom? No offense, but standing there glued to the floor is not 'handling' it. The stupid spider's probably crawled to Emily's room by now."

I glance at Em, whose eyes look like they are about to pop out of her head. She starts to whine. "I don't want a spider in my room!"

"Quit crying," Christina demands. "How are we supposed to find the spider with you making all that noise?"

As if we might miss the sound of the spider making its getaway.

"What's the problem up here? Geesh, I could hear you all the way from the basement." Max speaks from the doorway. That he could hear Christina's mouth from the basement could mean two things: either my son has excellent hearing abilities, or my daughter has powerful vocal chords.

I choose number two.

"Mom is afraid of the spider." Christina rolls her eyes while maintaining her ninja stance.

Max laughs. "Good thing she's got such a brave daughter, then."

I grin.

Christina glares.

"Where is it?" Max passes me and gets on his hands and knees in search of the nasty little intruder. I have never been more thankful that Max inherited his father's fearless warrior tendencies.

"It was right there on the floor, and now it's gone." Christina makes a sudden leap off the bed in my direction, apparently attempting to distance herself from the spider that has likely already made its way to a dark corner somewhere. I flinch, waiting for her ninja sword to pierce my side. Instead, her real weapon, the *Seventeen* magazine, smacks me in the head.

"Ow!"

Christina doesn't offer an apology. She is too preoccupied with escaping the grasp of her evil opponent, Big Black Hairy Spider.

"Found it. It's on the baseboard." He grabs the torn photo of Blake from Christina's nightstand and smashes it against the spider.

Emily wails.

Max smiles and triumphantly holds out the paper, now decorated with brown spider guts, for all to see.

"Ew! Mom! Max smashed Blake's face into a spider!" Christina screeches.

Emily struggles to catch her breath. "He...k-killed...it!"

Max shrugs at Christina. "You guys broke up anyway. You should thank me. The jerk got what he deserves."

"We broke up, but that doesn't mean I want his face covered in spider guts!" Christina is still shouting two octaves above her normal pitch. Makes me cringe.

"Christina, stop. Max, take a tissue and wipe off Blake's face. Emily, come here, sweetie."

Emily hops off the chair, runs into my arms, and buries her face in my sweater.

"I am so not sleeping up here tonight." Christina tentatively reaches for her pillow and shakes it before hugging it to her chest. She storms out.

Max sets the photo back on Christina's nightstand. I can see from where I'm standing that Blake's face is still slightly smudged.

"I say he deserves more than spider guts. The jerk." Max glares at the photo. Aw, despite all of his teasing, it's obvious Max feels protective of his sister. The thought is deeply touching.

"I won't argue with you on that one, honey. But you could have as easily grabbed a tissue. The box was right next to you."

Max's eyes twinkle. "It all happened so fast..." He shrugs.

Now it's my turn to shake my head. It wasn't very nice of Max to use

Blake's photo to squish the spider, but I can't help feeling—to a certain degree at least—that justice has been done.

There's no denying I'm more than relieved that Max found the spider and pummeled it to death. I mean, I'm aware there are probably dozens more where that one came from, but knowing they are there, and actually *knowing* they are, are two completely different things. I can't blame Christina for heading downstairs to the couch. I've been known to do the same after seeing a spider in my bedroom. Even after Richard smushed it and flushed it down the toilet.

"Mommy?" Emily sniffs. "Do spiders go to heaven?"

I look down at my daughter, whose eyes are red and lips are trembling. I want to tell her what she wants to hear. I want to assuage the guilt she probably feels for standing by while a living creature—however icky it might be—was bludgeoned not six feet away. I want to assure her that what Max did wasn't murder, per se; he was simply doing his part to control the spider population. But the words won't come. And, before I can stop myself, I blurt out, "Oooh. I hope not."

Because how fun could heaven be with spiders lurking under every gold brick on the road?

Emily starts to cry again. Max drops his jaw and frowns at me like I'm the meanest mother in the world. As if he's not the one who caused Em's pain and suffering in the first place by squashing the eight-legged monster.

Max turns a sympathetic gaze toward Emily, then entices her into forgiving him for the part he played in the spider's untimely death by offering her a giant bowl of Candy Confetti ice cream. And, lo and behold, at the mention of ice cream, Emily's tears miraculously dry up. She totally takes after me. Ice cream does the trick every time.

Emily doesn't even look at me as she follows her brother out of the room to retrieve her bribe.

I sigh. Even after fifteen years, sometimes I can't get the hang of this motherhood thing.

As I brush my teeth and remove my makeup, I think again about the invitation from Anita Langerak. With that thought, I yawn—my body's way of telling me to sleep on the idea of getting together with people who have barely crossed my mind in twenty years, and also let dreamland extinguish any persistent (and yucky) thoughts about my brother and Anita Chiquita hooking up.

Tomorrow is Thursday, and I am meeting Sylvie for our weekly ten o'clock coffee date at Beanie's Coffee Café. Once loaded up on caffeine and sugar, I will be better able to process this whole reunion thing. That is, after Sylvie grills me incessantly about where things stand with Richard.

An audible moan escapes as my head hits the pillow. I say a prayer that the images of dancing banana-nosed children with my brother's face will not follow me to my dreams.

♛

My breaths are coming in short, heavy bursts. No doubt about it—I've got to start exercising more. Being outrun by a bunch of bananas is not acceptable. I may be pushing forty, but still.

Suddenly, my feet are killing me. No wonder—I'm wearing stilettos. Make that, one stiletto. My other foot is bare. Oh, no. I'm Cinderella! Not only have I lost a stiletto, I have to get home before midnight, or my brother will marry Anita Chiquita and make lots of little banana babies.

Sarah Price appears in front of me in a light blue fairy-godmother gown and snakeskin boots. She pumps her wand in the air. "You can do it, Madi! Just a little farther! Remember, you're a princess!" Her voice is gentle, encouraging...I pick up the pace.

The clock starts chiming. Dong...dong...dong...dong...

Someone is standing next to Sarah. Oh great. It's the Wicked Witch, holding a poisonous apple. Doesn't she know this is Cinderella's story and not Snow White's? Oh, wait. It's not the Wicked Witch. It's Mom! She shakes a finger. "You might as well quit right now, Madi Lee. You'll never make it. And you're right. Your husband did cheat! He's a big, fat cheater-pants, that's what he is. Don't you ever forget it!"

Dong...dong...

"Don't listen to her, Madi. You are a princess. You can do anything you set your mind on. Stay positive!" Sarah stretches out her hand. I focus on her fingers, knowing if I can grasp them, all will be well.

Dong...dong....dong...

Then, before my eyes, Sarah transforms into Fawn Witchburn.

"You're no princess at all, Madi! You're only a poor peasant girl. Prince Charming is mine...all mine!" She breaks off in a fit of evil laughter.

"I AM a princess!" I shout. "I am not listening to you!" I stick my fingers in my ears. "La la la la la la la la la..."

(Muffled) Dong...dong...dong...dong...

And I'm there! I'm home! And just in time, too. My mother and Sarah have disappeared, and there will be no banana nieces and nephews for me! I raise my hands in celebration.

The clock sounds again, and with groggy disappointment, I realize it is no clock at all. It's the phone ringing in my ear. I peer at the real clock on my nightstand, red numbers glowing in the dark: 11:58.

P.m.?

It slowly dawns on me that I've been sleeping for only an hour. I groan.

All my kids are safe in their beds, so I'm thinking either it's a wrong number or Sylvie. Sylvie is the only person I know who is both a morning person and a night owl. I swear that woman gets by on no more than four hours of sleep a night.

I grab the receiver before the answering machine has a chance to pick up. "Hello."

"Oh, did I wake you?" Sylvie asks innocently, as if after thirty years she doesn't know my typical bedtime is between ten and eleven.

"You interrupted my celebration." My voice comes out thick and hoarse. "No Chiquita babies in my future."

There's a pause. "I'll pretend I know what that means."

"What do you want?"

"You never called me back, missy. I've been worried about you."

I exhale. "I'm fine. I promise to fill you in tomorrow morning when we've got hefty doses of caffeine with huge dollops of whipped cream in front of us. Okay?"

"Deal." She pauses, and I sense there's something else on her mind. "So, did you get a chance to read your mail?"

Another groan. "Yes, I got the invitation. And no, I'm not interested in going."

"Oh." Her voice is laced with displeasure.

"Sorry, Sylv, but rehashing old times with people we used to mock behind their backs doesn't sound all that exciting to me."

"You have to admit it would be interesting to see what they've been up to after all these years," she points out.

Sometimes I wonder how Sylvie and I can be best friends. She is ever the social butterfly. I, the recluse, would rather stay holed up in my office and play hours of computer Solitaire. I suppose we balance each other out that way. She brings me out of my shell, and I restrain her from venturing too far out of hers.

"We'll talk about it in the morning. I'll see you at Beanie's."

"Ten o'clock sharp," she reminds me, as if I'm a ninety-year-old with Alzheimer's.

I toss and turn all night and my alarm goes off way too soon, but I have to get up and get the kids off to school. Well, Em, anyway. Christina and Max can pretty much manage dressing themselves and pouring their own cereal in a bowl. Emily can, too, although she still asks me to brush her hair and get her breakfast. I'll admit I don't mind babying her a bit.

When the kids are out the door, I down a huge mug of coffee and hop—okay, drag myself—into the shower. Before closing the shower curtain, my eyes are magnetically forced to my Bible, sitting in the basket next to the toilet. It may seem gross and maybe even a bit irreverent to keep a Bible next to the toilet, but reading God's Word while soaking in the tub relaxes me. However, I haven't opened my Bible since Rich left. Now it taunts me. As does the thin layer of dust sticking to the cover—a blatant reminder that nothing has been cleaned since my husband left. I'd rather focus on cleaning the house than my heart, so I decide to give the furniture a quick dusting and maybe even run the vacuum before leaving to meet Sylvie for lattes.

After dressing and doing my hair, however, the computer calls my name. Unable to resist, I sit down and check my e-mail. One from Richard jumps out at me. The subject line reads, *Please take to me.* I assume he means, *Talk to me.* His typing has never been any good. I maneuver the arrow so it hovers over the message title. I swiftly move to the *Delete* button and click it before I can change my mind. I'm in no mood to hear what he has to say.

I sign off the Internet and onto My Games for a quick hand of Solitaire. An hour and nine games later, it's time to go. I toss a fishie treat to Charlie, grab my purse, and head out the door, calling over my shoulder to the dust bunnies that the carrots are in the fridge.

8

A true friend is one who thinks you're a good egg,
even if you are half-cracked.
AUTHOR UNKNOWN

Beanie's parking lot is bustling and jammed with SUVs and luxury company vehicles. Typically, Beanie's is the place where bosses send their secretaries on coffee runs, business people sit with their laptops and hip moms meet for cappuccinos after dropping the kids at school.

Sylvie would fit into two of those categories: Hip Moms and Business People. Totally put-together and happening mom is an understatement for Sylvie Williams. Just ask her two boys, Sage and Ryder, whose classmates regularly tell them how lucky they are to have such a hot mom. So "ew" to them—she is their mother, after all—but so ego-boosting for a woman pushing forty.

The Business Person category is also suiting. Sylvie works as a professional makeup artist/skin consultant for Royal Rejuvenation, a national Spa chain. Finding herself a widow at thirty, Sylvie put herself through Frederico's School of Esthetician, with a little help from her beaucoup-bucks stepfather. She worked her way up to become South Haven's beauty go-to girl and has made quite a name for herself.

As for me fitting into Beanie's patron categories? Well, unless you count my mom administrative duties, Business Person doesn't quite fit. If I land a job soon, however, that may change.

I like to think I fit into the latter category: Hip Mom. I may not be as put together or as "hot" as Sylvie, but hey, I try.

Outside my windshield, it's starting to snow again. The wind is gaining momentum, causing the snow to stick to the cars like powder to doughnuts. Ugh. Parking at the farthest point from the door and walking a hundred miles across the parking lot in this blustery weather, even if it is for the oh-so-yummy Snickerdoodle latte, does not appeal to me.

Maybe I won't have to. An elderly man is getting into his car near the door, and I wait patiently in my burgundy Dodge minivan for him to leave so I can snag his space. A blue sports car that has no business being out in the snow whips around the corner. The bleached-blonde behind the wheel spots the pending open space, too. I flick my turn signal to claim my spot. The woman scowls and presses on the accelerator. I can't help smirking. "I saw it first. Na, na, na, boo-boo."

The old man is taking his sweet time. I see him struggling with his seat belt and am stung with a pang of compassion. I so don't want to get old.

Sylvie's black Buick is coming toward me ,and she pulls up next to my car, window to window.

I do a double take. "Oh, Sylvie—it's you! I could have sworn Nicole Kidman was driving your LaCrosse." And Angelina Jolie is driving my minivan.

Sylvie laughs. "It's uncanny, isn't it?" She smooths the back of her new red bob, then nods toward the building. "This is crazy. Did you see the line inside? I don't mind a short wait, but standing in line for an hour isn't how I want to spend my morning off."

I follow her gaze. A zillion people are crowded into the thirty-square-foot area by the counter, pressed together like the ants I found on a half-eaten chocolate bar I unearthed in Max's room last summer.

Sylvie continues, "I think there's some business thing going on. Should we try somewhere else?"

"How about The Golden Brown Bakery Café, over on Phoenix?" I suggest.

"Sure. I'll meet you there." She flips her new auburn locks and drives away.

The old man is adjusting his rearview mirror and running his windshield wipers. I take off, passing the blue sports car that is making its second lap around the building. The woman quickly turns on her signal. I look up at my rearview mirror and notice the man is starting to back out. Wouldn't you know...

My eyes linger a fraction too long on the rearview mirror and by the time I refocus my gaze on the windshield, there's something in front of my van. I gasp and slam on the brakes, the seatbelt cutting into my shoulder.

A man dressed all in black jumps back, then composes himself to glare at me.

But wait. It's not a man. It's my brother-in-law.

We recognize each other at the same time. His glare softens into something like a smirk. I want to crawl into the back seat of my van and start hunting for my gloves—or anything—to avoid talking to Raymond.

But it's too late. Ray now stands at my window and makes the signal with his hand, silently telling me to roll down the window. He's a car salesman. He should know my windows are automatic.

I hesitate, hoping a vehicle will pull up behind me and I'll have an excuse to move my van. And then I'll keep going—right out of the parking lot. But suddenly the Beanie's parking lot has gone from bustling to lifeless. I push the button, and my window slides down.

"I know you want me dead, Mads, but I didn't think you'd try to kill me with so many witnesses around." The smirk grows.

"I definitely should have stomped on the accelerator, not the brake."

"Honest mistake. You are a woman driver, after all. It's easy to mix up those pedals."

I grit my teeth.

"So…are you meeting Rich?" He snaps his fingers. "Oh, that's right, I forgot. You're having marital problems."

"Good one, Ray. Why Rich would choose to move in with you, though, is beyond me."

"Looks as though Rich is beyond you, too."

"Hey, Ray? Can you move back to the front of the van for a sec?"

He chuckles. "Have a good day, Madi." With that, he strides off toward the entrance, where Miss Bleached-Blond-Sports-Car-Driver is waiting. Figures. The blonde gives me the evil eye before grabbing hold of Ray's arm.

He's all yours, sweetheart.

The Golden Brown Bakery is much less crowded, only a few cars parked on the street outside the front door. More of a mom's kind of place, where screaming babies and sweat pants far outnumber the laptops and business suits. I pull into a spot between Sylvie's LaCrosse and a van identical to my own.

The Golden Brown Bakery serves the best pastries in the state, and I'm thinking of splurging. Gotta remember to do some stair-climbing later.

Sylvie is waiting for me inside. She glances at her watch. "What took you so long?"

"On my way out of Beanie's parking lot, I ran into Ray. Literally."

She gives me a sympathetic look. "I'm sorry."

"Not as sorry as I am." So cliché. But so true.

We stand at the counter and order our coffee. I add a cinnamon roll to my order, not because they are so delicious I am practically salivating as I see a fresh batch on a tray, right out of the oven. And not because I am so weak-willed I couldn't resist. I merely don't want to drink coffee on an empty stomach.

Yeah, right. I almost convince myself.

Big surprise, Sylvie bypasses the cinnamon roll and grabs an orange from the fruit bowl on the counter. Hence, the reason she is a size four and I am...not.

Trying to balance my cinnamon roll on top of my coffee cup, I plod along behind Sylvie, who is *click-clacking* away in her black suede Gabriella Rocha boots, to a table next to the window. Not one to waste time, she sets down her coffee and orange, then rummages through her purse, pulling out the letter she received from Anita Chiquita.

"So, are we going?" Her caramel-colored eyes are sparkling. This is a new adventure for her, and she is anxious to begin. Sylvie thrives on anything new, interesting, and potentially exciting. I, not so much. To me, change is like going to the dentist. You know it has to happen and it's for your own good, but you put it off as long as possible.

"Sylv, please. Can I take some sips of my coffee before talking about this ridiculous letter-slash-Pampered Chef solicitation?"

Her brown eyes soften and the sparkle disappears. "I'm sorry. Could I be any more selfish?" She grasps my hand, studying my face. "What's going on with you? Are you okay?"

"Don't the bags under my eyes say it all?"

"Haven't been getting your seven hours, huh?" She frowns.

I resist injecting a sarcastic comment about how I might have gotten seven hours last night except for the midnight phone call.

"When you get home this afternoon, place a couple slices of raw potatoes over your eyes for ten minutes. You'll be amazed at the results. Those bags will disappear just like that." She snaps her fingers. Beauty tips roll off Sylvie's tongue like decorating tips off Martha Stewart's. It's more a habit than anything else; she can't help herself.

"The only potatoes I have at my house come in a box. Do you think dumping heapfuls of flakes over my eyelids would work?" I pull my hand away. I'm dying to dig into my cinnamon roll. Forking off a large chunk, I shove it into my mouth and concentrate on not moaning. It really is that good.

"So spill it. What's going on?" She remains focused on my face as she digs a nail into the orange peel. A stream of juice squirts onto the table and Sylvie dabs a napkin over it.

"Rich moved in with Ray."

Sylvie's eyes widen. "What? Why? What happened?"

I fill her in on the events from the last couple of days.

"So you haven't sat down and talked to him about the lipstick?"

"No. Unless you call blowing spit bubbles at him in Fred's parking lot 'talking.'"

She raises her eyebrows. "Okay....don't think I want to know what that means. But, come on, Mads. Give the poor guy a chance to explain himself."

I slam my fork down a little too hard and a chunk of icing from my cinnamon roll is airborne. In slow motion, I watch as it *kerplunks* into a perfectly coifed head of blue hair. The woman puts a hand to her head, and I quickly look away. Normally I'd laugh, but right now I'm more focused on my best friend defending my husband.

"He cheats on me and you refer to him as a 'poor guy'? Please tell me I have too much wax in my ears and heard you wrong."

She puts on her innocent face. "I'm only saying...what if he didn't really cheat? You know Fawn. She's been around town so many times her nickname should be 'the city bus.' You're telling me you believe that woman over your husband of eighteen years?"

She has a point. Fawn Witchburn is not exactly the credible type. Rumor has it she proclaimed affairs with three married men from church that she later admitted did not happen. Two of those marriages ended in divorce and, last I heard, the third one is on the brink.

The saddest part is the example Fawn is setting for her daughter. Lexi is nine, the same age as Emily. They go to different schools, but know each other from Sunday school classes. The girl is messed up. One Sunday after church, Emily asked me what a "ho" was. After I got past the shock, I asked her where on earth she heard that word. Emily said Lexi told her she overheard her mother's boyfriend call her mom "a stupid ho" during an argument.

All righty, then.

I quickly explained to Emily that a hoe was a garden tool and told her no, I didn't know why he didn't call her a normal garden tool name like shovel.

As Lexi's fourth-grade teacher, Richard has witnessed a few behavioral issues. He says Lexi has seen the school counselor more times than my mother has been to her psychiatrist. I'm no mathematician, but that's a lot of counseling sessions.

I lean over the table and lower my voice. "Those lip-shaped, chocolate-colored marks on Rich's shirt don't lie."

"I think it's called 'russet roulette.'"

"Quit with the beauty stuff, okay?"

"Sorry." She sits back in her chair and plays with her orange, then sets it on the table and grabs my hand. "Mads, we've always been honest with each other, right?"

I narrow my eyes and wait for it.

"Hate me if you want, but I have to bring this up again." She pauses, as if weighing her words. "I'm well aware that I have insecurities of my own, so I'm not trying to sound like Miss Know-It-All. Neither of us had great role models for marriage. But your mom..." She shakes her head. "Your mom instilled some ideas in you that you can't seem to shake. Ideas about men. Your mother loves you—in her own way—but she did you a huge disservice by convincing you that men aren't trustworthy. That isn't true. I mean, my father wasn't exactly honorable either, but then Ike came along and proved to me that all men are not the same. There *are* good guys in the world, Mads." She brushes a wisp of hair from her eyes. "You and Rich have dealt with this issue time and time again. Your suspicions and accusations over the years have always proved to be unfounded. And Rich has stuck by you for eighteen years. He's one of those good guys. So, no. I don't believe he cheated on you. Not before, and not now. Your insecurities are destroying your marriage. You need to deal with this stuff once and for all."

I can't stop the tears. They come tumbling out, unbidden. I know she's right. Not necessarily about the cheating, because something in me is convinced he's been unfaithful. But Sylvie's right about needing to deal with it. In a weird way, I think it might be easier if I find out Rich is having an affair. At least then I can say, "Aha—I told you. It's not all in my head!" I could deal with it and move on. Confronting the demons within me, however, will take much longer and require a whole new level of energy.

I reach for a napkin and wipe my cheeks. "I appreciate your thoughts, Sylv. I really do. But I'm not in the mood to talk about Richard or my marriage or deal with my deep emotional issues right now. Right now, I want to enjoy my cinnamon roll, pump myself full of caffeine, and talk about this little reunion thing."

It's a sad day when I'd rather talk about high school classmates with names like Anita Chiquita than my marriage.

Noticing Sylvie's frown, I murmur, "I *will* deal with it, okay? But not right now. Come on, you've been dying to talk about this reunion. You know you have."

"Let me know when you're ready to talk about your marriage, Mads. You know I'm here for you." She squeezes my hand.

"I know." I take a moment to look at my friend of thirty years. Like

Sylvie's hair color, we've experienced a lot of changes together. This is simply another one to add to the list.

"So let's talk about next Friday. Do you really want to go to this thing?" I blink away the remaining moisture and reach for the invitation, sliding it to the middle of the table. I can't help noticing the sparkle returning to Sylvie's eye as she scans the letter from Anita.

"My sister invited Sage and Ryder over for the weekend. It's been awhile since they've spent time with their cousins, and they're excited about it. Which means I'll have the night free. It might be fun, you know. And it could be what you need to get your mind off...things...and let loose a little bit."

I ponder this for a moment. "I have a serious question, Sylv."

Her forehead creases in concern. "What is it?"

"Do you think Anita Chiquita's nose has grown back to its original size?"

Sylvie giggles. "Let's hope not. There may not be room for everyone at the table."

"So why do you think we were invited, anyway? Well, I know why *you* were invited. I mean, who can pass up the chance to socialize with the now-famous Sylvie Williams? The Sylvie Williams who has performed spa services for Lady Gaga, four *American Idol* finalists, and an assortment of celebrities passing through town on concert tours? I'm probably invited by association alone."

Sylvie pooh-poohs me. She doesn't blush often, but a hint of pink spreads across her cheeks.

"Then again, maybe I was invited so Anita can grill me about Zach."

"Zach?" Sylvie raises an eyebrow and tears off a piece of her orange.

"Don't you remember what a huge crush she had on Zach in high school? But he wasn't into the perky, cheerleader-type like her. He went for the punk rocker girls, like Miranda Barr. Remember Randi? She wanted to be called 'Iron Girl' and wore fifty chains around her neck and a huge silver nose ring." I laugh. "So shudder-worthy."

"Hmmm." Sylvie looks off into space and rests her chin on her hand.

"Anita's married now, you know—or was, anyway, if her last name is any indication. But I'll bet you a chocolate bar that she asks how Zach is doing within sixty seconds of saying hello. She had it bad for my brother."

"I thought you were giving up chocolate."

"I am. Starting tomorrow." I think about the full carton of Dibs in my freezer, then glance at my empty plate. "Giving up cinnamon rolls, too."

For the next fifteen minutes, we talk about what we'll wear and who might be included in the intimate, "lucky" guest list of twenty-five. I'll admit it is kind of fun to rehash old times, although some of them I'd like to forget. Sylvie brings up the time I wasn't feeling well and ended up barfing all over Mr. Haskins, my drop-dead-gorgeous eleventh-grade English teacher. I was mortified back then but am now smiling at the memory.

"You gave new meaning to the term *lovesick.*" Sylvie smiles.

"I think *lust-sick* was more like it. Remember what we used to say? 'When Mr. Haskins rules, girls drool'?" This reminds me of the T-shirt Emily wore today that says *Girls Rule, Boys Drool.* Probably due to my emotions being all over the place, this strikes me as hilarious, and I start laughing uncontrollably. The old woman behind Sylvie cranks her head again, shoots me a sour look, which only makes me laugh harder. My hilarity seems to be catchy—Sylvie starts giggling, too.

As our laughter fades, Sylvie puts on her serious face and plays with the last section of her orange. "Hey, Mads, there's something I need to talk to you about."

"So you've said. I sure hope you're not considering changing your hair color again. The Nicole thing you've got going on is adorable." I smile.

This time, Sylvie doesn't mirror my lead. Her mood remains sober. "It's nothing like that." Her gaze wanders out the window.

"Okay…"

Sylvie is in la-la-land. She stares vacantly for several seconds until finally I wave a hand in front of her face. She doesn't flinch, but her lips draw tight. I follow her gaze, squinting into the bright snow.

Across the street, next to his Ford Explorer, stands my husband, Richard. And not two feet away from him is Fawn Witchburn.

9

When life hands you lemons,
Toss them to Claudia Boeve and reach for the Dibs.
ME, WHEN I'M HAVING A BAD DAY

My first thought: *How can Richard humiliate me like this?*

My second thought: *I need another cinnamon roll.*

As I stare out the frosty window through the snow, I feel like my mother. Lord help me, I know. But what I mean is, for the first time in my life, I can identify with her. How she felt when she found out my dad was cheating on her. The times when she saw him with another woman. Why she is the way she is. I can even understand why, afterwards, she turned bitter and cold, unloving.

Okay, maybe not that. Because no matter what Richard does to me, I would never withhold love from my kids. I would rather die than have them feel unloved by me.

I am not my mother. But today I can relate to her more than ever before.

Sylvie turns toward me, her brows knit in a V. She opens her mouth, then closes it again. You know it's bad when Sylvie is speechless.

"Yep, it's all in my mind, isn't it?" I snap. My heart rate quadruples, and I can't tear my eyes away from the window for more than two seconds. I watch as Fawn touches Richard's arm. He pulls away but doesn't get into his car.

I say a prayer. I ask God to supernaturally turn my husband around, shove him into the car, turn the key, and gun it, leaving Fawn in the dust—or at least in a pile of muddy snow that his tires kick up as he squeals away. That would be the only thing that might cause me to wonder if his pleas of innocence might be true. The operative word here being *might*.

But he doesn't. He stands there like a trained monkey and listens as Fawn flaps that chocolate-pudding-colored mouth of hers. Her arms follow suit as they thrash in the air, clearly trying to convey or convince or at least make her point, whatever that may be.

I desperately want to jump up from this table and march outside to confront them both. But the truth is, I don't have the confidence or the energy to go up against Fawn Witchburn. Or my husband, for that matter. So I masochistically sit and watch the scene play out, my emotions running rampant.

Sylvie tries to help by reaching up to pull the blinds on the window.

"Don't even think about it," I hiss.

She drops her arm to the table in defeat. "Mads..."

I ignore my friend and, with concentrated determination, will Richard to get in his car and leave.

Lo and behold, it works! My husband makes his way around to the driver's side and gets into the car. Fawn is standing there, black leather-gloved hands that moments ago were flailing through the air now stilled and positioned on perfectly shaped hips.

A spark of hope ignites in my heart. God is answering my prayer. I wait for the engine to start and the snow to fly onto Fawn's white sheepskin coat and matching UGG boots.

Then I watch as the passenger window slides down. Richard says something to Fawn. She opens the door and climbs in. He backs the car up and takes off.

The spark of hope flickers and dies. My heart has been smashed like the spider Max squashed yesterday against Christina's wall.

Sylvie tries her best to offer words of comfort. Her mouth is moving, but the words don't register in my brain.

Suddenly I'm sitting at the kitchen table again. Mom is angry—no, furious—and spewing horrible things about my father. He has hurt her badly, and she wants to lash out. Since I'm the only one there, she treats me like a best friend or her counselor instead of a daughter. She doesn't merely complain about my father cheating, she spills all the sordid details of his sexual indiscretions. Details a daughter has no business knowing about her dad.

I bite my lip to keep it from quivering.

"Madi?" Sylvie's voice interrupts my thoughts and I blink several times. "Do you want to leave?"

Leave. Yes. I need to get out of here. I push myself away from the table and huff toward the door, not even bothering to pull on my jacket.

Once outside, I hop into my van and drop my head to the steering wheel with a *thunk.*

Breathe in. Breathe out. In. Out.

"Yea, though I walk through the valley of the shadow of death..." For

some reason, this verse pops into my head. I do feel like I'm walking through Death Valley. The hottest place next to hell—right here on Earth. Yep. That's exactly where I am. And it certainly doesn't feel like I'm going *through* it. The tent has been pitched. Two days and counting…

I want to cry. But this time the tears won't come. For now, anger overpowers my tear ducts.

The minute I think it, I make a fist and smack the dashboard. That felt pretty good.

So I do it again. And again. Hey, it's my van. And it's not like I'm Arnold Schwarzenegger and will punch holes through my dash. I'm not even making a dent, in fact. Except maybe in my hand. It's starting to throb. I've got to remember to look for my gloves, still under the seat somewhere.

A loud knock on the window startles me. Sylvie.

But it's not Sylvie. It's that woman from the table behind us. The lemon-sipping one with the puckery lips, permanent lines set in her forehead, and a chunk of cinnamon roll in her blue hair. Is it my imagination, or does she look even more crotchety than before?

The woman is pointing to the door. "Unlock the door!"

Okay, now she's really getting on my nerves. Her crankiness may have been funny minutes ago in the restaurant, but not so much anymore.

I pop the lock and swing open the door. The woman scrambles out of the way as she didn't wear her ice skates and probably isn't interested in getting flung across the slippery pavement and landing on her rear.

"What is your problem, lady?" I step down out of the van. It's not normal for me to be so confrontational and direct, but whoever said I am normal, anyway?

"I'm going to call the police." Only she isn't reaching into her bag for a cell phone. Probably doesn't even have one.

"You're going to call the police? You're the one harassing me! I'm minding my own business, trying to have a quiet moment in my van. You've been giving me the evil eye since we sat at the table behind you. I should be the one—"

Click-clack. Click-clack.

Momentary distraction. I look over to see Sylvie carefully stepping her way across the sidewalk, making a knife-slicing motion across her neck with her finger. I frown. What is she saying? Is she warning me that the woman is a serial killer? The blue-haired, crotchety, serial killer?

"That's *my* van you…you…crazy woman!" A purse the size of a cement truck comes barreling out of nowhere and smacks me on the arm. As my body is forced sideways, my foot catches an ice patch, and I'm airborne. I land with a thud on the ground, pain slicing into my right butt cheek. A moment later, my own purse, which the woman has retrieved from the front seat, clunks my leg and the contents spill out onto the pavement.

Stunned, I sit there on the cold, icy cement. The woman is now inside her van and glares at me through the window, mouth still looking as if she just finished the world's most sour Skittle. She backs up and takes off, nearly running over my foot.

"Are you okay?" Sylvie grabs my hand and hoists me up off the ground.

I struggle to maintain my footing while at the same time hold the tears at bay. In silence, Sylvie and I retrieve the scattered items from my purse, jamming them into random compartments that will have to be reorganized later. Despite the cold temperatures, my cheeks are burning.

"It looked like my van, Sylv. Same make, same color...it was an honest mistake." And don't forget that temporary insanity thing I had going on....

Sylvie pulls me in a hug. "I'll follow you home," she says, probably to make sure I don't decide, in a moment of utter despair, to drive off an icy embankment. I accept her offer, not because I'm worried about my suicidal tendencies, but because I don't want to go home to an empty house.

The afternoon goes by in a blur. Sylvie stays for a couple of hours and tries to get me to talk about what happened. But I've gotten pretty good at pushing aside bad thoughts and pretending everything is okay. Sooner or later, the time will come when I have to face my feelings and deal with them appropriately. But I prefer later. For now, I choose to talk about other things and Sylvie obliges. She even makes me laugh about the old lady incident, which is pretty funny in hindsight.

The conversation eventually returns to the reunion and, horror of horrors, by the time Sylvie leaves to make her 2:00 appointment, I find myself looking forward to the silly little get-together next weekend. As usual, my best friend is right. It will be good to get my mind off things, even if only for an evening.

I watch through the curtain slit as Sylvie backs out of the driveway. As soon as she's out of sight, I race to the freezer and yank out the carton of Edy's Dibs. If I've ever needed a reason to pig out on chocolate, this morning's event is it. And since I'm laying off chocolate and sweets starting tomorrow, I might as well finish what's left today. That way, there won't be any left in the house to tempt me.

The thought of temptation brings more unbidden visions of Richard and Fawn. I dwell on them as I finish off the Dibs. My thoughts venture into the dark territory of the *D* word. I always vowed I'd never end up like my parents. That no matter what obstacles my marriage faced, I would always plow through them and never—ever—consider divorce. But I'm thinking adultery is a tad more than just an obstacle. If I had any doubts about Rich cheating, they disintegrated today.

Okay, so Sylvie is right. I've never been the world's most secure person. I'll even go so far as to admit that, when Rich and I first got serious, I bordered on "jealous psychopath." If a girl showed Rich any interest, I knew he would fall under her spell and forget about me. I've had issues with his college lab partner, various coworkers he's had over the years, a couple women in the neighborhood, even the bank teller. In my defense, these women were all gorgeous and showed obvious interest in my husband.

The worst bouts of jealousy came during the first several years of our marriage. After a rocky five years, God grabbed hold of both of our hearts. But my insecurities held on. I've gone through long periods where they didn't show up, but then popped up out of nowhere. Particularly after I've spent a bit of time with my mother, or during specific times of the month. But in the last several years, when doubts about Rich have surfaced, I've gotten better about openly sharing my feelings with him and, as a result, he has usually been able to put my mind at ease.

When Sylvie brought up the idea that maybe Richard is telling the truth, that maybe there is a valid explanation why my husband had chocolate lipstick marks on his shirt right after his parent-teacher conference with Ms. Witchburn, I wanted to entertain the idea. Embrace it, even. But seeing them across the street from The Golden Brown Bakery cinched it for me. Even if he's never cheated before, there is no doubt in my mind that he succumbed to temptation with Fawn. I am now the wife of an adulterer. I will probably soon be divorced. My children will be the victims of a broken home. I will gradually evolve into my mother.

Okay, shaking that last thought…

The carton of Dibs is empty, much to my displeasure. I forcefully slam-dunk it into the trash. I could easily give any pro-basketball player a run for his money. Granted, my "hoop" is closer to the ground, but hey, so am I.

I head to the computer to do what I always do when depressed, bored, or have some minutes to kill. Right now, Solitaire gives me something else to think about besides my cheating husband and his lover. Plus, I need to get my computer fix before the kids come home and hog it for themselves.

I can't resist checking my e-mail. Two jump out at me. Immediately, I click on the one from Sarah Price, my psychologist.

Hi, Madi,

I wanted to remind you that if you ever need to talk, don't hesitate to call or e-mail. I'd be happy to meet you for coffee or lunch. I'm here for you, not only as a counselor, but as a friend. No extra charge. I figure I charge enough for your normal office visits (smile).

Sarah

616-555-8790 (cell)

Ha! Ain't that the truth. I'm thankful Rich has excellent insurance. So I'm thinking some people would take advantage of Sarah's offer. Maybe even cancel the in-office appointments altogether and suddenly attempt to become best buds. But I'd never do that and Sarah knows it, hence, the probable reason she made the offer to give me a little extra counseling on the side.

And with all that has happened today, I could use some advice. I love Sylvie to death, but all she does is try to make me see things from Rich's perspective. I don't need that.

I grab the phone and dial Sarah's cell. It goes straight to voice mail. I leave a long-winded message, explaining what happened earlier at The Golden Brown Bakery. After leaving my cell number for her to call me back, I turn my attention to the second message in my e-mail inbox.

It's from Richard. This time the subject line reads, *I'm sorry*. Definitely deleting that one. Once it's gone, I regret it. Part of me wants to torture myself by seeing what he has to say. There's no way he knows I saw him with Fawn this morning, so his plea is most likely an extension of the one he tried to make in the grocery store parking lot.

But if I read it, I would feel compelled to reply and I refuse to dignify his "apology" with a response. Frankly, I'm not ready to deal with that yet. At least I can be thankful he sends typed (however badly) messages to my personal e-mail account instead of leaving voice mails on the answering machine where the kids might hear them.

Eerily, the phone rings. I screen the call and a nasally voice cuts into the silence of the kitchen. It's Kathy Stickler, Max and Christina's high school secretary. "Mrs. McCall, I am here in the office with Christina—"

I grab the phone off the hook. "Hello, I'm here."

"Oh, yes. Mrs. McCall. Uh, there's been an incident. Would you be able to come to the high school and speak with Ms. Jameson?"

The principal. She wants me to come and speak to the principal.

"Is Christina okay?" The only times I receive calls from the secretary are when my kids are sick or hurt, so I'm not holding out hope that the principal wants to personally inform me Christina won the "Student of the Year" award.

"She'll be fine. She's here with me now."

"Can I speak with her?"

Mrs. Stickler sighs rudely into the phone. A rustling follows.

"Mom?" Christina's voice cracks a bit.

"Honey, are you all right? What happened?"

"I'm fine. But please come right now, okay?"

"I'll be right there."

My mind goes into overdrive. I call Sandy Long, mother of Emily's best friend, Jessica, and arrange for Em to hitch a ride home with her. Then I dial the elementary school to let the office know Emily won't be riding the bus home today. I remember Max informed me this morning that he's catching a ride home from someone named Sam, a friend I've never heard of. I scribble a note telling him the girls and I will be home soon, then I dig through my purse for my keys for three whole minutes, only to finally find them in the very first pocket I'd searched.

Since princess slippers aren't practical today, I jump into my frumpy snow boots and I'm on my way.

10

You can learn many things from children…
how much patience you have, for instance.
FRANKLIN P. JONES

It usually takes about fifteen minutes to get to Lakeshore High but today, in spite of the snowy roads, I make it in ten minutes flat.

The halls are virtually empty, the last class of the day still in session for another—I check my watch—twenty minutes. My boots clunk their way along the shiny tiled floor.

I fling open the office door. There sits Christina, holding an ice pack to her eye. I gasp. What is this? Did she smack into a wall or a locker or something? Was there an accident in gym class?

Christina looks up at me with one eye. It starts to tear up. "I sort of got in a fight." Her voice is shaky, and her gaze wanders to the floor.

So much for the Klutzy Moment theory.

My heart swells for my sweet Christina, who is obviously the innocent victim of assault! What kind of barbarian would attack my daughter like this?

As I take a step forward to wrap my arms around my precious, wounded child, a dull moaning causes me to turn. There, several feet away, sits a girl I recognize as Paige Hardaway—*aka,* boyfriend stealer.

I can't hide my shock. Paige's pale blue shirt is stained with blood, a three-inch blob of red covering the two *L*s in Hollister. She holds a white— well, what used to be white—washcloth under her nose. Fresh scratches are visible on her bare forearms and her hair looks like it took on Hurricane Katrina and lost.

Deep inside my mind-socket, a light bulb flickers. As much as I don't want it to be true, the idea settles in my head that Paige might be the actual victim. Although I reason that, if Paige hadn't gone and kissed Blake in the first place…is it absurd to try to justify the fact that my daughter beat the pulp out of another human being?

Upon further inspection of my daughter, I note scratches on her arms as well, along with a doozy on her cheek. I do and I don't want to see underneath that ice pack. I am about to ask Christina to remove it when a husky voice sounds.

"Mrs. McCall."

I look up to see Ms. Jameson. "Look up" is an understatement. The woman is over six feet tall when she wears flats, not the three-inch chunky heels she is wearing today. She has on a smart, brown tweed skirt and jacket undoubtedly from the Big & Tall shop. The outfit, plus the straight line of her mouth, indicates that the principal is all business.

Smiling, I attempt to crack her stony exterior. "I hope you placed your bet on Christina."

Ms. Jameson does not smile back. "Follow me, please. Christina, you, as well." She turns and stalks off.

My daughter stands, and I place an arm protectively around her shoulder. As we make our way down the hall, I hear the office door burst open behind us. A strident voice I recognize as Celeste Hardaway sounds off. Great. She's going to make a fuss. I cringe as Paige starts bawling, and her mother threatens to sue.

Oh, boy.

Once inside Ms. Jameson's office, she motions for us to sit and takes her place behind a large oak desk. After shuffling some papers around, she pushes her red-framed glasses to the top of her silver-streaked head. I marvel that the woman is younger than I am. A box of Nice 'n' Easy would do her wonders.

"I'm sure you can guess what happened here today, Mrs. McCall. Christina, would you care to explain?"

"Not really," she mumbles. She slouches in her chair, glances at me nervously, and clears her throat. "I got into a fight with Paige Hardaway."

"Duh," I say, using one of Christina's favorite terms.

"Elaborate, please." Mrs. Jameson folds her hands.

Christina bites her lip and looks down at the floor.

"Answer, please."

I shoot a dirty look at the principal. I don't know Ms. Jameson all that well, but feelings of intense dislike toward her are rising up in me. No wonder her hair is so gray. The woman needs to lighten up.

"She provoked me." Christina straightens in the chair. The hand holding the ice pack comes down.

I can't help taking in a small gulp of air at the sight, although it's not quite as bad as I imagined. I had envisioned her eye completely sealed shut, skin puffed up to triple its size. I am relieved to find that although she sports a pretty good shiner, at least the kiwi green color is still visible. "It doesn't hurt that bad," Christina assures me.

"Anyway…" Ms. Jameson takes a long and obvious glance at her watch, clearly annoyed at the time it is taking to get to the point. She's probably got her granny undies in a bunch because she has yet to deal with Mrs. Hardaway. Can't say I blame her.

"How did Paige provoke you?" I ask my daughter.

"That is beside the point," Ms. Jameson interjects. "Striking a fellow student—"

I put up a hand. "Can we hear what Christina has to say? Please? I'd like to know the whole story."

The principal purses her waxy lips but remains silent.

I raise my eyebrows at Christina, encouraging her to continue.

"Paige cornered me in the girls' bathroom. She started saying things…" She glances at Ms. Jameson. "Nasty things."

Hmmm. How might Paige have provoked Christina? Could it possibly have to do with a certain boy named Blake?

Mrs. Jameson completely ignores Christina's account. "Mrs. McCall, we do not tolerate this kind of behavior at Lakeshore High. Fighting is strictly prohibited. You do understand we usually suspend students for fighting. In this case, I have decided to graciously allow an in-house suspension, so Christina will be more able to keep up with her schoolwork. But note, also, that the Hardaways have every right to press charges."

I return the principal's stare. "Do you have any sort of policy against name calling and harassment?"

"Of course. But this is physical assault, and Christina admitted to taking the first swing. She must be dealt with appropriately, and, as I mentioned, possibly even criminally."

"So Paige Hardaway won't be punished for her part in this? As you can see, Paige left a few distinguishing marks on my daughter, too." I clench my teeth and try to remain calm. Need to set a good example for my daughter.

"Being verbally provoked does not constitute an excuse for Christina physically assaulting another student. Miss Hardaway was only acting in defense."

Okay. So I'll give her that this is a little more serious than a verbal ping-pong match between two hormonal teenage girls. My sweet daughter scratched the tar out of someone, single-handedly drawing blood.

Richard and I have always taught our children to walk away from verbal attacks, but apparently we haven't done a good enough job. I am angry with Christina, yet part of me understands her inability to turn the other cheek.

For a moment I entertain thoughts of what I would do if Fawn Witchburn spewed venom at me. I don't consider myself a physically strong person, yet I suspect I could leave some distinguishing marks of my own. At the very least, I might be able to land a couple jabs in that chocolate pudding-colored mouth of hers.

"So how will Paige Hardaway be dealt with?" I ask. I happen to know that Paige's uppity mother, Celeste, besides being a pain in the neck, is a member of the school board. Her daughter will probably get off with a slap on the wrist.

"We will deal with Miss Hardaway accordingly."

"I bet you will," I say under my breath.

Ms. Jameson stands, towering over Christina and me. Not wanting to feel smaller than I already do, I quickly rise as well. At my prompting, Christina does the same, wincing in the process. Her eye once again disappears behind the ice pack.

"Christina will serve four days of in-house suspension, starting tomorrow and lasting through Wednesday of next week. This will bring us to midwinter break, which begins on Thursday. We will collect all of her work and expect her to complete it in the suspension room during school hours. My secretary, Mrs. Stickler, has a form for you to sign. And Christina." She turns her attention toward my daughter as she pulls her glasses back over her steely eyes. "I sincerely hope your mother encourages you to apologize to Miss Hardaway. You're fortunate you didn't break her nose."

And Christina is fortunate she's not blind in one eye.

It annoys me that Ms. Jameson is speaking about me to Christina like I'm not even in the room. With the day I've had, it takes every ounce of self-control to refrain from slapping her in the face to remind her.

Christina slides a glance in my direction. She's undoubtedly thinking ahead to the car ride home. What mother will she get today? The easy-going, cool mom or the psycho who flies off the handle?

Hard to tell.

We stop at Mrs. Stickler's desk and I take my time reading the form, which states that I am aware of Christina's in-house suspension, yada, yada, yada. Much to my relief, Paige and her mother are nowhere to be seen.

As we exit the office, I peripherally note that Christina is eyeing me again (with her good one), probably searching for some indication as to my emotional state. But I stare straight ahead and don't make eye contact with my daughter. I don't want to tip her off.

Besides, the verdict's still out as to which Madi I want to let loose.

To her credit, Christina keeps her mouth shut for five whole minutes. The inside of my lip is sore from chewing on it, but I'm not taking any chances. I don't trust myself to speak.

"Mom, quit biting your lip," Christina finally says.

"Would you rather I say something we'll both regret?"

"You're not going to tell Dad, are you?"

My laugh comes out more like a puff. "Sweetheart, unless your father had some kind of accident in the past two weeks where he's gone blind, there won't be any need to tell him anything."

"Oh, yeah, I guess my black eye will kind of give it away."

My daughter, the genius.

"I stuck up for you back there, Christina, but I'm angry. Give me some time to think about what I'm going to do about this whole thing."

Christina obeys for once and looks out the window.

We ride in silence for a couple of minutes until I can't resist any longer. "So what's up with the birth control thing?" I keep my eyes fixed on the road.

"Never mind. It was stupid."

"Honey, you don't say something like that without a reason. Have you...did you...are you...? "

"No, Mother. We didn't do it."

I expel a long breath I didn't realize I was holding. "But you've been thinking about it?"

No answer.

I glance over. "Christina?"

She avoids my gaze. "I told you, my periods are ridiculous. Tara and Jen's doctors prescribed them the pill, and they said it helped a ton. Barely any cramps at all."

How to answer? I swallow and breathe through my nose, attempting to slow my heart rate, which has doubled its pace. "Well, I don't know how I feel about that. You're not even sixteen. Allowing something like this would be like giving you a license to have sex. Which I will absolutely *not* do. You know our position on premarital sex. But more importantly, you know what God says about it."

"But my periods—"

"Is this really about your periods, Christina? I was a teenager once, too, remember? I know all about hormones. And sexual pressure. Is Blake pressuring you?"

Silence.

"He is, isn't he?"

Her shoulders rise in a slight shrug.

"Christina."

Nothing.

"Are your friends having sex?"

"Only two that I know of."

I can't help gasping. "Only two? That's a relief. Anyway, I thought you and Blake broke up."

"Blake said Paige came on to him. He said he loves me. And I love him." Pause. "Besides, Blake's not a virgin."

"And now that he's experienced sex, he can't be with someone who won't give him some? That's not love, Christina, that's manipulation." I try to keep an even tone, although I'm seething inside.

She sniffs, and I feel my anger give way to compassion.

"Honey, please be strong about this. You can only give away your virginity once. God has reserved a guy for you, I promise. If that guy is Blake, then he'll wait. And he definitely won't pressure you to do something you're not ready for. Look how upset you are *now*. If you have sex, it will only connect you and Blake more, complicating things even more. Trust me, there's a reason God designed sex for marriage."

Christina responds by focusing out the window again. I hope she's in the processing mode and truly considers my words. And better yet, God's Word.

Oy. Motherhood is not all it's cracked up to be.

I drive a couple of blocks past my street and turn down Honeybrook Lane to pick up Emily. She'll probably be bummed that she didn't get much, if any, time to play with Jessica after school. I consider inviting Jessica to our house to play for a while before dinner, but that thought flies out the window when I pull into the Longs' driveway.

Emily stands on the porch, shoulders hunched, purple backpack dragging on the ground. Jessica's mother, Sandy Long, crouches in front of her. I frown. What's up with that? The minute Emily spots my minivan pulling into the driveway she takes off running toward me. Sandy rises, turns around, and waves.

Emily runs so fast that she trips and is treated to a nice snow facial. She loses her grip on her backpack, and it soars through the air and into the slush.

Before I can open the door to rush out and see if she's okay, Emily jumps up like there's a colony of ants in her pants. She reaches the van in seconds and practically throws herself in and onto the seat.

I inspect her face. Not too much damage, other than being completely crimson from the cold. Nothing a warm washcloth won't cure. She's not crying, so I know it can't be that bad. I am taken aback, however, by the anger flashing in her eyes.

"Are you okay, honey?"

"Why did you call Jessica's mom to pick me up? Why couldn't you call Kelsey P.'s mom? I don't like Jessica anymore. Kelsey's my new best friend now." She slams her backpack onto the floor and chunks of slush go flying in the air. A few land on the back of the seat and one splats me on the cheek. I wipe myself off while Emily buckles her seatbelt, folds her arms over her chest, and scrunches up her normally cute face.

I try to remain calm. "I don't know Kelsey P.'s mom. And you, young lady, are coming with me to thank Mrs. Long for picking you up from school."

Emily pouts the whole way up the driveway, but pouting will not get her off the hook today. I stand by and wait while she addresses Sandy Long, who is now positioned half in and half out of the front door. Emily mutters, "Thanks for bringing me home from school." She sounds anything but thankful.

I send Em back to the van, along with an advisement not to run, and turn back to Sandy. Over her shoulder, Jessica lies on the living room floor, munching away from a bag of chips. She stares at the television, where several teenagers are dancing a hip-hop routine. It's obvious how torn up Jess is over her friendship with Emily. Not.

"Sorry about that. Em's not herself these days." I don't elaborate that it might have something to do with the fact that her mom and dad are separated, and Emily's emotional state is anything but normal.

"Oh, they're typical fourth-grade girls. They'll probably go back to being best friends tomorrow." Sandy chuckles.

I trudge back to the van. Nothing sounds better than another hot bath and a good night's sleep to forget about how pitiful my life is, even if only until the next morning.

"Why couldn't Dad pick me up?" Emily asks as my seatbelt clicks into place.

"Em, give it up. I'm sorry I forgot that you and Jessica had a fight and that I called her mother to pick you up from school. But your rudeness is inexcusable." Then, despite my resolve, I let her off easy. "Maybe I'll call

Kelsey's mom and arrange a play date." I smile weakly into the rearview mirror.

The scowl remains planted on Emily's face. "Daddy could have picked me up."

"Dad works, dorkweed," Christina chimes in with her two cents, without turning her head away from the window. She's likely trying to hide her bruised eye from her little sister to avoid having to make any explanations. "And quit whining!"

"Dad did not have to work today. He told me yesterday that he's taking a couple weeks off, through midwinter break. I can't wait until break starts. I'm sick of school."

"I'm sick of you whining," Christina shoots back.

"Please, you guys. Enough!"

Is this day over yet?

We round the corner of our street, and I groan. My father's car is in the driveway. Company is the last thing I need at the moment. As sweet as my stepmother, Candice, is, I have a feeling her kind and gentle personality will grate on my nerves. And, as much as I love my father and believe he is now a different person than he used to be, I suspect that today he will have a great big, invisible-to-the-rest-of-the-world-but-clearer-than-ever-to-me sign on his forehead that says *Adulterer!*

With all that's been going on, it hasn't dawned on me before this minute that today is the first Thursday of the month, when Candice and Dad come over and we all eat dinner together before going to our monthly Bible Study classes at church. The kids head to their own youth classes and Candice and I join the women, while Dad and Richard meet with the men. Afterwards, we go out for dessert and talk about what we learned.

This little tradition began about a year ago and has Candice's fingerprints all over it, though she makes it seem like my father came up with the whole idea. They both insist this is a great way for us to stay connected. Because what could bond a family better than an evening studying God's Word? I silently berate myself for forgetting to call and cancel tonight.

Overall, the monthly Thursdays have been a good thing. My kids have enjoyed spending time with their grandfather and stepgrandmother and my relationship with my father has warmed. Any other time, my dad's car in my driveway would be a welcome sight.

Problem is, I'm not going to church tonight. And telling my dad and Candice isn't high on my want-to-do list. Because they'll want to know why.

Enough said.

There are two reasons for my decision not to go. One, I am still a little angry with God, which could present a problem during praise and worship. Two, I do not want to run into my husband. And somehow, I know I would. It may be a huge church, but that's how God works. He would undoubtedly place us in the same place at the same time. I refuse to let that happen. I'm not ready.

As I pull into the driveway, I mull over excuses I can give about why I'm skipping out. Another question I consider: what will my response be when Candice asks where Richard is? Because she will.

Of course, one of the kids will probably blurt out the fact that he's moved out before she has a chance to ask. Dealing with the questions sooner or later is inevitable. Looks like it will be sooner.

Emily hops out of the van and runs inside to greet her grandpa and Candice, while Christina and I take our time.

"What do I say about my eye?" Christina asks.

"Uh...how about the truth?"

She clamps her mouth shut and steps ahead of me. As she enters the kitchen, I hear Candice gasp. Christina assures her stepgrandma she's fine. When asked what happened, she hems and haws before it finally comes out that she got socked in the eye.

Emily runs to her sister's side. Until this moment, she has been so wrapped up in her little world of friend-spats that she didn't notice her sister's face. "Did it hurt?"

"Duh."

"Please tell me the other guy looks worse." Dad grins, a dimpled crease spreading across his cheek.

"Ron!" Candice swats him on the arm. "Are you okay, sweetheart?" Candice slips into her nurturing mode and ushers Christina to the kitchen table.

"Hi, Dad." I take off my jacket and sling it onto the counter, nearly knocking over the same vase Christina did a couple days ago.

"Rough day?"

"You could say that."

"Hope it's nothing some good food and an inspiring Bible study won't help."

Here we go.

I take a deep breath. "Dad, about Bible Study—" The back door opens, and voices flood into the house. Irritation and relief emerge simultaneously.

A moment later, Max appears, wearing his famous lopsided grin, followed by Amy and another girl I've never seen before.

Amy is looking very cute in a hot pink ski jacket and matching cap. Her blond hair sticks out of the bottom, flipping up on the ends. She smiles. "Hi, Mrs. McCall."

So sweet.

"Hi, Amy." I smile back before fixing my gaze on the other girl. She is the exact opposite of Amy, starting with her hair, which is pitch-black and lined with pink streaks. The top sticks up, porcupine-like, in every direction. Her eyes are the color and shape of chocolate-covered almonds, set deeply in her olive-toned face. I have to say she is striking and exotically beautiful. Well, except for the gold ring protruding from her bottom lip. And the six hoops in each ear. And the black eye shadow. And nail polish. And lipstick.

Because of the grin taped to Max's face, and his trance-like state, somehow I suspect she is the girl who happens to think my son is "hot."

Oy.

"Mrs. McCall, this is Sam, a friend of mine. She recently moved here from Tennessee," Amy says.

Sam. Max's ride home.

"Hi, Sam, it's nice to meet you." I look at Max, a little perturbed that he isn't the one to introduce the girl who thinks he's hot. But Max is too busy drooling on himself to say anything at the moment.

"Hey, Sam, I'm Max's grandpa." Dad steps forward and extends his hand. "But since I'm much too young to be a grandfather, you can call me Ron." He winks and I roll my eyes toward the ceiling.

Sam grins and the lip ring wobbles.

I cringe. That's gotta hurt.

She shakes Dad's hand, then looks back at me. "It's nice to meet y'all."

So looks can be deceiving. She may not ever compare to Amy, but at least her parents taught her some manners. My initial impression is that she's a nice girl. Even with her spiky black and pink hair and multiple piercings.

Christina says hey to Amy and Sam and the four teenagers huddle together, talking about Christina's black eye, which she's suddenly proud of.

We decide on Chinese takeout for dinner.

"Emily, wanna come with me to pick up the food? You can select the fortune cookies for everyone." Candice motions to Em, who hops up from the kitchen chair. They head out while I pour sodas and get out the plates.

Max has invited Amy and Sam to stay for dinner. Max and Amy chat about the youth Bible Study but, from what I'm witnessing through keen observation and eavesdropping, Sam is uncomfortable at the mention of church. She is hesitating, not sure she wants to tag along. I'm thinking Sam could have a valid reason for not wanting to go, like piles of homework, a long list of chores, or another piercing appointment.

"I don't know that I want to go to church with my eye looking like this," I hear Christina say. "Sam, do you have any good makeup tips to cover up the bruise?"

Since the only color on Sam's face is black, I am curious as to what sort of advice she'll offer.

Before she can answer, my dad pulls a chair up to the table next to Sam and tries acting like he is one of them. "So who do you think will win *Survivor?*" he asks.

I shake my head. The man refuses to grow up. But the kids think he's cool. To them, Grandpa Ron is one hip old dude.

The doorbell rings. I leave the chaos of the kitchen and open the front door.

Blake the Snake stands there, looking strangely green.

Oh, boy.

"Is Christina home?"

Hmmm. This could get interesting. I am tempted to give Blake a piece of my mind. I am further tempted to lie and say Christina can't come to the door right now. But he peers over my shoulder across the house and spots her sitting at the kitchen table with Max, Amy, Sam, and Grandpa. I follow his gaze. Christina is laughing about something. I hate to ruin her good mood, but it doesn't seem I have a choice.

"Christina!"

She's still grinning when she gets to the door. Once Blake comes into view, however, her smile dies and her face ices over. Blake's eyes widen and then soften at the sight of Christina's eye, which is beginning to turn purple.

"Can we talk?" He resembles a puppy that has piddled on the floor.

After thirty seconds of serious contemplation, Christina invites him in. I stand back as they brush past me and wander off to a corner of the living room.

What is she thinking? As much as I want to throw Blake out the door and into a snow bank, I want to give my daughter the opportunity to make a mature decision on her own. I only hope that decision includes breaking it off with Blake for good.

Before turning to go back to the kitchen, I glance out the window and catch sight of another car—this one a familiar white Buick Century.

Mom!

11

Stress not only kills,
it adds years to your face.
SYLVIE

As Mom pulls into the driveway, I consider faking a panic attack, running outside, and begging her to rush me to the Emergency Room. Anything to keep her from coming in, as I'm not in the mood to referee a verbal boxing match between my parents. Then I realize the possibility that I'll have a real panic attack. Due to all of the stress from the past several days, I may die from anxiety right here in my living room.

I head her off at the door. "Mom, isn't Thursday your work day? And what are you doing driving around in this weather?" I block the doorway and, more importantly, her view of my father.

"Good grief, Madi, I'm not a hundred years old. I do know how to drive."

That statement could easily be debated.

"Let me in, would you? It's freezing out here. I traded days with Gloria. She has an appointment with the colon doctor tomorrow, so I'm picking up her shift for her. Isn't that nice of me? And you say I'm not considerate." She shoves past me and struggles with her jacket and boots. Following in Mom's considerate footsteps, I lend a hand and hang her coat in the closet.

Christina and Blake give a wave from the couch. I am thankful my daughter didn't turn her whole head and that the bad eye is not noticeable from where she's sitting.

Mom squints. "Is that the same boy Christina brought over for Christmas?"

"Blake."

"Right. There's something about him I don't like," she whispers. "He's gonna break her heart."

Too late.

"Where's my girl?" Mom hollers for Emily, the only one of her grandchildren who is ever the least bit excited to see her. It's then that she spots my father, sitting at the dining room table with Max, Amy, and Sam. They are chatting animatedly amongst themselves, oblivious to Mom's presence. Or maybe they're merely hoping she'll go away. That's not very nice to say, I know. But I can't say I blame them. She's not a very fun person to have around. My dad, however, is a complete riot and is currently impersonating Napoleon Dynamite. I have to say it's not half bad. Give the man a curly brown wig and some big nerdy glasses, and he'd have the character nailed. "What's your father doing here?" she whispers harshly.

"It's the first Thursday of the month, Mom. He and Candice come for dinner and then we all go to Bible study together."

Maybe, just maybe, she'll develop some manners and excuse herself from this little get-together.

And maybe I'll develop a love for spiders.

Mom glances around, obviously anxious.

"Candice isn't here. She and Em went out for the food."

"Why don't you ever invite *me* for dinner?" Mom is sullen and pouty. "Oh, never mind. You want to spend time with your cheating father and his bimbo, that's your business." Her shoulders lift and fall in a dramatic heave. "It's okay. I'll get over it. At least your brother invites me over on a regular basis."

Yeah, when his laundry starts piling up.

I am used to Mom's passive-aggressive behavior. She's nothing if not predictable.

"Mom, you're more than welcome to come for dinner any time—you know that."

She dismisses me with a flip of her hand and shuffles to the kitchen.

Heads turn as she enters. This could be due to the sudden "tickle" in Mom's throat, which causes her to cough continuously for thirty seconds. She makes a big show of grabbing a glass from the cupboard and filling it with water. She gulps it down like she has spent the past week in a desert.

"Hello, Maxine," Dad says with a tight smile. It wasn't all that long ago when even attempting to smile while saying hello to my mother was impossible for him, so I respect his attempt to be civil. Since he recommitted his life to the Lord, and with Candice's loving encouragement, a lot has changed. He's trying, I'll give him that.

Mom, on the other hand, hasn't changed a bit. She glares. She hmmphs. She scowls. I'm hoping she chooses the passive part of her disorder today and simply takes her leave without stirring up its aggressive partner.

"Do you think you're one of them?" she asks. She looks at the kids. "You do know he's pushing seventy, don't you? He's no spring chicken."

Max throws his head back and emits a hearty laugh. Good old Max, Mom's namesake, yet nothing like her—thank goodness. "Yes, we know, Grandma. But I don't know any other seventy-year-old who even *knows* Napoleon Dynamite, let alone how to impersonate him like that."

Amy and Sam laugh and Mom grunts.

Max suggests to the girls that they go downstairs to play pool until Candice gets back with the food. Again, my heart swells for my son. He might be a big goof much of the time but he has a good head on his shoulders. He's witnessed enough spats between his grandparents and doesn't want to subject his friends to the drama.

Mom stares at Sam as she follows Max through the kitchen. I wait for it. But surprise of surprises, Mom keeps her mouth shut.

Christina calls from the living room that she and Blake will be outside. I call back and remind her to put on her coat. I envision the eye roll coming from the other side of the wall. I don't know why I waste my breath—she won't do it. She's worn her coat maybe three times so far all winter.

Oh well. At least it should stay in good enough condition to get a nice chunk of cash on eBay next fall.

Dad gets up from the table and approaches Mom. "Maxine, Candice will be back any minute. Maybe it will be best if you're not here when she returns." He doesn't say it in a mean way. Anyone can tell he's just trying to prevent things from turning ugly. But my mother is not anyone.

"Fine. Throw me out. It's always been like this, hasn't it, Ron? I'm the one left out of everything."

Here we go...

"I'm all alone, and you have everything—a nice house, a dependable car, an 'in' with the teenagers. You even have your pocketful of 'Candice,' and get all the sex you want." She pauses for effect. "Oh—that's right—you've always had all the sex you wanted. With everyone except your wife!"

Dad's face reddens. "Maxine, let's not go there again. Please. It was a million years ago—"

Mom huffs and folds her arms across her abundant, heaving bosom. "No, it's been twenty-eight years, three months, and fourteen days."

The world momentarily stops spinning. For fifteen seconds, all goes silent as we process what Mom said. I know my mother has bitterness issues, but actually keeping track to the day? That's sick.

I suddenly feel acute sympathy for this woman. She needs help before she is completely destroyed by her unwillingness to forgive.

Dad stares at Mom. What can he possibly say?

As I scrape my jaw up off the floor, Mother stomps out of the kitchen, toward the front door. "Oh—did Madi tell you?" she spontaneously shoots over her shoulder. "Her husband cheated, too. I knew it was only a matter of time. You men are all the same." She steps into her boots and grabs her jacket from the closet. "Have fun tonight."

I can't believe she blurted it out like that! I take that back. I can easily believe it. But understanding it is a whole other matter. My father's eyes are burning the back of my head and I avoid turning. Instead, I watch as my mother plods through the snow to her car. She doesn't even say good-bye to Christina and Blake, who stand huddled together on the front porch. She starts up her car and backs out of the driveway, barely missing the mailbox.

And then, when I think it can't get any worse, a blue Ford Explorer comes barreling down the road, remarkably resembling Richard's.

Oh, look! It is!

12

There must be quite a few things that a hot bath won't cure,
but I don't know many of them.
SYLVIA PLATH, *THE BELL JAR*

I want to be Princess Jasmine—independent, strong, and brave. I want to hold my head high and stand up to my opponent. (This would be Richard.)

But I'm not Jasmine. At the moment, I'm Princess Pathetic, struggling to fight back the tears. Crying is normally not my thing, but there's only so much a woman can take!

Christina walks out to meet her dad, Blake lagging behind like a three-year-old. Richard climbs out of the driver's seat and smiles. His smile flips upside down when he notices his daughter's black eye. He inspects it as Christina gestures with her hands, likely explaining the afternoon's events.

As I observe them talking, I feel...something. Regret? Sadness? Anger? Love? I'm not sure. But I want to disappear and not have to deal with this.

I glance over my shoulder. Compassion flashes in Dad's eyes. It only lasts a moment, though, before it is replaced with a simple understanding.

"I've got this, sweetheart. Why don't you go on to that great big bathroom of yours and soak in some bubbles or something?"

Choking out a "Thank you," I sprint up the stairs to my room. Once inside, I lock the door, thankful that my room is at the far end of the house, and the door is thick enough so it muffles most everything. But, just in case, I take my father's advice and start the bath, letting the running water completely wash out all sound. I busy myself with adding bubbles and retrieving the red nail polish from the cupboard. It's about time my piggies are pampered.

If there is ever a time I need my Bible, it is now. But as I soak in the tub, painting my toenails, trying not to think about what's going on downstairs, the dust from my Bible taunts me from the basket behind the porcelain throne. I come up with a million reasons I can't read it at the moment. A few being:

1. It's too far out of reach.
2. I have to wait for my nails to dry.
3. I'm too tired.
4. I'm too exhausted (is that the same as tired?)
5. I might be interrupted.
6. I don't wanna.

Okay, I'll admit that last one is the reason that resonates through my head. I simply don't want to. And, because no one is here to make me, I don't.

I soak for about an hour, adding hot water as it cools. By the time I climb out, my skin resembles my ninety-three-year-old grandmother's. I generously apply lotion to my skin, which is now red and completely dried out from scalding hot water.

At least something good came out of this—my toenails are finally painted. If my feet had a mouth, they would be grinning from ear to ear. That is, if they also had ears.

I slip on my robe, pad to my bedroom, and press my ear to the door.

All is quiet.

I crack the door and listen again.

Nothing.

The short winter day has sapped all of the sunlight from the house even though it can't be past six. I've made the trek through my house in the dead of night thousands of times so it doesn't bother me in the least to make my way down the hall in the dark. Charlie startles me from the shadows. He brushes up against my leg before sprinting toward the kitchen.

"Sheesh, Charlie, do you want the kids to come home to find me dead on the floor from a heart attack? Sneaking up on me like that is not going to earn you any extra fishie treats, that's for sure." As I enter the kitchen, I reach around the wall and slap around for the light switch.

And then there was light.

And a man. Sitting at my kitchen table.

For the second time in two days, I let out a piercing scream. And, for the second time, the scary man is my husband.

Distracted by the shock of seeing Richard, it takes me a second to realize I jumped so hard, the tie on my robe has come undone and I'm standing there, exposed. And Richard is…well, Richard is doing what any man would do in this situation. Staring. With a slightly dazed yet satisfying expression, I might add.

My hands have never moved so fast. Pulling the sash around me, I shoot eye daggers at my husband, hoping to intimidate him into looking away. But he doesn't. A smirk plays at the corners of his mouth and the hint of a twinkle appears in his eye. A twinkle! How dare he twinkle at my humiliation!

"Sorry I startled you, but I figured since this is my house, too, I have every right to be here." He leans forward and rests his elbows on the table. For a second, the light reflects off his wedding ring and it flashes, lightning-like. Automatically, my right hand moves to my left and I finger my diamond.

"You should be at church."

My hypocritical comment is not lost on Rich. It's obvious he wants to laugh, and I can't blame him. "I think God understands," he says.

"Seriously, Rich. You could have called to say you wanted to talk. Showing up unannounced—twice in one week, at that—and scaring me to death seems rather immature, don't you think?" My tone comes out harshly, exactly the way I intended.

He cocks his head. "This coming from you?"

I ignore the comment and breeze past him. I note that the counter is clear, the dishes done. That Candice. Was there even a doubt that she would leave my kitchen cleaner than when they arrived? She even lit the apple-cinnamon scented candle that sits on the stove.

My dad will get an earful, that's for sure. How could he leave Rich in the house without warning me?

"Don't blame your dad," Rich says, as if reading my mind. "I explained things to him. He's a good judge of character, Madi. He knows me. Better than you do, it seems."

I hmmph. Since it irks Rich to no end when I ignore him, I keep silent and open the fridge in search of leftovers. I pull out leftovers from the Chinese takeout—a carton of rice and some sweet and sour chicken. Once nuked in the microwave, I take a seat at the snack bar, my back to Richard, and start chowing down. I love Chinese food and I'm sure it tastes good, but the truth is, it could be a dirt pie and I probably wouldn't know since I can't really taste anything. It's a little hard to concentrate on food while my cheating husband sits three feet behind me at the kitchen table. At the moment, he's drumming his fingers on the table, waiting patiently—or not—for me to finish my food. The drumming is annoying, and I debate whether to hurry so he'll stop and we can get this confrontation over with or to chew even slower to prolong his agony.

Oh, whatever. Might as well be done with it.

Shoving my cartons away, I swivel toward him on the bar stool.

"Don't rush dinner on my account," he says.

I frown. "Let's do this, Rich. Say what you came to say. Tell me what you want."

He scoffs. "What do *I* want? The question is, what do you want, Madi?"

I place a finger on my chin. "Hmmm. What do I want…"

"Yes. Please tell me. Because, in eighteen years, I haven't been able to figure it out. I've put up with your insecurities and accusations. I've—"

"I'm so sorry you've had to put up with me for so long," I spit.

"That's not what I meant."

"Oh. I didn't know there was more than one definition for 'put up with.'"

"What I meant was—"

"You know what? Never mind. Back to your question. I believe you asked what I want. Well, how about this? How about a husband who loves me? Or, hey. At least one who doesn't cheat. That would definitely make up my top two. Let's see…what else do I want? How about a great marriage? How about romance? How about flowers or a sappy Hallmark card once in a while? Or even a 'how was your day today, Madi?' I know I'm only a stay-at-home mom, but a little appreciation would be nice. I never claimed to be Martha Stewart, but I keep the house looking pretty nice. Would a 'thank you' be too much to ask? Or how about a compliment? Hey, there's an idea! You don't even compliment me after sex anymore. At least then I was good for something. Oh, well, you've got Fawn. I'm sure she appreciates your compliments."

I start crying and hate myself for it. The last thing I want is for Rich to see me break down.

Where is all this stuff coming from anyway? This fountain of emotions that spewed forth from deep within? The feelings themselves are not necessarily a revelation to me, as I'm well aware that I haven't been happy in my marriage for a long time now. Rich certainly knows what it's like to get a piece of my mind. But normally it's disguised in snappy, sarcastic comments and not with such blatant raw emotion. And it almost never includes tears.

Richard doesn't say anything. But his eyes are moist and I can't bear to look at him, so I turn away and watch Charlie as he paws at something under the table.

The moment goes on forever—or what seems like forever—before Richard finally speaks.

"I don't know what to say."

"How about 'good-bye'?" The words are out before I can stop them. I fold my arms across my chest and turn my back again. I focus on the Chinese takeout containers.

"That's really what you want?"

"I told you what I want."

Rich's Lagerfeld cologne invades my space as he steps closer. I can feel him standing behind me. A tiny part of me wants to turn around and bury my head in his chest and allow him to hold me for hours while I cry. To beg him to stay so we can work on our marriage and rebuild the trust.

But I can't. How can I forget what he did? How can I shake the memory of my husband and Fawn Witchburn standing face-to-face across from The Golden Brown Bakery? Right now, I can't handle the stress and inevitable pain of dealing with everything from the cheating to my anger issues. The reality of how much work and effort it will take to forgive and learn to trust again outweighs the pain of being without him. So, instead of turning around, I do what I do best. I walk away.

As I make my way around the table and head back toward my bedroom, Rich heaves a heavy sigh. I stand in the darkened hallway and listen as his footsteps sound on the kitchen floor. For one brief moment, all is silent. And then I hear the faint closing of the back door.

And a little piece of my heart closes with it.

13

Eat as much chocolate as you like.
Your problems will still be there in the morning.
CLAUDIA BOEVE, DIET WORKSHOP LEADER

Because I'm a stressed-out woman, the first thing I think of after Rich leaves is chocolate. The thought of a couple of Edy's chocolate Dibs for dessert makes my mouth water, but having finished those this afternoon, the two fortune cookies Candice left for me on the counter will have to do. I toss the fortunes without even reading them. Even if I did believe in fortune telling, I wouldn't risk it with the way my luck's been lately.

I'm so lost in my thoughts that when the doorbell rings, I almost choke on my cookie. My heart palpitates as I consider the possibility that Rich has returned. But after the brush-off I gave him, he'd have to be crazy to come back for more rejection. Besides, he's probably halfway to church by now to attend the last half of Men's Bible Study. Or who knows? Maybe he'll look for comfort in Fawn's arms.

The bell sounds again and another thought hits me. What if it's Mom coming back to either finish her verbal tirade or lay on some more guilt? Dread courses through my veins. Given the choice, I'd almost prefer to see Richard standing on the front step.

Almost.

Swallowing the last of the dry fortune cookie, I drop to my hands and knees and crawl to the picture window. Charlie watches me from the green leather recliner in the corner. I put a finger to my lips, even though I know he couldn't make a sound even if he wanted to. I move the blinds a quarter of an inch and peer through the slat.

Zach.

Relief washes over me as I struggle to my feet. I never thought I'd say this, but my brother is a sight for sore eyes.

I open the door to Zach's finger in the pointing position.

"I was just going to ring again," he says. "I knew you were in there."

"And you would know that...how?" I step back and Zach enters, kicking off his snow-covered Vans skate shoes. "Wait. Let me guess. Mom called you?"

He smiles and brushes a long lock of blond-streaked hair from his eye. It looks like he just stepped out of *Surfer* or *Skateboarding* magazine and belongs on the beaches or skate parks of California instead of a small, snow-laden town like South Haven, Michigan, although there are plenty of hills nearby to accommodate his love for snowboarding.

"Nope. Well, she did call. But only to complain about her hip. She didn't mention you."

"Why doesn't that surprise me?"

He follows me into the kitchen. I grab two clear glasses from the cupboard and fill them with ice, then foaming Dr. Pepper—his favorite. I slide one glass across the counter and guzzle from the other.

"It was Dad. He was on his way to Bible study and called to ask if I would stop by and pick up his reading glasses. He said he left them on the counter."

I do an eye-sweep over my tan Formica countertop. Then I scan the table and the desk by the phone. Hmmm. No glasses.

"In other words, he wanted you to come and check on me. What do you bet he'll 'find' those glasses as soon as he gets to church."

Zach puts on his confused face. "Why would Dad want me to check on you? Are you sick or something?"

"Man, those acting classes sure paid off, little brother. You're good."

He shrugs. "Okay, so he told me you and Rich are having problems. And that Rich stopped by tonight and that Dad sent you off to bubble heaven so you didn't have to deal with it, but then Rich stuck around while Dad and Candice took the kids to church. He is gone, isn't he?" Zach glances around as if Richard may suddenly pop out from behind the refrigerator.

"Yes, he's gone. And I think I may have to buy a muzzle for Dad next Father's Day. What *didn't* he tell you?"

"How would I know if he didn't tell me?" Zach grins.

I roll my eyes.

"He also said he wishes you'd joined them for church."

I half expect a *tsk-tsk* to follow. But I know better. Zach doesn't "do" church or Bible study or anything like that. He says he believes in God, but the whole church thing isn't for him. But I have to say, he's been asking a few questions lately, making me wonder if God is working in his heart somehow.

"Yeah, well. He says that about you every week," I point out before taking a big swig of Dr Pepper.

Another shrug. "You wanna talk about it?" He glances at the clock. Zach isn't exactly a talking kind of guy.

I blow right past the question. "Don't you have better things to do than hang out with your sister? Why aren't you out on a date with what's-her-name?" I am talking about a girl he works with who, awhile back, Zach mentioned was cute. I can't, for the life of me, remember her name. Sienna...Sierra...Serena …

His eyes shift sharply into mine. "Who do you mean?"

Because I am an expert people-reader, I note that he says this a little too quickly. This only means one thing: Zach has a girlfriend.

I place my hands on the counter and smirk. "You're so busted."

"So you know?"

"Of course I know. A sister always knows."

Zach jerks his head, flipping his hair out of his eye, and reaches up to tug at his collar. "And you're okay with it?"

I narrow my eyes. "That depends. If she's anything like your last girlfriend—Valley Girl Vicky—then, *like*, no, I'm not okay with it." I badly impersonate his last irritating girlfriend. "But if she's like Angela—what was she, four girlfriends ago?—I'm all for it. She was a gem. I still want to kick your butt for letting her go without a fight."

He swallows hard and avoids my eyes. Not a good sign. I purse my lips at the good possibility she's another Valley Girl Vicky. Like, gag me with a spoon!

"Well, now that I've done my brotherly duty and checked on you, I'm outta here." He drains his glass and plunks it onto the counter. "Thanks for the Dr P."

"Wait a minute. You asked me if I want to talk, and now you're leaving." I follow Zach to the door, where he slips his feet into his snow-soaked Vans and zips up his jacket.

"Yeah. I'm willing to talk if the conversation centers around *your* love life—not mine."

"How about we don't talk about love at all? I need some legal advice, Zach."

He raises an eyebrow.

"I might be sued."

Okay, so Zach probably doesn't know a lot about real-life legal matters. But he's had more experience with the law than I have, as he was busted for smoking pot right after high school. Plus, I know for a fact he's a huge fan of *Law & Order*—has the DVDs from every season. You'd never guess by looking at him. You'd think *Baywatch* reruns, *Survivor,* maybe. *Law & Order* seems a little, oh, I don't know…intelligent…for him.

I can say that since I'm his sister.

I fill him in on the details of Christina's fight, the principal's warning that the Hardaways could sue. Zach inserts a few nods, "hmmm"s and "wow"s. When I'm finished, he can't offer me anything except a little sympathy.

"Sorry, Sis. But I wouldn't worry about it until you get a legal notice. Maybe the whole thing will blow over."

I hope he's right.

By the time Zach leaves, I realize the events of the day have drained me—in the mental *and* physical capacity. Maybe I'll go lay down for a bit, grab a few Zs until the kids get home. I trudge to my bedroom, pull back the covers, and crawl in. Sinking against my pillow, I pull the plum-colored down comforter up to my neck. I close my eyes. Just a…little…nap.

♛

Someone is peering at me in the dark. I haven't yet opened my eyes but know someone is there. Now that I'm conscious, I can hear him or her breathing. I've heard that breath before. It's Em. I reach out and feel for her hand. It's there, and I cover it with my own.

"Sorry, Mommy," she says.

"Sorry for what, sweetie?" Squinting against the darkness, I can barely make out her face but see a slight glistening of tears on her cheek.

"I couldn't help it. I was dreaming that I was going to the bathroom and when I woke up, I was going." She starts weeping. "I wet my bed, Mommy."

I sit up and pull her into my arms.

"It's okay, honey. It was an accident." I brush her hair with my hand, intertwining my fingers in its silkiness. "Let's go get those sheets changed."

I'm trying to make it sound like no big deal. Truthfully, it doesn't bother me in the least to change my daughter's sheets in the middle of the night. My greatest concern is why she is suddenly wetting her bed at nine years old.

Her hand slips into mine, and she walks awkwardly beside me, the way one does when their underwear is soaked. I change her sheets while she goes to the bathroom and changes into dry pajamas.

The clock reads 4:00 a.m., meaning Emily still has a couple of hours to sleep before it's time to get up for school. She is now tucked under fresh sheets, the turquoise and lime comforter pulled up to her neck, her blinks long and heavy. It's obvious she's sleepy, yet I don't want to let this moment pass without making sure my baby girl is okay.

Before I can speak, Em whispers, "I miss Daddy."

"I know you do, sweetheart."

"I got to see him last night. He took us out for ice cream after Bible study. He let me have a root beer float—a large. I drank it all, too," she says, a smile tugging at the corners of her mouth.

"No wonder you had to go to the bathroom so bad. Didn't your mother ever tell you not to drink so much right before bed?" I wag a finger and give her my best scolding look.

Em mega-grins, displaying the gap where one of her teeth is starting to come in. "Daddy brought us home and Christina helped me get ready for bed 'cause you were zonked out. She said you probably took a sleeping pill or something."

I shake my head. "I didn't take a sleeping pill. I was just super-duper tired." I use one of Em's kid words. "That was nice of Christina, though. I'll have to thank her in the morning."

"It is morning."

I glance at the clock in her room. "You're right—and you, young lady, have to get up for school in a few hours. Better get some sleep, or you'll be falling asleep at recess."

"No way! During math, maybe..." The toothless smile reappears for a second and then fades. She is quiet for a moment. "Mommy?"

"Hmmm?"

"I asked Daddy when he was coming home. He said he didn't know. Why won't you tell Daddy to come back home?"

I weigh my words. "You know how you and Jessica aren't getting along?"

Em nods.

"Well, it's like that between Daddy and me right now. We need a break from each other for a while."

"But me and Jessica aren't married. You guys have your kids to think about."

Okay, now my daughter is sounding a little too wise for her age.

"Yes, we do. And remember, your dad and I both love you very much." My voice is getting higher and I swallow the lump in my throat. "Don't ever doubt that, okay?" I touch her nose.

"I know, Mommy. I love you, too."

I sit with Em and stroke her silky hair until she falls asleep, the whole time thinking how sometimes life isn't fair. In fact, sometimes it just plain stinks.

And it's definitely no fairy tale. This is the real world, where people do bad things…hurtful things. And nobody rides in on their white horse to save the princess. Things don't always end happily. And even when they seem to, they most certainly don't stay that way.

But it's not fair to the innocent kids who are subjected to consequences beyond their control. Consequences suffered due to poor choices made by their parents. The longer I sit there, the angrier I get at Richard for doing this to our family. Then the anger transfers to myself and, finally, to God.

I know I can't go on like this forever. These roots of bitterness need to be pulled out and dealt with so I can move forward—with my life and in my Christian walk.

I know the roots go deeper than Richard's unfaithfulness. In fact, they almost certainly go back as far as my childhood and the heartbreak I experienced over my parents' divorce. Add to that my father's indiscretions and my mother's sadistic need to disclose them to me, and there is some major weeding to be done.

I am furious with Richard for shoving the pain of my childhood into my face and forcing me to deal with my issues once and for all. I wonder if anyone is ever truly ready to face the demons within themselves. Or to confront the ghosts of the past that continue to haunt the heart in spite of every effort to shoo them away. It seems every time I think I'm over it and can move on with my life in a healthy way, something happens to assure me that I am anything *but* over it.

I lean over and kiss Em on the forehead. Because there is no way I will be able to fall back to sleep, I move to the kitchen and start a pot of coffee. Then I do what I sometimes do when I'm angry or frustrated or worried or simply restless. I dig out the scrub brushes, dust rags, and cleaners and finally get to work on the dust bunnies that are multiplying faster than I can say, "hippity-hop." Perfect timing, too, because I'm pretty sure we're all out of carrots.

"Do you think I did the right thing?"

I'm talking to Sylvie on the phone, my hands immersed in soapy water. The kids are off to school, and I've finished my stint as a Molly Maid on steroids. For a moment, I seriously entertain the idea of applying to a couple of cleaning services. A toned physique while earning an income sounds good to me.

So now the floors shine, the toilets sparkle, and the dust bunnies have been conquered. I have only the breakfast dishes to clean before I will finally be able to sit down with a gigantic cup of coffee and relax my weary muscles.

"I think you did what you felt you had to do."

I scrub jelly from Emily's breakfast plate. "That did not answer my question."

On to Max's orange juice glass. Surprise of surprises, he used one this morning instead of guzzling right from the carton. He must be working on his manners for when he finally gathers the courage and asks Sam out on a date.

"Madi, you already know how I feel. If Rich did cheat, I'm not saying it was okay. I just wish you'd talk to him."

"I did talk to him."

"You know what I mean. Dealing with something like this is never easy. But you'll have to do it sooner or later."

"I'll opt for later."

"I missed you at Bible study last night." Sylvie smoothly changes the subject. "I ran into your dad and Candice. They said you weren't feeling well."

"How good would you feel if your husband cheated on you? Wouldn't you want to avoid any place where you might run into him?"

"Even if avoiding Richard means avoiding God, too?"

"God is everywhere, Sylv. I don't need to go to church to spend time with Him."

A pause. "So have you? Spent time with Him?"

I cluck my tongue like I'm appalled that she'd even ask such a question. Then I pop up the sink stopper, watching the bubbles swirl down the drain— much like my life right now. "So I haven't spent much time in prayer lately. My Bible is collecting dust. Cut me some slack, Sylv. I'm going through a thing, here. Let me go through my thing in my own way. Please. No lectures."

"I'm not going to lecture you, Mads. But you know I love you. I'm worried about you, that's all. And I want you to know you're at the top of my prayer list."

I mutter thanks because, well, what else can I say? I do appreciate Sylvie's prayers, though I seriously wonder how much good they're doing. Then again, Sylvie is a champion interceder, I'll give her that. A true prayer warrior. By the world's standards, she may be a tiny woman, but in the spirit realm, demons tremble. It certainly couldn't hurt to have her sending up a prayer or two on my behalf. Someone needs to.

"So what are you wearing to the *reunion* next weekend?" This time it's my turn to change the subject. I sarcastically stress the word *reunion* because, to me, this is no reunion at all. It's more like a curious gathering of virtual strangers who want to prove they didn't turn out to be as pathetic as the people they went to school with twenty years ago.

Sylvie perks up. "I'm wearing my black pants and a great wool sweater I bought from the mall the other day. Nothing fancy."

"Really? You mean we don't have to dress up for Reggie's Classy Diner?" Again, sarcasm rolls off my tongue. I've been to Reggie's a million times, probably the majority of those back in high school, which is probably why Anita chose it for tomorrow night's meeting place—to bring back those warm and nostalgic feelings.

Gag me.

There's no doubt about it. I'm getting old. Twenty years ago, Reggie's was the place to be. For cool kids and geeks alike. Today, I think of Reggie's as a greasy hangout for rowdy, obnoxious kids. It's bound to be swamped with wild and crazy high school and college students, out for a wild and exciting weekend. I guess I should be thankful that Anita reserved the party room where we'll be slightly distanced from the beer-guzzling and pizza-gorging crowd. At least Reggie's has followed the trend of going with smoke-free dining and I won't come home smelling like I've been hanging out all evening in a smoky furnace with Shadrach, Meshach, and Abednego.

"It'll be fun. I took the boys to Reggie's for pizza about a month ago. They love it."

"That's the point, Sylvie. *Kids* love it. In case you haven't looked in the mirror lately, we're not kids anymore."

"You are such a party-pooper, you know that? Loosen up and have some fun. Relax and let your hair down, Madi. And for the record, thirty-eight is not old."

"Well, of course it's not old to you, Miss Forever-Twenty-Nine. By the way, do you know who I saw this morning when I looked in the mirror?"

"Your mother?" Sylvie asks, her voice dripping with sympathy.

"Worse. My father."

Sylvie laughs.

"It's not funny. Not only do I have his deep-set eyes and nose with the slight bump on it, I'm getting his jowls. They waved at me this morning."

Sylvie's laugh includes a snort this time. "You do not have jowls, Madi!" she manages to get out between guffaws. "And besides—your father really isn't that bad-looking."

"Gee, thanks. What a compliment."

After she has some fun at my expense and gets her laughing fit under control, Sylvie says, serious-like, "Okay, here's what I want you to do, missy. I want you to march into that nice, big bathroom of yours, look in the mirror, and tell that woman how beautiful she is. Tell her that she is a child of God and that she is special. Call her 'gorgeous.' Call her 'pretty.' Call her 'fabulous.' But whatever you do, do not call her 'Dad.'" Giggles re-erupt from the other end of the phone.

"I give up. I can't confide anything to you. All you do is poke fun of me." I wipe my hands on a towel and lean back against the counter.

"Madi, seriously. You're beautiful. Have I ever lied to you?"

"Hmmm. As a matter of fact, what about the time you told me my panty liner wasn't showing?"

Sylvie laughs again. "Well, that wasn't technically lying. You asked me if it was showing through your pants. And it wasn't."

"No—it was only stuck to them, attached to the back of the hem. I must have dragged that thing around for an hour before Missy Clemens told me it was there." Despite my mood bordering on sour, I crack a smile at the horrid memory. I'd been so embarrassed that I feigned illness for two days after.

"Didn't Anita's letter suggest that we bring along some memories to share?" Sylvie asks. "Maybe I'll share that one. I'm sure everyone would get a kick out of it."

"And you, my dearest friend, would get the biggest kick of all."

14

> But Donkey, I'm a princess!
> And this is not how a princess is supposed to look!
> PRINCESS FIONA

On Monday morning, I sit at the computer to do some online job hunting. I spent the weekend on the couch with the stomach flu. I still can't stomach coffee, so I sip from my steaming mug of lemon tea. Before I begin my search, I scan my e-mail and delete a bunch of junk mails before coming to a message from an industrial trucking company at which I applied for an office position a couple weeks ago. They inform me that, after much consideration, they've given the job to another more qualified candidate.

Whatever. How qualified does a person have to be to file paperwork and answer the phones? I'm thinking office work may not be for me. I recall last week's Molly Maid moment and decide I'll apply to a few cleaning services. Not the most glamorous of jobs, but at least it's something I'm "qualified for." I regret not taking some before and after pictures of my house so potential agencies can get a better idea of how good I really am.

Moving on, I spot a message from Richard. Again. But this time, the subject is, *The Kids.*

Oh, he's good. Now he's resorted to using the kids to get my attention. Because how can I ignore an e-mail about my kids?

Tentatively, I click on the message. I expect a long-winded apology, love letter, explanation, or some other sneaky tactic to win my forgiveness. But surprise, surprise, it's only one short paragraph.

Dear Madi,

Dont worry. This e-mail is not about us its about the kids. I would like to take them to Clevland over mid witner break to visit my mom for the weekend. She misses them and Id like to spedn some time with them. If its ok, Ray will pick them up Friday morning because I have an appt. I will bring them home on Sunday evening.

    Please let me know if this is ok.

    Rich

Sighing, I reread the message. It never ceases to amaze me that he is a fourth-grade teacher. His typing is atrocious! Hasn't he ever heard of spell-check?

I will have to run his request by the kids first. Personally, I'm fine with it. As upset as I am with Richard, the kids could use some quality time with their father. And their grandmother, for that matter.

Not thrilled about the fact that Ray will be the one to pick up the kids, though.

Raymond. Raymond. Raymond.

The guy grates on my nerves more sharply than an orange peel down the garbage disposal. And it's not only because he treats women, in general, like they are one step down from a donkey, but the way he treats his mother is unacceptable.

Okay, so I'm not the perfect daughter and don't always treat my mother with the love and respect I should. But my situation is totally different. My mother is, well…I'll just say it's hard to respect someone who is so blatantly obnoxious most of the time. Someone who is so self-absorbed that the first thing she says when she calls is, "You haven't called lately. Don't you want to know I'm still alive?" Not, "How are you?" or, "I wanted to see how you're doing." No. It's all about her.

And when she's not talking about herself, she's complaining. And, as demonstrated at least twice in the past week, her complaints are frequently about my father and the "wonderful" life he has while she is all alone, poor and pathetic.

Wah. Wah. Wah. Pop the cork and break out the cheese and crackers.

As much as I'd love to see my mother change her bitter and self-destructive ways, I've accepted the fact that it's not something I can control, any more than the fact that Richard cheated on me. The only one who can change my mother is the Holy Spirit.

I really wish He'd get on that.

Sorry. I digress. Sometimes I go off on tangents about my mom. These anger issues pop up in all kinds of places.

Anyway, I was less than thrilled when Ray moved to Michigan from Cleveland three years ago, although I felt glad for Nancy. At least she wouldn't be subjected to daily ridicule or mounds of Ray's dirty laundry (pause to shudder). I don't make a habit of inviting him over but, at Rich's suggestion and my sense of obligation, Ray has invaded our dinner table a handful of times.

But the fact Rich is staying with his brother astounds me. Five minutes with Ray makes me crazy. I can't imagine living with him.

I type a quick reply, telling Richard I will talk to the kids, but I don't see any problem. I also mention that he might want to consider some course of action regarding Christina's recent unladylike bar-room-brawl behavior. I hope he will handle it, even if it's with a simple lecture. That's one less thing I'd have to worry about.

My sarcastic tendency causes me to struggle with the urge to add: "P.S. Say hi to Fawn," but I resist. Yay for me!

As soon as I hit *Send,* the phone shrills, making me jump.

It's Sarah Price. "Sorry I haven't called you back, Madi. I had to leave town on an urgent family matter. How are you doing?"

"I'm fine. Just a little weary."

"I have an hour for lunch. Do you want to meet somewhere? Or you can come in to the office and we can talk over sub sandwiches and chips."

Right on cue, my stomach growls. I think I could handle some turkey on wheat.

"I'll pick up the subs on my way."

♛

It's as if God is spitting from the sky. The sleet against my windshield sounds like the Pop Rocks I used to eat as a kid. Sitting in my van, I pray for God to part the sleet like the Red Sea so I can make it inside to Sarah's office without looking like I've stepped out of the shower.

Doesn't look like my day for a miracle, so I don't have much choice. I whip open my door and speed-walk to the entrance, trying to balance two bags and two sodas. I try pushing open the door with my back, only to be reminded that it opens toward me.

Hmmm. How to handle this? Meanwhile, my hair is getting stringier by the second.

Ha! No need to decide. Charles Manson appears out of nowhere.

"Need a hand there, lovely lady?" He grins and makes googly eyes at me. His beard hosts some sort of food item, brown and grainy.

I recoil, turning my head away from his face, now mere inches from mine. For a moment, I fear he'll shove me into the snow-covered bushes that line the walk. Nervously, I glance over my shoulder at the parking lot, which is empty except for one car pulling out of the drive.

Ugh!

Just as I consider shoving the bags into his chest to distract him while I run furiously back to my car, he pulls open the door so I can enter.

"Thanks," I mutter, scurrying past him to safety.

A receptionist I haven't seen before glances up from her computer and smiles at me. "Are you here to see Dr. Price?" she asks, ESP-like.

I nod.

"You can go straight in." She turns back to her computer screen.

No waiting room for me today. Hooray!

Looking around, I note that, oddly, Mr. Manson has disappeared.

I rap on Sarah's door and she calls me in. Papers are piled on her desk, and she slaps another one on top as I enter.

Food distributed, we make small talk while we munch. After our subs are consumed, we get down to business.

"So tell me what happened the other day," Sarah says, wiping her hands on a napkin. She doesn't even reach for her notepad, just rolls her chair around from behind her desk and crosses her legs. We're two friends about to have a heart-to-heart.

I had already left a recount of The Golden Brown Bakery incident on her voice mail, but I relay it again in more detail, adding to it the rest of that afternoon's events, including Rich surprising me in the kitchen after I came down from my bath. I tell her pretty much everything, minus the robe coming open. Somehow, I don't think that part is necessary.

"Did you tell Richard that you saw him with Fawn?"

"No."

"Why not?"

"He'd only deny it."

"And you know this because…"

"Because men always deny everything. This wouldn't have been any different."

"Have you considered the possibility that Rich might deny it because he's not having an affair?"

I stare, unblinking, at Sarah. "I thought you were on my side. Now *you're* going to start telling me it's all in my mind, too? I just told you. I saw them together. It's kind of obvious, don't you think? "

Sarah removes her glasses and sets them on the desk. "Madi, first of all, I *am* on your side. I want to help you. Not because it's my job, but because I'm your friend. If Rich was—or is—cheating, trust me, it will come out eventually. But I want to do more than help you find the truth. I want to help you discover who Madi is. If Richard has been unfaithful, I want to help you find the strength to deal with that and give you some tools to help you cope. But if there is a chance—no matter how small—that he didn't cheat, we need to explore the reasons you believe he did. Reasons like...lack of trust, feeling unloved, and past insecurities. And we need to discover where those insecurities come from. I'm looking at it from all sides. That's the only way I'm able to see the whole picture. It's the only way *you* can become whole. Does that make sense?"

Not really. "I guess."

She uncrosses her legs and rests her forearms on her knees. "Remember what I said last time about you being a princess? Have you given that concept any thought?"

"Yes. I've come to the conclusion that I am Princess Fiona. I'll always be an ogre and never fit in with the other princesses."

Sarah chuckles. "Ah, but you forget. Princess Fiona had the chance to fit in, and she chose to remain an ogre. She accepted and loved herself for who she was. She didn't waste time comparing herself to other princesses. The fact is, Fiona is a princess, simply because she is the king's daughter."

"But Fiona doesn't have my problems. Her dad didn't cheat on her mother—at least, not that we know, anyway—and Shrek didn't cheat on her," I point out.

Sarah sits back in her chair. "So let's talk about that." She reaches for her glasses and slides them back over her eyes. "Start by allowing Richard to tell you his side of the story. Give him a chance to explain. Once you hear what he has to say, you can take that information, process it, and move forward. Until then, you're merely torturing yourself with questions and assumptions."

I hate it that she's right. "But what if he says something I don't want to hear?"

She smiles. "That, Madi, is where God comes in."

15

Whatever...

MY DAUGHTER, CHRISTINA, EVERY DAY OF HER LIFE

It's around 1:30 when I get home. I unwind by seeing how many times in a row I can win at Solitaire. Before I know it, it's almost time for the bus to make its loud stop in front of the house. My back aches, and I'm slightly annoyed with myself for wasting the past couple hours on the computer. I've got to come up with a better way to *not* deal with my issues. On a sticky note, I jot down a reminder to myself to Google "computer addicts" the next time I log on. I stand up, stretch a bit, then settle into my chair again for one more quick game.

By the time Em slams the back door, I have beaten my record for Solitaire—eight wins in a row. Elated, I go to share my news with my daughter.

"Cool," she says, unimpressed.

"Hey, have you been setting any records lately?" I ask as I open the cupboard and take out the fudge-striped cookies. Emily recently went through a stage of trying to set world records. First she attempted the "world's largest bubble" record, which resulted in globs of sticky pink bubble gum stuck in her hair, and a trip to my hair dresser, Anya, who gave her a super cute (albeit super short) haircut. The new, shorter do is adorable, framing her heart-shaped face. It suits her personality much better than the longer locks. Plus, the cuteness came with a bonus: no more matted mess for the brush to get tangled in. That means less screaming in the mornings. I never thought I'd be so glad that Emily got gum stuck in her hair.

Next, she tried to set the "holding your breath the longest" record. She was majorly reprimanded for that one after almost passing out.

And, finally, she decided on the "go the longest without talking" record. Truth be told, I relished this one for about a day. But then I longed to hear my daughter's voice again and tickled her until she broke. After she stopped laughing, I received an earful of whining, moaning, and pouting about how I ruined her record. Within seconds I was kicking myself, wishing for a rewind button so we could go back to silence.

I felt bad for ruining her record-setting efforts so I suggested a new one: "see how long you can keep your room clean."

She rolled her eyes and told me my idea was lame.

Go figure.

"I'm not into setting records these days," Em is saying.

"You're not, huh? So, what are you 'into'?"

"You know…fashion, makeup…that stuff."

I narrow my eyes. "Hmmm. That's strange, I thought I had only one teenage daughter. Nine-year-olds aren't supposed to be into things like that. They're supposed to play with Barbies, video games, and American Girl dolls."

Em rolls her eyes. At this moment, she's a spitting image of her sister. "Oh, Mom. That is so yesterday." With that, she picks up her fudge-striped cookie and dunks it in her milk, evidence that she is, in fact, only nine and not a sixteen-year-old in a miniature body.

The door slams, and Christina and Max walk in together. They are arguing about something. My ears perk up when I hear the word "Sam." At the same time, they both notice me and abruptly stop talking.

"What are you two talking about?" I cross my arms.

They exchange a look they likely assume I don't notice. "Nothing," they say in unison. It's a twin thing—drives me crazy. They say the exact same thing at the exact same time like they've rehearsed it a dozen times.

"So how has in-house suspension been going?" I look at Christina but notice out of the corner of my eye the relief on Max's face that I've dropped the questioning. He is opening the fridge, in search of a carton to guzzle from.

"Just great." Christina moans and graces me with an eye roll. "It feels like prison, only worse. At least in prison you have a toilet in your cell. The rule is, if I have to go to the bathroom, I'm supposed to ring for Mrs. Stickler to give me a pass. If I'm caught in the hallway without a pass, I'm in even bigger trouble. Well, today I had to pee like crazy and Mrs. Stickler would not answer my call. I swear she was avoiding me on purpose. I almost wet my pants, Mom. I think you should call the principal and talk to her. I should be able to go to the bathroom when I need to. What if I had my period or something?"

"Gross!" Max wrinkles up his face. "Personally, I think it would have been cool if you peed in your pants. It would have made a great picture for the yearbook."

Christina glares at Max, and I shoot a glance at Em. She's chewing on her bottom lip. I suspect she is thinking of the wetting incident from the other night, probably wondering if I'll say anything, which, of course, I never would.

"So what's up with you and Blake?" I've been dying to ask but haven't wanted to hound her about it.

Christina shrugs.

"She took him back," Max says, snorting in disgust.

Christina swats him on the arm. "Do you want a black eye to match mine?"

I frown. So I don't want to be cynical here, but I'm thinking getting back together with Blake might not be such a good idea. Don't get me wrong—I believe people can change. But I have my doubts about Blake. Then again, all members of the male species are on my hit list right now. Particularly those who have been caught cheating. "Are you sure that's a good idea, honey?"

"Don't worry about it, Mother." Christina is irritated. It's obvious she has no desire to discuss the status of her relationship with Blake. "So tell her about Sam." She jabs an elbow into Max's back, cleverly diverting the topic.

It's rare that I see my almost-sixteen-year-old son blush. But here he is, turning an acute shade of pink. He turns away and opens the cupboard, pretending to be looking for something to eat.

"Don't be shy, Max," Christina goads. She eyes me. "He asked Sam out. And she said yes, can you believe it? The poor girl."

"Who else is going on this date?" I ask in a mom tone. The group-dating-only rule is very important to me. Particularly in light of the sexual pressure conversation Christina and I had the other day.

Christina answers for him. "Amy and Kyle and maybe me and Blake."

Normally, I would correct Christina's bad grammar, but I'm still stuck on the first part of her sentence. "Kyle?"

"Amy's boyfriend."

My hopes for acquiring Amy as a daughter-in-law are fading fast. I feel another sense of betrayal. Why can't they see what I see? That Max and Amy are perfect for each other.

Shaking away my disappointment, I try to act happy about the fact that my son is dating a punk rocker or Goth girl—or whatever kids call it these days—from Tennessee. "Sam seems like a nice girl, Max."

"You know, just because she has a lip ring, pink hair, and wears dark lipstick doesn't mean she's a bad person," Max says from behind the cupboard door.

"Honey, you don't have to defend her. I already said she seems nice. Of course, I only met her once. I'd like the chance to get to know her a little better. Maybe you can invite her over for dinner sometime next week." It wouldn't hurt to get to know the girl who thinks my son is hot.

Max's face reappears, looking worried. "You wouldn't cook, would you? We could get pizza or something."

My kids have little confidence in my cooking abilities.

"I could make mostaccioli. You guys like my mostaccioli."

"That's okay. Pizza is fine."

Ouch.

Since I have all three of my kids together, I seize the opportunity to talk to them about going with their dad to visit Grandma Nancy. Max is kind of nonchalant. He agrees, but without much enthusiasm. Of course, that could be because he's a guy and his emotions aren't exactly pinned to his shirtsleeve for all to see.

Christina moans for a second about being stuck in a cramped car for four hours with her—gasp!—family. She finally says something about listening to her iPod the entire trip to not only occupy her time but distract her from the fact that she's traveling with a car full of dorks. I wonder if she'll be able to get through all 980 songs she has downloaded on that thing before they reach Cleveland.

Emily has yet to say a word, which is so unlike her. I lean across the counter on my elbows and look her in the eye.

"Em? What do you think, sweetie? Would you like to visit Grandma Nancy for a few days?"

"You're not coming?" she asks quietly.

"Not this time. Sylvie and I have a high school reunion thing to go to on Friday night." As if that's the reason.

"But you'll be all alone." She searches my face for some kind of reassurance that I'll be all right while she's off having fun with her dad.

"I don't mind being alone. Really. And I'll have plenty to do—like the laundry." Okay, so that was lame. But what am I supposed to say? That I'll be playing game after game of computer Solitaire in hopes of breaking my new record of eight wins in a row?

"But I'll miss you." Her eyes are welling up.

I grasp her hands. "I'll miss you too, sweetheart. But it's only for a couple of nights. And I'll tell you what. I'll let you hold on to the cell phone this time."

I glance at Max and Christina, my eyes saying, "Work with me here." Em has asked several times if she could carry the cell phone. I've always said no, that a nine-year-old is too young to be responsible for a cell phone. But that was before I needed to come up with something to convince my daughter to leave my side to spend time with her father.

"And I'm sure Christina will let you listen to her iPod for a little while."

"Mom!" Christina cries.

I shoot her my best pleading look. She pleads back. Finally, I win the glaring contest and she stares at the ceiling and throws up her hands. "Whatever."

When I turn my attention back to Emily, the tears are gone. "I can call you anytime I want?"

"Anytime at all."

"I guess I'll go," she says.

I breathe a sigh of relief. Part of me is a tad bit hurt that an iPod and cell phone won out over her concern for me. But I remind myself that she needs this time with her dad. And even though Richard is a rotten husband, he's still a good father, no matter how hard I try to deny it. Although the little devil on my shoulder reminds me that if he really was a good father, he wouldn't have cheated on their mother.

Is it selfish to look forward to the time alone, too? It suddenly occurs to me that I can indulge in all the Dibs I want and nobody will know! Then I remember I have cut them out of my diet.

Bummer. I could really use the chocolate.

Somehow, my gut tells me that God will show up at some point this weekend. Yes, He's always around, but I'm becoming increasingly aware of the fact that I'm ignoring Him. And I am reminded of this every time I use the bathroom and see my Bible sitting there atop the pile of magazines. It's almost been a week now—the longest I've ever gone without reading my Bible since I became a Christian. I suspect God is frowning on me.

But, hey, I'm frowning, too. I mean, come on. He has allowed my family to be ripped apart in a million pieces like the picture of Blake that Christina tore to shreds. The stubborn side of me wants to engage in a battle of the wills to see who can out-frown the other. Okay, I'm not an imbecile—I know who will win. I'm merely giving Him a run for His money.

And if God does show up this weekend, that's exactly what I'll tell Him.

16

A father's love is like chocolate.
No matter how hard you try to resist, you'll always crave it.
SARA PRICE, MY THERAPIST

I t's Friday morning and the weather report is calling for a 90 percent chance of snow. Or, I should say, more snow. There are already a couple inches on the ground, but according to Mr. Weather Man, this is nothing. Mounds more are definitely on the way.

But I, a more accurate meteorologist, say chances are 50-50. Michigan weather reporters take a lot of heat—pun intended—because our state is bordered by the Great Lakes, and the weather tends to be pretty unpredictable. Many storm watches and warnings go by without a flake of snow or drop of rain. It's not that the storm isn't headed our way, but more often than not, it veers off at the last minute and completely misses us.

Truth be told, I love a good storm—snow or thunder. As long as I don't have to be outside in it and can cozy up indoors with a good book. So when I hear the weather report on Saturday morning, my first thought is that since the kids will be gone, spending the whole weekend snuggled up in my robe while losing myself in a couple of books I've been meaning to read sounds inviting.

My second thought revolves around my kids' safety. Should I even allow the kids to go away with Richard this weekend if the weather does, indeed, show its blustery face?

Then a third thought hits me. I might have an excuse to back out of the reunion! Driving in snowstorms or even blizzards normally doesn't bother me much. I've heard that, in Tennessee and Arizona, schools shut down when a trace of snow hits the ground. In Michigan, that's laughable. Twelve *feet* of snow barely keeps us home. But still, I could milk the whole snow thing and tell Sylvie I don't want to risk it. Wonder if she'd fall for it?

Doubtful.

The kids are glad to have a few days off, though Christina still isn't thrilled about wasting winter break with her dad and grandmother. She's made it perfectly clear she'd much rather spend it at the mall with friends. But, to use her favorite word, *whatever*. She'll get over it.

All three have packed their suitcases, which now sit neatly in a row by the back door. Max's is a manly black duffel bag. It doesn't even look like anything is inside—probably only his boxers and a couple pairs of jeans. Perhaps a picture of Sam. I briefly consider snooping but then think better of it. Maybe I don't want to know.

Christina's brown and turquoise striped bag is practically ripping at the seams. It's obvious she's packed enough for an entire week. She thinks she needs clothing to suit every mood. And, because she's almost sixteen and extremely hormonal, that means for the weekend she's probably packed at least twelve outfits.

Emily has carefully packed the only bag she has—a pink Strawberry Shortcake suitcase she got for Christmas four years ago. She's been begging for a new one, as this one is much too babyish for a nine-year-old. I can't argue with that. It looks very out of place next to the bigger, more grown-up bags. Mr. Snuggles, her stuffed lion, is propped on top, along with her hot pink and lime floral pillow.

Gloom overwhelms me. Emotions long buried rise to the surface. Standing in the kitchen gazing at my kids' weekend bags, preparing to say good-bye to them as they go off with their dad, is too much. I know how they feel, because I used to be them. My brother and I spent many weekends and Wednesday nights with my dad. He would take us out for dinner, to the movies, bowling. Dad always tried to make our time together fun—and it was, I guess—but there was always an underlying intense sadness because of the fact that he wasn't coming home with us.

Every time Dad dropped us off, I remember thinking he looked relieved our time together was over. He would walk us up to the house and try his best to hightail it out of there before Mom appeared at the door. Unfortunately, she was usually watching out the window for us to return and would be standing there waiting, stalker-like.

I can't blame Dad for trying to rush off, though. The second we got home Mom would start with the questioning. "What did you do?" or, "Where did you go?" or, "Did he make you brush your teeth every night before bed?" or her favorite, "He didn't bring home a woman, did he?"

The thing is, Dad rarely brought women to meet us. When he did, the ladies were always nice, or at least cordial. And even when his girlfriends spent the entire weekend, Zach and I would always answer with, "No, Mom. We just hung out with Dad." It didn't even occur to us to tell her the truth. We both knew if we did, she would keep us up all night to interrogate us about the "other woman."

Now I find myself wondering if there will come a time when Rich brings women home to meet our kids. When tears sting my eyes, I blink them back and look away from the bags.

The phone rings.

It's Dad. "Hey, kiddo. How are you holding up?"

"I'm okay. Hey, thanks again for taking the kids to Bible study last Thursday night. And for sending Zach to check on me," I add.

"What? Oh, I thought I left my glasses on the counter, and I asked him to swing by and see if—"

"I almost believe you, Dad. But I do appreciate your concern. What I don't understand is why you let Rich hang around without warning me first."

"Sorry about that, honey. I tried talking Rich into coming with us and giving you some time, but he was pretty insistent. He said he'd wait until you came out and that he only wanted to talk. And then it got late and we had to leave if we wanted to make it to church on time. I hope you're not upset with me."

"I'm not mad. Just tired." Time to change the subject. "So how was Bible Study?"

"Oh, it was great, as always. We missed you, though, especially during the praise and worship time. You know Candice...she can't carry a tune." He chuckles. "At least when you're on the other side of me, I can focus on your lovely voice. I know this sounds terrible, but I kept getting distracted by Candice's screechiness."

I can't help but smile. Candice has a lot of great qualities, but singing isn't one of them.

"Bible study was great, though. Candice said the women talked about forgiveness," he adds.

Somehow this doesn't surprise me. "Sorry I missed it."

"So...about what Maxine said the other day...you know, about Rich. Is there anything you want to talk about, sweetheart?"

So much for changing the subject. My smile fades as a strange feeling creeps into my soul. Talk about Richard's sexual indiscretions with my cheating father? No thanks. That would be like asking for child-raising advice from an abusive mother.

"Not really." I know my dad means well, but I'm itching to end this conversation. "Hey, Dad, I have to go. Raymond is picking up the kids and dropping them off to Rich. They're going to visit Nancy this weekend."

"Okay, kiddo. But if you need anything at all, please call. Candice is really worried about you. And so am I."

"I'm fine. But thanks."

"Hey, is Emily all right? She was pretty quiet the other night."

I grimace and, before my brain can catch up with my mouth, I blurt out, "Em will be fine, Dad. Max will be fine, Christina will be fine, and I'll be fine. Okay?"

Boy, I can sound witchy at times.

There's a pause at the other end as my dad likely processes my sudden irritability. "Okay, honey. I love you."

"Yup," I say.

Click.

Uncouth, I know. But sometimes self-preservation comes at the expense of being rude to people you care about.

I know an apology will be in order—later, when I'm in a better mood. For now, I will put on my happy mask for my kids while I weep behind it.

The thing I can't stop thinking about is that I told my dad we will all be fine.

But will we?

"When is Uncle Ray gonna be here?" Emily's face is pressed to the window.

"Any minute, sweetie."

"It's starting to snow again, Mom."

So it is. Big, heavy flakes float down from the sky. Still, I doubt it will amount to much, even though the Weather Channel continues warning of potential blizzard conditions. I'll be surprised if we get three inches.

"Don't worry, honey," I assure Emily, who is regarding me with furrowed brow. "Even if we do get the snow they're calling for, you'll be far enough south. It's not supposed to reach you."

She frowns. "But what about you?"

Hello...could I be the star of *Dumb and Dumber,* or what? Emily isn't thinking about herself, she's thinking about me. Probably conjuring up visions of her mom stranded outside in a blizzard, lying in a snow bank somewhere, unable to call for help.

I crouch down so we're eye-to-eye. "Don't worry about me, sweetie. I'll be fine. You know me. I love a good snow storm. Think of me sitting here by the window with a good book, drinking my humongous mug of coffee, watching the snow come down." I smile. "You have the phone, right?"

She unzips her coat pocket and pulls out the cell.

"And you know my cell number?"

She recites it by memory.

"Try me at home first. If I'm not here, call my cell. And if I don't pick up, don't panic. Leave me a message, and I'll call you back as soon as I can." I pull her into a hug. "Okay?"

"I'll miss you," she says, voice quivering.

My heart cries. "I'll miss you too, babe. But it's only a couple of days. Besides, Grandma Nancy will keep you so busy you won't have time to miss me too much."

"Do you think she'll let me give Champ a bath, like last time?" Emily perks up at the thought of her grandma's cocker spaniel.

"I'm sure of it."

Emily turns back to the window as Raymond pulls into the driveway in a sporty, red, Mustang convertible.

I do a double take. *What is he thinking? It's snowing, for goodness' sake.* That thing should not even *see* snow. It should be locked up in storage somewhere for the winter.

Emily's eyes expand, and she squeals, "Max! Christina! Uncle Ray is here! And look at his car!" She takes off in search of her siblings.

I fling open the door and meet Ray with a glare.

Sunglasses cover his eyes. His light brown hair is slicked back in normal fashion, and his white T-shirt pokes out the top of his black leather coat. It looks as if he stepped out of the fifties, sans the rolled-up jeans and penny loafers, which he's substituted with blasted Levis and a pair of Timberland work boots. Actually, he's a replica of my husband, but from another era.

"Hey, Mads," he says with a grin. His effort to appear charming falls flat on me. Ignoring my scowl, he ambles up the front steps, coolly removes his glasses, and slides them, along with his hands, into his leather coat pockets.

"What do you think you're doing, Ray? There's a blizzard warning. My children are not getting into that—that—car with you." I can't believe I couldn't come up with something better than "car," but Ray's got me flustered. I'm relieved to escape the stress of seeing Richard today, but still, a blood-pressure pill would do me good about now.

"Mads," he says calmly, irritating me even more. "You and I both know there won't be any blizzard. I took Red Rider out just for the kids. So sue me for wanting to add some excitement to their lives. Lord knows they can use it right now."

"They don't need excitement, Ray, they need to live another day. You might as well put them on a sled greased with oil and shove them into oncoming traffic."

"I took it easy. I'm not stupid." He pulls his hand from pocket and holds it up. "Don't say it."

I clamp my mouth shut and glare some more, letting my eyes do the talking.

Max, Christina and Emily traipse to the door, luggage in tow.

Max looks out and his eyes increase by two times their normal size when he sees the car. "Cool! When did you get the Mustang?"

Raymond slides his eyes toward me before responding. I could swear they're laughing.

"I got it from the lot. Pulled a few strings to get the boss to let me take it on an overnight. I wanted to surprise you guys. "

"Sweet," coos Christina. "You should buy it, Uncle Ray."

He grins. "As soon as I sucker another dozen people into paying too much for their cars...hey, talk about sweet. How'd you get that shiner?" He looks impressed.

Christina's eye is turning a nice shade of green.

"She got in a fight," Em blurts out.

"I hope the other guy looks worse."

I roll my eyes as Christina confirms that Paige Hardaway does, in fact, look much worse than she does.

"Oh, speaking of," Christina says, turning to me, "Paige says to expect a call from her mom's lawyer. They're definitely going to sue."

"What?"

"Bye, Mom!" Christina is out the door as her words struggle to fully register in my brain.

"It'll be okay, Mom," Max says, patting my back. "I'll ask Dad what to do. He knows more about this stuff than you do." He grabs Emily's Strawberry Shortcake suitcase, says good-bye, and makes his way out the door.

"Who's Sue?" Em asks.

"What? Oh—nobody. Never mind."

I'm officially going to be sued by the boyfriend stealer's parents. Oy.

I say good-bye to Em. I hug her tightly and try to take enough to last the weekend. She pulls away and bounces off toward the Mustang, Mr. Snuggles under one arm, bright floral pillow under the other.

"Sounds like you have a few things on your mind these days," Ray says when we're alone.

For a moment, I can't tell whether he is being sarcastic. As I look at Ray, his face says he is genuinely concerned, but his tone sounds mocking. As a sarcastic person myself, and knowing Ray like I do, I know not to let my guard down. But I soften my tone.

"I'll be fine."

"You know, Max is right. Rich will know what to do. Men always do."

I shoot eye daggers at my brother-in-law. I knew the genuineness was too good to be true.

"Just like they always know how to tear their families apart?"

Raymond considers me for a long second and feigns a frown. He puts a hand to his chest. "That really hurts, Mads. I'd take it as a personal attack, but I don't have a family. So you must be talking about Richard."

Why do I allow Ray to get under my skin?

Glancing out the window, I watch the kids as they check out the car. It's still snowing, but not as hard. "Okay, here's the deal. Do not even think about letting the speedometer get above thirty miles per hour. And call me as soon as you get home to let me know you arrived—my *kids* arrived—safely. Can you do that, Ray?"

He shrugs. "Sure I can. But will I?" He smirks, then turns and walks to the car. Is it wrong to pray for Ray to slip and fall on the ice…just to humble him a bit? And because I could use a good laugh?

I motion for Max to roll down the window, which he interprets as waving. He smiles and waves to me in response.

My kids are good about buckling their seatbelts but, in case, I cup my hands around my mouth and, like a madwoman, yell, "Fasten your seatbelts!" as Red Rider rolls backwards down the driveway.

But they don't hear me above the rock music blaring, the pulsating bass loud enough for me to hear fifty feet away. I shake my head at Em, who is doing some head-banging in the backseat, her fists pumping the air.

I utter the first prayer I've said in over a week. "Oh, Lord. Please keep my kids safe."

17

Quit complaining! When I was your age,
I had to walk three miles to school
through fourteen feet of snow.

MY MOTHER

I finally pull that box of Nice 'n' Easy from my bathroom cupboard and color the gray right out of my hair. A good half inch of gray roots—gone! I feel ten years younger, at least. I'll never understand those ladies who let themselves "go gray." I am in no hurry to show the world my real age. It's bad enough that most of the time I feel almost forty—I certainly don't want to look it, too.

Sylvie calls around eleven to confirm one last time that we're still on for the reunion. She knows me too well and is worried she'll arrive to pick me up only to find me glued to my computer chair in my leopard-print jammies.

"You know we're supposed to get dumped on, right?"

"Good try," she says. "That storm has about as much chance of hitting us as Ryder has of bringing home an A in algebra." She speaks of her fourteen-year-old son and creative genius. *A*'s in English and Art are a given. Algebra? They throw a party when he gets a *C*.

"Are you really going to make me go?"

"Quit whining. It'll be fun."

"Yeah. Like a pap smear."

I'm beginning to think I really am Sybil. But my emotions emerge and retreat at a much faster pace than Sybil's alter-egos. I keep going back and forth about tonight. I don't want to go. I do want to go. I guess I'll go. Don't make me go. Ugh.

Sylvie listens as I fill her in on Rich taking the kids this weekend.

"Even one more reason to go tonight. I know you, Madi. If you stay home, you'll wind up sitting on that stupid computer playing Solitaire until your fingertips go numb. You need to get out and socialize. Take your mind off things for a while."

See what I mean? Sylvie does know me. A little too well sometimes. But, as usual, she's right. I swallow my pride and admit it. "Whatever," I say, sounding annoyingly like Christina.

"I'll tell you what. If you're not having the time of your life by nine o'clock, I'll bail with you."

Reluctantly, I accept Sylvie's offer and agree to give her two and a half hours. "But be prepared to leave Reggie's promptly at nine."

"I'll pick you up at six." She hangs up before I can change my mind.

I spend the next couple hours putzing around the house. Around four o'clock, I open my closet to select an outfit and settle on a pair of dark-washed denim jeans and a red turtleneck sweater.

On to the bathroom to apply my makeup. At first glance, it looks as if I've morphed into a raccoon. The shadows under my eyes make me regret not picking up a bag of potatoes to see if Sylvie's suggestion really works. I guess concealer and powder will have to do.

Forty minutes later, I'm ready to go. My final evaluation is a mixture of good and bad. Although I'm glad I colored my hair, I'm in need of a cut, so the volume is squashed beneath the heaviness, and my bangs hang in a heavy chunk across my forehead. Should've called Anya for a trim days ago. And although I like my outfit, the Dibs are definitely taking a toll. My jeans and sweater hug me a little too closely. I suck in and turn sideways. Not bad. But the thought of holding in my tummy all night does not appeal to me. I let out my breath and watch as my belly returns to its previous bloated state.

Oh well, no one to impress anyway.

With still an hour until Sylvie arrives, I hesitantly pick up my Bible and head to the living room. One look out the window tells me that, for once, the weather people may have gotten it right. Snow is falling at a rapid pace. Wow. Tearing my eyes away from the snow-globe-like scene is nearly impossible. Not sure if that's because of its beauty, or I'm avoiding opening my Bible.

I play "speak to me," a game that my pastor once warned the congregation against playing. It's that game where you open up the Bible and see which verse jumps out at you. Not that it's bad to randomly read Bible verses, but sometimes we expect God to speak to us this way. It's as if we want a "magic message from God." He may speak to people that way sometimes, but most of the time He'd probably rather have us dig into His Word and study it because we want to know Him better. Not because we're trying to get a quick and easy solution to a problem.

And really, we can turn God's Word into anything we want it to be.

Many verses can be interpreted in a way that makes us assume it's a response to our current situation. What it comes down to is listening for the Holy Spirit's voice, not merely what we hope—or expect—to hear.

But right now, I don't know where to start digging. And honestly, I'm not sure I want to hear what God has to say. Probably because I know it won't be pleasant. Because I'm thinking He won't be sympathizing with my "right" to be angry with my husband. More likely, God will bombard me with verses on forgiveness and love.

Mmmm, nope. Can't go there yet.

So I close my eyes and thumb through the pages before letting it fall open onto my lap. I open one eye and peer at the book. Ephesians. Figures it would land on the book loaded with discipline and admonition.

My gaze rests on the fourth chapter.

> You were taught, with regard to your former way of life, to put off your old self, which is being corrupted by its deceitful desires; to be made new in the attitude of your minds; and to put on the new self, created to be like God in true righteousness and holiness.

Verse 23 won't let me go. "To be made new in the attitude of your minds." Okay, that's something I can take to heart. My mind has been misbehaving for years. It can definitely use an attitude adjustment. Maybe God decided to play "speak to me" after all. Then again, maybe His Word is always speaking to me—it's simply a matter of opening my ears.

I place the attached ribbon-slash-bookmark in the crease of the page and close the Bible. Ephesians 4:23. I think I'll make that my new motto. I want to be made new in the attitude of my mind.

♛

"I can't believe I let you talk me into this."

The snow is really coming down now, and large accumulations seem probable. The winds are picking up, and visibility is decreasing. Tonight, of all nights, the weatherman has to be right.

"We'll be fine, thanks to Earl letting me borrow his Land Rover." She pats the dash of her stepfather's vehicle. "This baby can get through anything. Anyway, chances are the snow will let up by the time we're ready to leave."

I gape at my friend. "I don't know, Sylv. Look at the way it's coming down. The weather report is calling for blizzard conditions at least until midnight." I rest my head against the seat. "We're risking our lives to attend a reunion with people we don't even like. I don't get it."

Sylvie laughs. "You know, I remember a time when you were fearless. Remember when you practically drove through a tornado to get to my house?"

"That day, my mother was more of a threat than any tornado warning. You'd have done the same thing if your mom was acting like a crazy person."

"Of course I would have. But my point is you've turned into a wimp, Madi. When did that happen?"

"When I became a mom?" I ask, as if Sylvie can confirm it was, indeed, at that moment when I lost my backbone. Honestly, I don't know exactly when I lost my risk-taking spirit. Maybe Richard's safe, practical ways have rubbed off on me over the years. Maybe I've been losing it little by little and that's why today I am, as Sylvie said so plainly, a wimp.

Sylvie has eased up on the gas. She's concentrating now as gusts of wind lift the snow off one side of the road and toss it violently to the other.

My thoughts turn to my kids. Emily called before I left to let me know they had arrived safely at Raymond's house. She went on and on about Uncle Raymond's car and how cool it was, assuring me he only spun out twice, when no cars were around. Gee, that made me feel so much better. As I wound down the call, Em asked if I wanted to talk to Richard, who was outside at the moment, packing the Ford Explorer (much safer…thank goodness…than the tiny Red Rider) for the weekend trip to Grandma's. Emily was clearly disappointed when I declined her offer to speak to her dad.

I hope that by this time they are far enough south that they're missing the storm. Reaching into my purse, I check my cell phone. No missed calls.

In between momentary concentration pauses, Sylvie chatters away. She talks about her boys, Ryder and Sage, who are at Ike's sister's house for the weekend to spend some time with their cousins. I think it's nice that Sylvie still keeps in close contact with Ike's family.

The conversation eventually turns to the salon.

"Hey, I may have a job opportunity for you."

I raise my eyebrows.

"Shelly quit today."

"Who's Shelly?"

"You know, the receptionist. The one with the purple spiked hair."

I nod. "Wonder if she's any relation to Sam."

"What?"

"Never mind. So why did she quit?"

"She's moving to California. Says she's destined to be working on Rodeo

Drive. Next Friday's her last day. You should apply."

"Why? Because I have such a perky nature and cheerful phone voice?"

She laughs. "Well, you may need to work on that. But, really, you'd be perfect. It's not a hard job at all."

"That was a compliment, right?"

Sylvie goes on to say how fun it would be to work together. But I'm thinking I would spend most of my time comparing myself to all the size four spa girls with shiny hair, constant root-lift, straight white teeth, flawless skin, and eyebrows waxed to Barbie doll perfection. I can't picture myself fitting in with my not-size-four figure, hair that falls flat in temperatures above forty degrees, PMS pimple-prone skin, and eyebrows that, when neglected (which is often), have been mistaken for caterpillars.

But let's be realistic here. Finding a job may soon be necessary. And I have to say, being around gorgeous women who know all of the outer beauty secrets might not be a bad thing. Who knows? Maybe I'd even be asked to appear on the local television show, Total Transformation, where they take an ugly duckling and turn her into a beautiful princess. I may not look like an ugly duckling all the time, but during those times when I peer in the mirror and see my dad's jowls waving back at me, I definitely qualify.

On that note, I tell Sylvie if it comes down to it, I may polish up that résumé and pop over to the salon very soon.

Sylvie turns the Land Rover down the last three-mile stretch of long, winding road that will soon dead-end into Reggie's Classy Diner. On a sunny day, the drive down this road is breathtaking—especially in the fall, when trees line both sides of the road and turn brilliant shades of orange and yellow and red. I often take a detour down this stretch for no reason other than to enjoy the scenery. Every time I do, I know I'm getting a glimpse of the brilliance of heaven. Tonight, however, even illuminated by the Land Rover's headlights, I can barely make out the shapes of the leafless trees behind the blowing snow.

We plow ahead toward Reggie's, sandwiched between two other restaurants—an Italian Grill and an upscale (translation: high-priced) seafood place. All three restaurants have large decks off the back on which patrons can lounge, mill about, and, when the weather cooperates, enjoy the peaceful scenery and beautiful sunsets. The eateries are close enough together that if you speak loudly enough, you can carry on a conversation with someone dining at one of the other restaurants. Since all three have liquor licenses, many people restaurant-hop—particularly after nine o'clock, when families are replaced with young married couples, college singles, and slimy men on the prowl.

Reggie's is a hangout for the younger crowd, mostly because their menu offers a variety of food choices, including teenage and young adult favorites: pizza and burgers. They also have live entertainment—namely, a karaoke stage—where kids can prove they are the next *American Idol,* and adults make fools of themselves. Once, when they were twelve, Max and Christina dragged me onto the stage and forced me to sing "Love Stinks," by the J. Geils Band. How appropriate that, four years later, that title would turn out to be my life's theme song.

My stomach growls, interrupting my nonsensical thoughts. I squint into the snow as the Land Rover inches along. At this rate, the five-minute drive to the end of the cul-de-sac will take a good half hour.

"Well, we aren't the only ones to venture out tonight. There are several sets of headlights following behind us," Sylvie says.

I glance over my shoulder. "Wow. There are people as stupid as we are. Go figure."

Sylvie dares to take her eyes off the road for a second to shoot me a dirty look. "We are not stupid, Madi, just adventurous."

"You are such an Ariel."

"Huh?"

"I've been seeing Sarah Price and she says—"

"Sarah Price the psychologist from church?"

"Yes."

Sylvie glances at me. "I think that's great, Madi. Really, I do. She did wonders for me after Ike's death."

Memory jog. I had forgotten that Sylvie saw Dr. Price for about six months after her husband died.

"But Ariel? What's up with that?" Sylvie asks.

"Sarah is trying to convince me that I'm a princess. She wants me to see myself that way, anyway. And if I could compare you to a princess, it would definitely be Ariel. She was curious...adventurous...always seeking thrills. You remember the story."

"I have boys, remember? They never really got into the whole princess thing. But I totally agree with what Sarah said about being God's princess. We are daughters of the King, you know."

"That's exactly what Sarah said."

Sylvie leans forward, squinting into the snow. "What's that?"

I follow her gaze to a car on the side of the road. The hazard lights are flashing and a woman is flailing her arms, obviously trying to flag someone down.

"Oh, that poor woman. Only a mile to go, and she breaks down."

"Maybe she's stuck."

"I'm pulling over," Sylvie decides.

Okay, forgive me here, but the last thing I feel like doing is stopping in the middle of an oncoming blizzard. First of all, I'm not dressed for snow, as I am wearing fashion boots and a denim jacket. Sylvie may have been smart enough to wear her down jacket and furry white boots, but she looks cute in snow garb. It only makes me look frumpy. At Sylvie's suggestion, I did throw my frump-o-matic boots and my winter coat into the back of the Rover, in case, but I don't feel like climbing over the seat to retrieve them.

And then there's the hair thing. My black wool pea coat doesn't have a hood and I spent a half-hour wrestling with the curling iron, getting my hair to flip just right. Not that I care what my "friends" from high school think or anything.

But although bypassing a stranded motorist is something I might have done ten years ago, now I know better. Helping fellow citizens in times of peril is definitely the Christian thing to do, even when I don't feel like it. *Especially* when I don't feel like it. Wonder if I'll collect any bonus points for this nice gesture of Christian love even though I opened my Bible today for the first time in a week.

As our headlights illuminate the woman, my mouth drops. I thought *I* was inappropriately dressed for the weather. The only sensible piece of clothing she is wearing is a heavy, olive green coat with a large, fur-trimmed hood that overlaps her head by a good two inches, concealing her face. Two things that are visible are her long, spidery thin legs, covered seductively (to put it nicely) by black, fishnet stockings. Just the tip of her cut-off denim mini skirt hangs about a quarter of an inch below the hem of her jacket. And boots? Pfft. But why wear boots when spiked four-inch heels do such a better job of completing the outfit?

Sylvie puts the Land Rover in park. The woman, wobbling in her heels, schleps toward us through the snow. Gloveless hands hold her hood in place, and I'm thinking surely both her hands and feet have acquired frostbite by now. I brace myself for the sight of blackened fingers and toes.

Sylvie slides down her window. "Get in, girlfriend! We'll give you a ride!"

As the door bursts open, an invasion of bitter, gusty air assaults us. The woman climbs in, followed by a heady scent of musky perfume that fills the vehicle like a fog. She tosses her suitcase-sized purse onto the seat.

Unbidden, my mother's warning about picking up strangers wafts through my mind. I've seen enough *Law & Order* episodes to know the dangers lurking out there. For all we know, this woman might not be a woman at all. I mean, we have yet to see her face. Maybe she is a man, albeit an awfully skinny one, dressed in women's clothing to lure unsuspecting victims to their torture and—gulp—death.

I wonder what's in her/his bag. It's definitely large enough to hold a gun. Or duct tape and rope. Or body parts.

A chill tickles my spine. Fear invades my soul, and my heart pounds against my wool sweater. Within ten seconds, I am entertaining the idea that this "woman" is the FBI's most wanted, bloodthirsty, serial killer!

In slow motion, she pushes back her hood.

I gasp. It's even worse.

It's Fawn Witchburn!

18

Quit screaming and just breathe.
RICHARD, THE NIGHT EMILY WAS BORN

God is punishing me, I am sure of it. I haven't given Him the time of day lately and He is making me pay.

Had I said that out loud, Sylvie would argue with me. She says God doesn't work that way. He doesn't punish us for ignoring Him. That ignoring God results in enough punishment—like lack of peace, discontentment, and fear (all three of which I have been experiencing). But, right now, I am convinced He is, indeed, working like that. I mean, out of several hundred women traveling this road tonight, the one who happens to get stranded and *we* happen to pick up just happens to be the woman my husband is sleeping with. A little too "coincidental," in my opinion.

Fawn lets her long auburn hair loose and it tumbles over her shoulders, reminding me of the shampoo commercials I see on television. Before she looks directly at me, I quickly turn around in my seat and stare out the passenger window.

A car passes. The woman driver slows and turns to gawk. Despite the twenty-year lapse, there is no mistaking that it is my former classmate, the one and only, Anita Chiquita. I attempt a cheerful wave, trying to take my mind off the "other woman" in the backseat. Anita obviously doesn't recognize me. She mistakes me for a lunatic and guns it, tires spinning.

I notice in the side mirror that several more cars are coming. Yep, there's no doubt about it. In Michigan, people are used to driving in nasty weather conditions. Even a blizzard warning can't keep them away from the lobster dinner they crave or a night of cheesy karaoke at Reggie's Classy Diner.

As Sylvie pulls onto the road again, she pretends to reach for her purse and punches me in the leg. I refuse to look at her, partly because I don't want Fawn to recognize me and partly because if I do, I will punch her back. Sylvie is strong for a tiny woman, and I suspect my leg will show signs of bruising in the morning.

"It's freezing out there." Fawn's voice is low and sultry. "I should have dressed warmer."

Ya think?

"Are you flat?" Sylvie asks. Normally, we would both get a good laugh out of that one. But the last thing I can do right now is laugh. And Sylvie is too good a friend to make light of this so-not-funny situation.

The implication is lost on Fawn. "No, I ran out of gas. I knew I should have filled up this afternoon."

"That stinks." Sylvie tosses me a sideways glance.

Speaking of "stinks," I catch another whiff of Fawn's perfume, which is quickly giving me a headache.

"We're on our way to Reggie's. Which restaurant are you headed to?" Sylvie asks. I sense the tension in her voice, but that's only because I know her so well. Fawn probably thinks Sylvie's voice is always high and screechy.

"I'm meeting a friend at The Whitefish. You can drop me at the door." As if it will be a privilege.

I hear Fawn rummaging through her purse-slash-suitcase. She clucks her tongue. "First, I can't find my cell phone, now my lipstick. Do you think they ran off together?"

Must be her attempt at humor. Again—so not funny. I resist the urge to remind her that if her cell phone and lipstick have run off together, it's probably because she has taught them well, considering she runs off with things all the time. Namely, other women's husbands.

A long, sharp fingernail taps my shoulder. I flinch and feel a hot flash coming on.

"Hey, do you have any lipstick I can borrow? Preferably brown."

As if! Like I would let Fawn Witchburn borrow something as personal as lipstick. Like I would let her lips touch something mine touch every day.

Okay. Poor choice of words.

In spite of myself, I dig through my purse and pull out the darkest lipstick I can find, which is more of a burgundy than brown. I am acutely aware that Sylvie is giving me her "Are you nuts?" look and probably wants to punch me again.

"You can keep it." I hand it over my shoulder without turning my head.

"Do I know you? You look familiar."

"I don't think so. I must have one of those familiar…backs of the head."

Sylvie lets out a noise resembling a snort.

"I don't know…there's something about you that seems…oh, wait!" Fawn snaps her fingers. "I know."

I close my eyes and wait for it. For Fawn Witchburn to blurt out the fact that she knows I am The Wife. The Wife of her daughter's teacher and her current man-flavor of the month. My hot flash has escalated to burning-up-flash and—horror of horrors—there is perspiration trickling down my cleavage. If the pits of my sweater end up with sweat stains, Fawn will definitely be getting the dry cleaning bill.

"Have you recently been a guest at the Renaissance?"

The Renaissance is a local, privately owned hotel on the shore of Lake Michigan. It boasts upper-class accommodations, mainly for wealthy business people or well-off couples from nearby cities who want to escape the hustle and bustle for a weekend of serenity and a breathtaking view of the water.

I have stayed at the Renaissance once—and only once—on my tenth wedding anniversary when Rich and I couldn't afford to take a real vacation and settled for two nights away in a Jacuzzi suite at the Renaissance. We wouldn't have been able to afford even that, but an envelope mysteriously appeared in our mailbox, stuffed with six hundred dollars cash and a note demanding we use it for a weekend away. The handwriting looked oddly like Candice's, but with an upward slant scribble-ness to it, as if she'd purposely tried to disguise her writing. She vehemently denied leaving the note, but if I'd had a fingerprint kit handy, she would have been totally busted.

"I haven't been to the Renaissance in a long time," I say flippantly, as if I now prefer the five-star Hilton.

"Oh." She sounds disappointed. "I work there. I'm the night manager."

"How convenient for you." My sarcasm spews forth with a vengeance.

"Excuse me?" She leans forward, and I fight the tickle teasing the back of my throat as her perfume invades my space.

I cough and turn around, giving her full view of my face. "What I mean is, it must be nice to have the full use of..." I'm tempted here to insert "available men," but then I realize not all of the men she uses are truly available. At least, not in the single vs. married sense. So I go with "workout facilities." "You can probably use the fitness room for free, right? That is, if you don't get your exercise another way."

Before I can say, "Oops, that last part just slipped out," my blood begins to boil. I realize that, for the past few minutes, it has been simmering quietly as I have been in a state of semi-shock that my husband's lover is sitting two feet behind me.

The fact she doesn't recognize me as Richard's wife is downright infuriating. She mistakes me for a guest at her hotel? Whatever! I have passed her in church a million times. Our daughters are in the same Sunday school class. Plus, Richard has a picture of me on his desk. Then again, during that "parent-teacher conference," I'm sure Fawn wasn't taking inventory of his desk accessories. Or maybe that photo happened to get shoved in a drawer five minutes before Ms. Witchburn arrived. In fact, I bet that's exactly what happened. At the moment, I wouldn't put anything past my husband.

"We're here!" Sylvie chirps in an octave higher than normal.

Fawn opens the door. "Thanks for the ride, ladies. Maybe after dinner my friends and I will head over to Reggie's for a drink. We'll stop and say hi." I am still staring at Fawn, trying not to focus on what she has that I don't. Besides the obvious. She cocks her head toward me. "I will figure out where I've seen you before." She swings a daddy long leg out of the Land Rover, then leans back as her fishnet stocking dangles out the door. "Oh, here." She holds out the lipstick. "Burgundy isn't really my color."

I take it from her and watch as she gracefully exits. I hope she'll take her heady perfume scent with her but it lingers like a rotten egg, a sickening reminder that the last five minutes weren't a bad dream.

I turn and smash the lipstick into the dash, envisioning—bad girl that I am—that it is Fawn's face.

"I'm gonna throw up." I grip the white porcelain sink and stare at myself in the mirror. My face is pasty. I desperately need a tan. Maybe I'll get a job at a tanning salon. It may not pay a lot, but at least I'll always look healthy. At least, until skin cancer sets in.

A middle-aged woman bustles out of a stall and tosses a nervous glance my way. She obviously heard my comment and is probably hoping I don't barf all over her red and white striped blazer and matching red shoes. The woman leaves without washing her hands. Talk about gross.

"You are not going to throw up. Madi, look at me." Sylvie takes me by the shoulders and physically turns me to face her. "It's okay. It's over."

"Over? It's over? It is definitely not over, Sylv! It's right here—all the time." I tap my newly colored hairline. "Right up here, Fawn Witchburn and my husband are doing the nasty. Constantly. Do you know what it's like to have those images play over and over and over in your mind? And then to have her in the same car with me…" I cover my face with my hands. "I can't take this."

Sylvie pulls me into a hug. "I know," she says.

But she doesn't know. Not really.

I pull away and take a couple deep breaths. I glance down at my jeans, which still have smudges of burgundy lipstick on them, the result of my psychotic lipstick-smashing moment on the dashboard of Sylvie's dad's Land Rover. I can only hope it comes off the leather seat.

I stare at my friend, who is speechless for a change. "Let's go over the facts, shall we? Number one." I hold out a finger. "My husband's been cheating—with a woman who looks like she belongs in a brothel instead of sitting on the pew behind me in church.

"Two. In one week, my fifteen-year-old daughter asked to go on birth control pills and got into a cat fight over a the boy who's pressuring her to have sex, and I'm going to get sued over it.

"Three. My son is salivating over a girl with spiked hair and multiple facial piercings, which probably don't end with the facial part, but, really, do I want to know?

"Four. My mother has been keeping track of the days—the days, Sylv—since my father left. She should probably be locked up in a mental institution.

"Then, when I think it can't possibly get any worse, number five comes along." I wave my stiff open hand in front of her face. "My husband's lover, the Wicked Witch in my life's princess story, sits twelve inches behind me, looks me in the eye, and has no clue that I am the woman whose husband she's sleeping with. She even borrowed my lipstick!"

"I can't believe you gave her that lipstick." Sylvie's hand flies to her mouth. "I'm sorry. That was a stupid thing to say."

Sadness and anger collide. I am not one to break out in hysterical sobs, especially in public, so the anger part is winning. I'll save the tears for when I'm home, alone. Closing my eyes, I take some deep breaths.

"Do you want me to pray with you?" Sylvie takes my hand.

I pull my hand away like it connected with a hot oven burner. Normally, I would jump at her offer to pray for me. But I can't bring myself to do it.

"I appreciate your offer, Sylv—I really do. But I'm not in the mood to pray right now." In the back of my mind, I'm thinking how very glad I am that Christ's dying on the cross for me didn't depend on His mood. "Thanks, though, for being a great friend. At least I have one person in this world I can trust. One friend who will never let me down. Not counting that lipstick comment."

Sylvie looks away and fidgets with her necklace. She clears her throat. "You know what? Let's leave. Let's rent a movie or something and ditch this whole reunion idea. You were right—it's silly to waste our time with people we haven't seen in twenty years. Come on, let's go." She turns on her heel and starts to walk toward the door. After a few steps, she stops and peers over her shoulder. "Are you coming?"

"No."

"Why not? I thought you'd be sprinting out of here."

I lean against the sink and cross my arms. "Spill it."

"What do you mean?" Sylvie's caramel-colored eyes gaze everywhere but at me. Totally atypical Sylvie.

"You forget. I've known you for thirty years. I think I know by now when you're having a Sybil moment. I mean, you've been practically jumping out of your skin to get to this reunion thingy. Now that we're here, you're suddenly going to bag it? I don't think so, Sylv. Something's definitely going on with you."

She swallows hard and tries to pooh-pooh it away. "My best friend's sanity is more important than this silly reunion."

That answer is so weak.

"Good try. You've said several times recently that there's something you want to talk to me about. Does that 'something' have anything to do with why you're acting so weird? Why you suddenly can't look me in the eye?"

"I am not acting weird. And it's nothing." She struggles to maintain eye contact with me to prove she can. "Really. Let's go, Mads. I'll talk to you about it over popcorn and a huge glass of Diet Coke."

"That confirms it. You don't even drink pop."

The bathroom door opens, and Sylvie steps aside as a mother and daughter enter.

The little girl is staring at me. "Mommy, why does that lady have spots on her jeans?"

"I don't know, sweetie," the woman says quickly. "Come on, I thought you had to go potty." She practically shoves her into the stall.

I stare down again at my jeans. "Sylvie, I can't go out there like this. Help me get this lipstick off my pants."

Clearly glad that I've abandoned grilling her about her strange behavior, Sylvie helps by pulling paper towels from the holder and running them under water. I forcefully dab them at my jeans. All this accomplishes is smearing the lipstick around on the now-soaked denim.

Eventually, most of the lipstick comes off. But now it appears I wet my pants. I stand under the hand dryer and let the warm air blow at my jeans. I get a couple of strange glances from bathroom patrons, but at this point, I'm beyond caring.

"See? Good as new," Sylvie says, trying a little too hard to be cheerful. "So are you ready to go?"

I sigh. "Fine. We'll go. But you are going to tell me what's going on with you. It'll be refreshing to hear about *your* problems for a change."

"Uh, right." Sylvie averts her eyes again.

I narrow my eyes. Although I doubt anything Sylvie has to talk to me about could rival my current situation, I brace myself for the worst. I wouldn't rule out anything right now. If there's one thing I've learned, it's that when you think it can't get any worse, it usually does.

19

There is nothing like returning to a place
that remains unchanged to find the ways
in which you yourself have altered.
NELSON MANDELA

"You aren't going anywhere, Miss." The host of Reggie's Classy Diner blocks the door, preventing us from walking out. His nametag reads *Matthew.* He's clean-cut, with boyish features, and resembles Justin Bieber. I'd be shocked if Matthew is more than eighteen years old. I doubt this kid could stop even a determined five-year-old from leaving.

"Excuse me?" Sylvie says.

"They've closed the road due to the weather. Nobody's leaving. At least, not for a couple hours until the snowplows can come through." Matthew is trying to be professional, but really. His baby face makes it tough to take him seriously.

Sylvie laughs and glances at me. She makes a face. "What a jokester." She looks back at Matthew. "You are joking, right?"

The boy solemnly shakes his head.

Oh, what I'd give to go back in time, to my moment of insanity when I agreed to come to this reunion for two hours instead of staying home, snuggled up in my robe with a trashy romance novel. Okay, maybe romance wouldn't be the best genre for me right now. Mystery...suspense...historical... Anything would be better than this.

It was bad enough ten minutes ago when I was here of my own free will. But now I'm trapped for God-knows-how-long in Reggie's Classy Diner, forced to dine with high school has-beens. This must be what prison is like.

I try not to think about the fact that Fawn Witchburn is next door at the Whitefish and that at any moment she might "pop in to say hi." That would be just the thing to top off my evening.

Taking a minute to scan the place, I see it's pretty crowded, particularly the bar area surrounding the karaoke stage. Several teens mill around the microphones, waiting for the clock to strike seven so they can show off their singing abilities. Or, more probably, lack thereof. But there are twenty more minutes till show time. A group of four girls huddles around the song list, deciding which one they want to perform. One of them looks a lot like Amy.

I squint. Wait a minute—it *is* Amy.

Before I can excuse myself to go say hello, Sylvie grabs my elbow. "Well, it looks like the movie and popcorn will have to wait. At least for two hours, anyway. I guess we don't have a choice. We *have* to stay."

Sylvie is glancing around, her eyes darting here, there, and everywhere.

"What on earth is the matter with you, Sylv? I think I've only seen you act this way twice in thirty years. Once when you didn't want to tell me that Eddie Reynolds hit on you a month after he and I started dating, and the other time when you borrowed my Cyndi Lauper album and scratched the tar out of it."

"I told you—my cat got hold of that album. If you'll recall, I offered to buy you another one. And the Eddie thing was not my fault. He hit on everybody."

"I'm not looking for an apology. I'm only saying you look like you did then—nervous. Like there's something you want to tell me—need to tell me—but don't know how."

"Yeah, well." Her eyes flicked away again.

"That's it? 'Yeah, well'?"

Suddenly, I feel my neck get warm. Someone is breathing down it. Literally. Sylvie's eyes move to the breathing source, then narrow. Her brow creases.

"Madi Sanders…," the breath says. Beer and onions. Ew.

I turn around and quickly back up, stepping on Sylvie's foot. She yelps, but I'm too caught up in my repulsion to apologize. "Oh, hi!" My smile is tight. Acting happy to see someone when you really would rather be locked in a cage with a wild boar is not easy. But when I think about it, I am locked up with a wild boar. And his name is Eddie Reynolds—*aka,* high school boyfriend and class octopus. He never could keep his hands to himself.

It seems not much has changed.

Eddie eyes me like a trough of fresh slop. "You look…so…" He licks his lips.

"Old?" I joke.

"If old means sexy and hot, then yes. You're old, baby." He laughs loudly—drunkenly—and steps closer. Now I'm getting uncomfortable, almost to the point of resorting to fourth-grade behavior and kicking him where it counts.

What on earth did I ever see in this loser? I must have been desperate for attention back then—even grossly negative attention. I shudder at the thought that I'd let the eight-armed octopus get to second base. I make a mental note to repent of that later. You know, when I'm on better terms with God again.

Sylvie grabs my arm and yanks on it. Eddie's face falls as I am pulled away. I flash my wedding ring at him and shrug. Hey, at least the ring's still good for something.

Sylvie and I make our way toward the back of the restaurant to the party room, which Anita supposedly reserved for our get-together.

No one notices us as we make our grand entrance. A few people are seated around the three long tables, but most are standing in small groups. I get a strange sense of déjà vu, as the scene remarkably resembles the hallways of our high school twenty years ago. Best friends and student council members Pamela Cromwell and Wendy Perkins solemnly converse with two men I assume are their husbands. Class clowns Ben Adams, Dirk Dryer, and Shawn Weston are imitating the Three Stooges, while their significant others roll their eyes and shake their heads. Fellow former dweebs Stan Trudeau and Phillip Fryberg hover over their technical gadgets, pushing buttons and undoubtedly talking "Geek."

And there is Anita Chiquita herself, making animated facial expressions as she chats with...I blink a few times in case I'm hallucinating...Bobby Stanton?

Back in high school, Bobby was one of the Grungers. He and his thankfully small group of friends used to brag about the fact that they took showers only every other week and never—ever—threw their clothes in the laundry. Good for their mothers (less laundry to do), but appalling for those of us stuck sitting next to them in class.

I am happy to report that the grunge days appear to be over for Bobby Stanton. Showering and shaving have evidently been added back into his daily routine. Dressed in crisp Levis and a green rugby shirt, the guy has cleaned up well. The thing that strikes me most about Bobby, however, is that his eyes have yet to rise above Anita's chin.

When Anita glances our way, she flashes a smile bigger and brighter than any dentist's ad I've ever seen. She touches Bobby's arm, throws her head back, and laughs flirtatiously before excusing herself. She walks—er, bounces—our way.

As she perkily makes her way across the room, I don't have to be a man to notice that her nose isn't the only thing Anita's had fixed since high school. And the turquoise, deep V-neck sweater she's wearing is proud to announce it to the world. Hence, Bobby's inability to focus on anything other than the main attraction. Or, should I say, double feature.

"Helloooo, ladies!" she squeals, then lowers her voice. "Can you believe that was Bobby Stanton? I almost didn't recognize him without the five o'clock shadow and long, greasy hair. Amazing, isn't it?" Before we can reply, she gushes on. "I'm soooo glad you both could make it. I'm honored to be in the presence of the town Spa Girl." She takes a second to half-bow before Sylvie, who blushes appropriately.

I'm merely hoping Anita's sweater holds up as she bends over.

I start to comment about the roads being closed, but I no sooner open my mouth than Anita continues. "And we arrived just in time, too! Did you hear? They closed the roads. Guess we're stuck with each other for a while. Like high school, right?" She giggles. "You might as well have a seat. Order a drink. Relax. Loosen up a bit. Let it all hang out, K?"

Like you are? No thanks.

"You two are both still so gorgeous." She's looking at Sylvie. "You haven't changed a bit!"

And I'm thinking the only thing that hasn't changed about Anita is her obnoxiousness. And her expert ability to fish for compliments.

"Well, you've changed," I say before I can stop myself. "In a *big way*."

An elbow connects with my ribs as Sylvie tries to suppress a snort.

"I hope that's a compliment," Anita tee-hees, completely clueless to my inference. "So…," she says, inching closer, "how's your brother doing? What's his name again?" She places a French-manicured fingernail to her chin, as if trying to remember.

What a faker! She knows exactly what his name is. I'm wishing Sylvie had taken my bet yesterday that Anita would mention my brother in the first five minutes. I'd be munching on a candy bar by now. If I hadn't given up chocolate, that is.

"Simon," Sylvie blurts out.

"Simon?" Anita looks confused. "It's Zach, isn't it?"

I turn to see Sylvie making her way toward Simon Becker, high school football quarterback whose rock-hard, baked potato arms have now been mashed and whose six-pack abs have dissolved into a pony keg that hangs over his belt.

"Yes, it's Zach. And he's fine." I try to get over feeling offended that Sylvie left me alone to deal with Chiquita. Then again, I forgive her because knowing Sylvie, she was about to erupt into a serious case of the giggles and probably wanted to hightail it out of there before she lost control.

"I'm sure some lucky girl has snatched him up by now, huh?" Anita grabs a drink off the nearest table and downs it. I'm not even sure it's hers, but no one else is around, so...whatever.

"Yep." She doesn't need to know that Zach was divorced six years ago. Besides, the last thing I want to do is sit around talking about my brother all night. Don't get me wrong. Even though I think my brother is a dweeb and has some major issues, mostly regarding his taste in women and his inability to commit to one, I still love him. Which is why I would never in a million years reveal any part of his personal life to the likes of Anita Chiquita.

Give it up, already, Chiquita. You are so not ending up with my brother!

"Aren't you married?" I ask, steering the focus back on her.

"Oh...I was, but, you know...it didn't work out. Chuck didn't want me to get implants. But I wanted them more than anything. I've always felt, you know...not right up here." She places a hand to her chest. "I knew that if I got the implants, I would feel so much better about myself. So I went ahead and scheduled the surgery for a weekend when he was on a hunting trip with his buddies. I figured he spends thousands of dollars over the years on hunting equipment, so why shouldn't I be able to spend a few thousand on something that would make me really happy? Plus, I make good money as a Pampered Chef consultant. Top seller this month," Anita says proudly. "I got two free stoneware pieces plus the double burner griddle. I've wanted that griddle for so long. It's great for entertaining—my absolute favorite thing to do."

She sets her glass on the table and reaches for another. I narrow my eyes and imagine the reactions of people who will come back looking for their drink, only to find their glasses empty.

"Sorry I got off topic. I can't seem to help myself. Pampered Chef is such a huge part of my life. Where was I?" She stares up at the ceiling. "Oh, yes. So when Chuck came home from his hunting trip, he was so mad. Walked out on me that very day and a week later informed me he wanted a divorce. Said I wasn't the same girl he married. Can you imagine? Most guys would love for their wives to get implants, don't you think?"

Okay...this is getting a tad too personal. Sylvie, say good-bye to Simon and come rescue me!

"Wouldn't your husband love it if you got implants?"

She doesn't give up! I toy with whether I should be offended by her question. I'm aware that I'm not well-endowed, even considered small to some. But I've never given it much thought. Rich has never complained.

"Zach always seemed to date big-breasted girls."
Whoa! Stop right there, sister!
Conversation halted.
"Hey, Anita. I think Sylvie is waving me over. Nice talking to you."
Not.

Sylvie is in her element. All evening, she has been flitting from person to person, ever the social butterfly. She expresses genuine interest in every one of our former classmates, popular and unpopular alike. Sylvie asks question after question about their jobs, their families, their struggles, and their dreams. And, of course, she slips in some beauty tips whenever she gets a chance.

Sylvie normally doesn't talk incessantly about herself but will gladly share her heart with anyone who asks. At the moment, she is relaying the details of her husband Ike's death to Chonda Peters. It seems Chonda also lost her husband several years ago. Sylvie lost Ike to a motorcycle accident, while Chonda's husband died from stomach cancer. They commiserate like long-lost friends and it's like I'm not even standing here. I might as well be invisible. If we were still in high school, I might get peeved that Sylvie is ignoring me.

Oh wait. This is like high school, isn't it? Maybe I should write a short hate note on a napkin, telling Sylvie she's not my BFF anymore.

As I stand on the sidelines, it's clear to me that something is amiss with Sylvie tonight. It's nothing a casual acquaintance would notice, but to me, it's as obvious as Anita Chiquita's fake boobs. Every once in a while, Sylvie glances around, her eyes coming to rest on the front doors of the diner. Since the roads are closed for the time being, I wonder who she could be expecting. Maybe she's being a protective friend and watching for Fawn Witchburn to come springing through those doors.

But instead of engaging myself with a guessing game, I choose to stand quietly, keeping a close eye out myself, not only for Fawn, but for Eddie Reynolds. He's approached me from behind three times now, the last time snaking one of his eight slippery arms around my waist, causing me to spill some of my drink on my sweater. Now my jeans and my sweater are stained. I've so far been able to slither out of Eddie's grasp and, as long as I remain in the crowd, I figure I'll be safe.

The problem is I have to pee. Badly. Perhaps due to the four Diet Cokes I've sucked down. It's no secret I tend to eat excessively when I'm bored, angry, or stressed. And right now I'm two of those three—both bored and stressed—although, if Eddie gropes me one more time, "angry" will join in. Since my burger and fries were consumed a half hour ago, I've resorted to downing glass after glass of pop. At least it's diet so my binge won't add extra inches to my waist.

Meanwhile, several of my former classmates have chosen other—not so soft—drinks to sip on or gulp down. And as their drink tabs increase, their voice volume does, too. Lo and behold, my headache has also grown.

With Sylvie deeply engrossed in her conversation with Chonda Peters and my bladder screaming for relief, I peer around the corner of the party room. Yes! Now's my chance. Eddie is currently on stage, singing an out-of-tune version of The Police's "Don't Stand So Close to Me." No problem complying with that one, buddy.

I wiggle my way through the maze of people to the hallway leading to the restrooms. It's dark and quiet, which is surprising considering how many drinks are being consumed out there. I take a deep breath, enjoying the solitude, if only for a moment. Pausing at the drinking fountain, I pop the two Tylenol I found at the bottom of my purse. I hope this sip of water won't send my bladder bubbling over the edge. But my headache is winning the pain contest at the moment, so it's worth the extra bladder discomfort.

Swallowing the pills, I turn toward the ladies' room and movement catches my eye. I squint into the short dark hallway leading to what appears to be the restaurant manager's office. Taking a couple steps forward, my ears are met with slobbery, kissing noises, and it hits me that I've intruded on a couple's secret rendezvous. All righty, then. Get a room, people!

So as not to interrupt, I tiptoe back a couple steps, hoping to make a silent getaway into the restroom. Suddenly, I smack into something solid and warm. And smelling oddly like beer and onions, with a hefty dose of sweat mixed in.

I yelp. Loudly enough to startle the two lovebirds in the hallway. As my brain tries to wrap itself around the realization that I've just backed into Eddie Reynolds, I hear a rustling and the girl emerges, face flushed, hair matted, clothes askew.

It can't be.

"Amy!" I sputter.

My former future daughter-in-law is speechless, so it seems. Her cheeks have turned from pink to crimson in a matter of seconds. She smoothes her blond hair and her eyes dart everywhere but into mine. As well they should. Promise ring on her finger or not, right now her actions are a little less than honorable.

I glance over her shoulder, waiting for presumed new boyfriend Kyle to emerge, so I can meet the boy who has stolen Amy away from my son and lured her into temptation. I half expect horns to be sprouting from his head and a pitchfork at his side.

As the figure appears behind her, it is my turn for vocal-chord failure.

"Hi, Mrs. McCall," he croaks.

Blake the Snake stands, cowering behind Amy. He really is cowering. And he has good reason, because I am ticked. In fact, I think I feel the water boiling at the surface of my ears. Any second now, the whistle will sound and the steam will shoot straight out into the air.

"Yeah, Blake! You da man!" Eddie cheers.

Eddie. He's still here. Breathing down my neck.

"She sure is a foxy little thing, isn't she?" He jabs me in the side a little too hard, causing me to wince. "Come here and give your dad a high-five. Way to go! I ain't raised no wussy, that's for sure."

My side pain disappears in light of this unexpected newsflash. I gape at Eddie in disbelief. "You're Blake's *dad?*"

"Takes right after me, don't you think?" He winks. "What's your name, sweetheart?" He's speaking to Amy, who, I realize, has tried to slink away during my exchange with Eddie. She stops in her tracks.

"Amy," she mumbles. She turns to me: "Mrs. McCall, please don't tell—"

I hold up a hand. "I don't even want to hear it."

Her lip quivers and she runs off, not even noticing her shirt is buttoned wrong.

"How are you Blake's father?" I demand, my hands finding their way to my hips.

"You jealous? He could have been yours, you know. If you'd let me get further than second base." He winks.

Can anyone in the northern hemisphere possibly be any more disgusted than I am at this moment?

He puffs out his chest. "Me and Blake's mom never married. She put her last name on his birth certificate. But I'm his dad, all right. Have the DAN test results to prove it." He puffs out his chest. "He's a good-lookin' kid, right? Real ladies' man. I taught him everything he knows."

"It's DNA, Dad," Blake mutters.

"Huh?"

"Nothing." Blake swallows hard and takes a step back. "Look, Mrs. McCall—"

My hand shoots out again. I step forward, invading his space. He's a good head taller than me, so I crane my neck toward the ceiling. "It wasn't bad enough to cheat with someone Christina doesn't get along with. You had to move in on her friend?"

Yes, I know that Amy is as guilty as Blake. And if she hadn't run off just now, she'd be getting an earful too.

"Unbelievable." I shake my head. "I'll make you a deal, Blake. I won't tell Christina about this little...whatever it was...you had going on here with Amy. But you have to promise me that you will break it off with my daughter for good. And, more importantly, you have to swear that you'll never—ever—call Christina again. You'll never ask her out. You won't flirt with her. You'll not so much as flash a dimple in her direction. Is that clear?" Sylvie would be proud. I've rediscovered some of that backbone she accused me of losing.

Blake nods and focuses on the wall.

"So we have a deal?" I hold out my hand. Part of me hopes he doesn't shake on it, so I won't have to fight the urge to flip him, karate style, to the hard floor.

A voice booms from behind my back. "Hang on a minute. You can't tell my son what to do. Kissing a girl's not a crime. At least the pretty ones, anyway—"

My backbone's on a roll, so who am I to stand in my own way? I spin around to face my archenemy. But my words catch in my throat as I notice none other than Fawn Witchburn breezing down the hallway toward us.

"Hey, Eddie," she husks in that annoying raspy voice.

Why does it not surprise me that Fawn Witchburn and Eddie Reynolds know each other?

Eddie turns and licks his lips, eying her up and down, much like he did to me earlier. Only Fawn has a lot more skin showing to lust over. "Fawn. You're lookin' mighty fine as always."

That's it. How dare he turn his back on my almost-outburst?

I imagine swinging him around by the shoulders and giving him a very large piece of my mind. But, spontaneously, my bladder starts convulsing. Must be that the adrenaline coursing through my body has held it at bay. Now it's about to spew forth with a vengeance. I turn and make a beeline for the ladies' room before I stain my pants yet again.

I hear Fawn call out to me, but I ignore her. I breathe a prayer that by the time I'm finished, she and Eddie will be gone.

👑

20

No matter how far behind the past seems to be,
it has a way of sneaking up on you and biting you in the butt.

ANITA LANGERAK, MY CLASS VALEDICTORIAN, AT OUR HIGH SCHOOL
GRADUATION

"So, Matthew, have you gotten a status on the roads?" I rest my elbows on the hostess...er, host...stand and massage my temples. I took my sweet old time in the restroom and, thank goodness, Fawn didn't follow me in. Maybe God *is* on my side.

I've so got to get out of this place. And preferably before Fawn catches sight of me again. At the moment, she is sitting at a table with her "friends," who happen to be a couple of rough, biker-looking dudes. It seems the two men are trying to coerce her into getting up on stage to sing. And Fawn is flirtatiously refusing their challenge.

When her head starts to twist my direction, I whip my head back toward Matthew. "So, how much longer, Matthew? You have no idea how much I really, really need to get home," I say, my voice laced with anxiety.

The host/boy glances at his watch. "I received word ten minutes ago that the snow has let up enough for the plows to come through. It shouldn't be too much longer now." He smiles, clueless to my desperation. Probably thinks I need to get home to get some beauty sleep or something. Not that I couldn't use an extra helping right now. Outside it may be blustery, but in here it feels like 100 degrees and my hair is getting flatter by the moment. That, in addition to my stained clothing...I'm sure I'm a vision.

A few people around me seem anxious to escape this restaurant-slash-prison, too. They cluster around the front entryway, biding time until they are permitted to leave. One man with long, black sideburns loudly complains about the singing. He expected more talent, and he could sing a million times better than the people up there. Um, then why aren't you up there, Elvis wannabe?

A woman is in tears because she needs to get home to her dog that's been locked up in the house all day. She is crying over the probability that her carpet will be in need of a good cleaning by the time she returns.

Several children are whining and/or screaming—an obvious indication that it's way past their bedtime. Usually, by this time, parents have taken their children home to allow a more mature crowd to take their place. You know, mature people like the man at the table directly in front of the karaoke stage, guzzling beer right from the pitcher and then seeing how loudly he can belch his ABCs. And his friends who are egging him on like it's the most impressive act they've ever witnessed.

A lady approaches Matthew and asks if she can get up on stage for a moment to use the microphone and make a plea for diapers. She's fretting over the fact that she has no extra Pampers for her three-year-old who has just had an accident. Okay...pooping in a diaper is not an accident. The kid is old enough to know he is wearing a diaper and still grunts any old place he chooses. How is that an accident?

Wetting the bed...now that is an accident.

Emily.

I pull my cell phone from my purse and check the display screen. I'm amazed to see there's still a signal, although only one bar remains. Hoping the kids aren't already in bed, I dial Nancy's number and make my way back to the quiet hallway leading to the restrooms.

Nancy picks up on the third ring.

"Hi, Nancy, it's Madi."

"Oh, hello, dear. How are you? I hear you're getting a lot of snow up there."

"Yeah...you could say that."

"It's been snowing a bit here, too. The weatherman says the worst of it is a bit to the north of us, which is quite a relief. Of course, Richard is here to shovel the driveway for me if needed." She chuckles. "Shoveling is getting to be too much for this old lady. My back's been acting up again."

As much as I love my mother-in-law, I'm not in the mood, nor do I have time, for small talk. I just need to hear my kids' voices before the phone battery dies. I feel a pang of guilt about having to cut her off and silently vow to call her tomorrow to talk.

"I hate to be abrupt, Nancy, but my cell phone is about to die. Are the kids around?"

"Oh. They're in the middle of watching a movie. We had a coupon for a free rental...the children seem to be enjoying it."

"That sounds nice. Can you get Emily? I'd like to say good night."

"Oh. Well, when the phone rang, Emily—sweet thing that she is—said if it was you calling, to tell you she'd give you a call back in the morning. She doesn't want to miss any of the movie."

Wow. So much for missing me. And last time I checked, DVD players had a pause button.

"Okay, then. I don't want to interrupt. Tell the kids I love them, and I'll talk to them tomorrow."

"Richard, too?" There is hopefulness in her voice. She clearly knows something's not right, but I doubt Rich has confided in her too much. I mean, would he really admit to his mom that he cheated on his wife?

"You're cutting out, Nancy. I'll try again tomorrow." My nose grows three inches as I click off my phone and slide it back into my purse.

My kids are safe. Watching a movie. With their dad.

And I am here, surrounded by a hundred people I can't stand—with the exception of Sylvie, wherever she is—in the midst of whining kids, drunk classmates, Amy (*aka,* Judas) and Christina's snaky, cheating boyfriend. Oh, yeah. And how can I forget about my husband's lover, who is forty feet away from me, at this very moment?

I look toward her table. Uh, make that twenty feet away and closing the gap.

For the second time in the past few days, I feel like Mulan. Disguising myself sounds pretty good about now, but somehow I don't think Matthew keeps any costumes behind his host stand. Of course, Mulan's reason for disguising herself was not because she was afraid; it was so she could fight without being detected.

Once again, it's confirmed that I'm no princess. I want a disguise so I can run and hide. Hey, I'm getting good at it. I've been running from God for the past week and walked away from my husband the other day. Why not escape from Fawn Witchburn? But really, where would I run? To the ladies' room? Outside to the nearest snow bank? Behind the karaoke stage?

It's too late, anyway. Fawn now stands directly in front of me and points a finger. "I figured out how I know you." She seems pleased with herself and is smiling like Charlie after he finishes his fishie treat. Too bad, though, that unlike Charlie, Fawn speaks.

My heart starts pounding a little too hard against my Diet Coke-stained sweater. Mental preparation is a must when facing a confrontation with the other woman. A month doesn't even seem long enough to gather the courage to speak with Fawn face to face. It's bad enough that earlier tonight she sat behind me in Sylvie's dad's car. But this is too much.

I never thought I would say it, but I want my mommy! Hard to imagine, I know. Yet I would take her nasty comments, negative attitude, and idiotic complaints in a second over standing in this spot right now.

But Mom is not here. Not to mention, I'm a thirty-eight-year-old woman who should be able to get through a confrontation like this without fear of a panic attack, or worse, dropping dead of a heart attack right in the middle of Reggie's Classy Diner. In front of former classmates, no less. Definitely not how I want to die. Particularly with my heart the way it is toward God.

At this thought, I briefly consider calling on my heavenly Father. But, as desperate as I am to cry out for Him to bail me out of this mess, or at least do something, I can't do it. I can't bring myself to pray.

Is it pride? Or maybe guilt over giving Him the brush-off for the past week and now that I need something, deciding that He's necessary after all? I picture Him shaking His head at my stubbornness.

"Did you hear me?" Fawn is saying. "I said I figured out how I know you."

I wait for it.

"You're Richard McCall's wife, right?"

Oh. My. Gosh. I am going to die. I put a hand to my chest. *Pound. Pound. Pound.*

"Mmmm-hmmm," I croak, not trusting myself to even open my mouth.

Fawn snaps her fingers. "I knew it!" She sighs. "You're a lucky woman. Rich is a great guy. Sweet, kind, gorgeous...great teacher too. My daughter, Lexi, is in his class. She adores him." Her sharp, angled cheekbones soften a bit and her eyes glaze over, a little like Max's when he talks about Sam. "I'll bet he's a great dad. A great husband."

Is she taunting me? I search her face for signs of sarcasm, but all I see is wistfulness and maybe a hint of pain and sadness behind her smoky, heavily madeup eyes.

"Richard is exactly the kind of dad I want for Lexi."

Okay, now I want to punch her.

The gall! How can Fawn stand here and so calmly relay her carefully laid plans to rip my husband away from me? To steal my kids' dad away from them so her daughter will have a father? Who does she think she is? And how dare she think for one second that I will let my husband go without a fight?

Wait a minute. That dirty rotten husband cheated on me. With *her,* no less. Why do I want to fight for someone who betrayed me in the worst possible way? Who couldn't have hurt me any more if he stuck a double-edged sword through my heart?

Why am I suddenly willing to fight? Why? Why? Why?

Maybe because Richard is that same someone who wouldn't give up until I agreed to a second date. Who has stuck with me throughout major jealousy phases and has never berated me for my insecurities but always reassured me of his love. Who—before last week—never walked out on me, even when it seemed I had multiple personalities. Which would be about once a month for the past eighteen years, minus two nine-month periods (no pun intended) when all I did was sit around and cry about how fat I was while eating package after package of Hostess Ding Dongs (because Dibs weren't yet invented). During those moments, I definitely could have given Sybil actress Sally Field a run for her money.

Maybe I want to fight because Richard stepped outside of his non-romantic comfort zone and surprised me on our eighteenth wedding anniversary with a private candlelight dinner followed by two tickets to the Dancing with the Stars concert tour even though he couldn't care less about going.

Maybe because he is the one who brushes the snow off my car in the winter. Who cooks—yes, cooks—me homemade chicken soup when I'm sick. Who has shared the last twenty years of his life with me.

Who fathered my children.

You know what? I am not going to give him up. And certainly not to Fawn Witchburn. Yes, Richard cheated on me. But I have a choice. I can divorce him and completely uproot our family and be bitter forever and turn out like my mother—yikes!—or I can deal with it, pay Sarah Price's mortgage with my months of counseling sessions, and move on. As difficult and painful and humbling as that would be.

Hmmm. Turn into Mother... or forgive? When I stop to think about it, it's not such a tough choice. Looks like the opportunity to make an attitude adjustment is here.

"Are you okay?" Fawn's sultry voice cuts into my thoughts. "You're crying."

And so I am. My eyes burn, and my cheeks are wet. I swipe at the tears. And then I find my voice.

"No, Fawn. I am not okay. And how you can ask me a question like that when…"

"Is there anything I can do?" She searches my face. Does Fawn even have a conscience? Trying to befriend the wife of the man you're having an affair with is...it's just wrong. Are her morals truly that warped?

"Yes. As a matter of fact, there is something you can do, Fawn." I grit my teeth and growl like a mother bear protecting her cub. "Stay. Away. From. My. Husband." *Grrrr.*

Fawn backs up a step. "What?" Her dark lips pucker in surprise. "From Richard?"

Okay, she's looking genuinely confused, and I'll admit this puzzles me a bit. I expected either one of two facial reactions from Fawn: mock surprise, resulting in blatant denial, complete with rapid eye-blinking and avoiding eye contact altogether, or a smug, in-your-face scoff that says, *Of course I got your man. And what are you going to do about it, frump-girl?*

What I didn't expect was confusion. Maybe Ms. Witchburn has taken acting classes. If so, she is very, very good. Academy Award good.

"Wait a second," she says. "You think...you think me and..." The corners of her brown-colored mouth lift in a smile. "Oh, honey. It's not like that."

I am tempted to turn and bolt for the ladies' room again. But my feet won't budge. I need to know what Fawn has to say. And even if I'd sucked down four more Diet Cokes and had an exploding bladder, I wouldn't miss this performance.

21

Moron: A very foolish or stupid person.
YOURDICTIONARY.COM

"Oh, there you are, Madi!"

I groan. Behind Fawn's back, Anita Chiquita is making her way toward me, pearly white veneers displayed proudly behind her enormous fake smile. I'm finding there's not much about Anita that isn't fake these days.

She gives Fawn the once-over, then puffs out her bosom, as if competing in an implant competition. "Hi. I'm Anita Langerak, a friend of Madi's."

Well, I wouldn't say friend, exactly…

"And you are…"

"Fawn." Fawn appears amused as her perfect, pencil-thin eyebrows arch heavenward.

Anita's face still has the enormous smile plastered on it. Only now her smile is joined by a hint of judgment. Or maybe it's jealousy. "Fawn. Hmmm. Interesting name. So how do you know Madi?" she asks.

I tap my foot. I am so done with this conversation. "Is there something you need, Anita?" I ask, butting in ever so politely.

Attention diverted, as planned. "Oh. We're getting out the old yearbooks, and I'm rounding everyone up. Bobby Stanton definitely gets the vote for Most Changed. Really, Most Improved is more like it. I never thought I'd say this in a million years, but…Bobby Stanton is hot, don't you think?" She fans her face.

I feel the urge to stick my finger down my throat.

"Of course, then there are those hideous pictures of me, before I was transformed from the Ugly Ducking to the Beautiful Swan." Giggle. Giggle. "I've blacked them out in my own yearbooks and I'm asking around for a black permanent marker so I can discretely confiscate everyone else's yearbooks and do the same to theirs. I mean, I don't want people remembering me like that." Anita turns to Fawn. "You don't have a marker, do you?"

Fawn shakes her head. I notice her starting to glance around the room, probably wondering how she can make her getaway. But that can't happen.

"Look, Anita. I'll be there as soon as I can. Okay?" My brown untweezed, not-so-arched eyebrows do some rising of their own. I suspect my expression resembles a toddler waiting expectantly for her mother to approve her request for a cookie.

For the first time, Anita's mouth straightens in apparent disappointment. "Oh. Okay. But hurry. You wouldn't want to miss all the fun."

The eye-roll is right there. But I resist, offering a tight smile instead. "Nope, sure wouldn't want that."

Anita gives Fawn one last look before half swaying, half bouncing off in search of another poor soul from the 1992 graduating class of Lakeshore Heights High.

"You were saying…" I tilt my head toward Fawn and quickly say a prayer for no more distractions.

Fawn creases her brow, appearing to either be considering whether or not to continue our conversation that was so rudely interrupted by Anita Chiquita or trying to recall what we were talking about in the first place.

As if she can't remember.

"About Richard…" I do the hand-rolling thing for effect.

"Ah, yes." She gives a throaty laugh. "Well, Madison, rest assured I am not having an affair with your husband."

"And I should believe this because…," I prompt, sounding like my therapist.

"Because it's true." Her voice is steady, and she looks me in the eye.

I've had plenty of experience with lying—I am the mother of three, after all—and know the signs: avoiding eye contact, ear tugging, lip biting, jaw twitching, voice cracking. But there is none of that. Fawn is staring me down. It's unnerving, really.

I look away first. Matthew has the door open a slit, and I see the snowplows making their way through the parking lot. A line of people desperate to escape has formed at the door. The woman worried about her dog piddling on her carpet is first. She stretches, like a runner getting ready for the 100-yard dash.

"May I ask why you think we're having an affair?"

Hmmm. How to answer. Should I hold back, or say what I'm thinking?

Aw, what the heck.

"Look, Fawn. We both know you have a sort of, um, reputation. Affairs with married men seem to be part of your daily routine. And look at you," I scoff. "A skirt so short it can't even be considered mini—*micro* is more like it. Fishnet stockings...four-inch heels...in the snow? God created men to be visual, and you certainly give them something to gawk at."

My backbone is really popping through, but now I'm not so sure that's a good thing. I've let loose my share of crude remarks in my lifetime, but since becoming a Christian, I've been trying to keep them to a minimum. Of course, I haven't done much to renew my mind lately. Not to mention the fact that I've never stood face-to-face with my husband's lover. If that's not enough reason for the crudeness to burst forth, I don't know what is. But something is pinching my conscience, making me almost wish I could take it back.

Too late now.

Fawn cocks her head and smirks. "Sounds like an insecurity issue to me."

And to think I came this close to regretting my previous words.

"Excuse me, but dressing to attract a man's attention seems more like insecurity to me."

"No, honey, dressing like I do requires confidence."

It's not lost on me that, as she says this, she glances down at my turtleneck sweater. I long to retreat by pulling my head into the neck hole. That would look pretty weird, so I tug at the collar instead. But I don't miss a beat. "I could stand here all day and argue the importance of modest dressing and even give you verses from the Bible to back it up"—*but please don't ask me because I can't, for the life of me, remember what they are*—"but you go to church, right? Modest dressing is a subject that's been preached on a hundred times. You should know by now what God thinks about it."

Fawn regards me for a moment. "I also know what He thinks about judging a person based on their appearance."

Ouch! And just when I thought I was winning.

"Can I cut to the chase, here?" I ask.

"Please." Fawn crosses her arms over her chest.

I take a deep breath. "You had a parent-teacher conference with my husband a few days ago. I saw the lipstick on his collar, Fawn. And I'm no detective, but I suspect it's yours. Because, frankly, I don't know any other woman who wears lipstick that dark or that...brown. And then I saw you together the other day on Phoenix, across from The Golden Brown Bakery."

Her eyes cloud over and she looks past me for a second, as if recalling each incident. Slowly, she nods. "Yes. That was my lipstick."

Having it confirmed makes me feel better and worse at the same time. Better, because I know I'm not losing my mind. And worse because, well, I may have lost my husband instead.

"But it's not what you think."

Oh, that's so movie-cliché. "Why don't you tell me what 'it' is, exactly?"

Fawn slips her purse off her shoulder and rummages through it. I can't help tapping my black-booted foot and checking my watch, mostly to make it seem like she is wasting my precious time. But really, what else do I have at the moment? I am dying to know what she's digging for.

After several seconds, she pulls out a black leather clutch, opens it, and slides a photo from a plastic protective sleeve. She holds it three inches from my face. Her voice is firm and steady.

"This is my nine-year-old daughter, Lexi. Take a good, long look. Then I'll give you one guess who her father is."

I swallow the watermelon-sized lump in my throat. I've looked at Lexi hundreds of times—at church, around town. Describing her to a stranger would be a snap. But I guess I've never really *looked* at her. Staring at the photo, the fog lifts and my eyes adjust. I notice the light brown pin-straight hair very unlike her mother's thick and curly auburn locks. Her eyes...huge and almond-shaped like Fawn's, but deep blue instead of smoky brown. The fairer complexion. The straighter nose. Thinner lips.

Richard. It's totally Richard. His eyes, his nose, his chin, his...everything.

My mind starts racing. Nine years ago. Where were we nine years ago? No, wait. It would have been ten years ago that Lexi was conceived. Rich and I were trying to get pregnant. I should say, still trying. After Max and Christina were born, we thought it would be easy to get pregnant again. But not so. We tried for six years. Six long years of heartache, disappointment, anger, hundreds of dollars wasted on pregnancy tests, fertility tests...

After a while it took a toll on our marriage. We stopped having fun. Sex became a chore—a means to an end. A dead end, at that. I withdrew. Rich started spending more time at church. Playing basketball. Golf. Anything to avoid coming home.

Is that when it happened? Is that when Fawn came along and dug her claws into my husband? Seduced him when he was most vulnerable?

Of course it is.

And I was so caught up in my obsession to get pregnant, I missed the signs. I am disgusted with myself for being played a fool for the past ten years. Ten years!

But Fawn wasn't even in town ten years ago. The first day I ever set eyes on her was two years ago when she and I were picking up our daughters at the same time from Sunday school. Most of all, I remember the looks the volunteers gave her as she stood at the classroom door looking like Julia Roberts in Pretty Woman. It wasn't long after that the rumors started flying and marriages started breaking up.

How could Richard have cheated with Fawn ten years ago, before she even breezed into town? I recall Rich's reaction when I told him I was pregnant with Emily. To say he was excited is a major understatement. Did a fifteen-minute happy dance right across the kitchen floor. For the next eight months, he doted on me like never before. Made midnight trips to the store for Hostess Ding Dongs, brought me breakfast in bed, even let me hold the television remote most nights and was sympathetic when I broke down in tears during *Extreme Home Makeover.*

Was Richard extra attentive because he felt guilty for cheating on me? If so, he did a bang-up job of it. The thought is heartbreaking. To think it was all a sham…

"So? Any guesses?" Fawn withdraws the photo and turns it around so she can take a look. "Uncanny, isn't it?"

I am totally at a loss for words. Bolting is my first inclination. To escape and find a dark and lonely corner where I can sit and rock. How far away is the nearest mental hospital? Because I'm losing it. Big time.

Fawn is still staring at the photo. I attempt to speak. "How-how did it happen?" It comes out as a whisper.

"I worked for a dumpy hotel in Cleveland. That's where we met." She tears her eyes away from the photo and looks at me.

My brain is in overdrive, searching through a bazillion bytes of memory to come up with a time when Rich went to visit his mother by himself—without me and the twins. There were a few times, but he always stayed with his mom—not at a hotel.

"He came in for a drink at the bar," Fawn says, as if reading my mind.

I can buy this. Rich gave up alcohol when he gave his heart to the Lord, but when we were going through our rough patch, I know there were a couple times Rich went out for drinks with his buddies.

Fawn stares off into space, then glances at her male companions. I follow her gaze. They are in the middle of an arm-wrestling contest, a pair of bulging tattoo-covered biceps on display, while a few patrons at nearby tables cheer them on. We both watch for a moment.

Fawn turns back to me. "We only saw each other a few times. When I found out I was pregnant, I panicked." She lets out a breathy laugh. "Believe me, panic was not something I was used to. But for the first time in my life, it wasn't just about me. I had someone else to think about. When I told my boss

I was pregnant, he fired me. Can you believe it? Said he didn't want no fatso working for him. I should have sued the scumbag. So I went home. To Mom and Dad, of all places. Big mistake."

She pulls a cigarette from her purse and holds it, unlit, between her fingers. Clearly, just the thought of going home ignites feelings of nervousness or maybe rebellion. I've never been more thankful Reggie's is smoke-free.

"Anyway, after Lexi was born, I moved around a lot. Waited tables to make ends meet. When she turned five, and it was time for her to start school, I decided we needed to settle down. Lexi needed more security—a place to call home. And I wondered if it wasn't time for my daughter to know her father. She deserved a better life than I could give her."

I can't help interjecting here. Oddly, my voice now comes out loud and clear. "Or maybe *you* wanted cash. Maybe you didn't care about Lexi's need to know her father, or for her father to finally have a chance at a relationship with his daughter. Maybe you kept them from each other until you ran out of options. Until you got sick of working your tail off with nothing to show for it. Maybe it wasn't about what was best for your daughter. It was about making your life easier."

Fawn's face hardens, her sharp, striking features turning stony, making her appear ten years older. "What do you know about being a single mom?"

I laugh, but it's not so funny. "I grew up with a single mother and my best friend is a single mom. And now—thanks to you—I'll be one very soon. How many families have you demolished, Fawn? How many kids' lives have you turned upside-down? Five? Ten? Fifty?" I am no longer thinking about my own personal pain. That my husband did something horrible to me by betraying our marriage vows will be dealt with later. But now my heart expands for Lexi. And for my kids. The innocent ones who will ultimately pay for the sins of their idiotic parents.

"What are you talking about?" Fawn rams her fists into her sides. The unlit cigarette breaks in half and falls to the floor.

Clueless doesn't even begin to describe Fawn. "Hello...families! You know, those things made up of a husband, a wife, kids. Doesn't it bother you at all to rip them apart? To destroy marriages and traumatize children?" My own fists are now rammed into my sides and I'm in her face. I'm like a lion defending her cubs, as well as all the other lion families in the jungle. "My family will never be the same, Fawn, because of you!"

Fawn steps back. Something flashes in her eyes...I'm not sure what it is, exactly, but I hope it's a light bulb flickering with sixty watts of sense.

And then she laughs. Not merely a nervous snicker. A full-blown belly laugh. She holds her sides while I stand there—in shock. I so wasn't expecting this reaction.

My emotions do a flip-flop. The anger is too much, and I do what I vowed not to. My lip begins to quiver like a jackhammer. And then I break down in tears.

Across the room, through the fountains sprouting from my tear ducts, I see a blurry Sylvie hurrying toward me. Fawn has stopped laughing and is saying something I can't hear over my blubbering sobs. People are staring at me. Eddie. Blake. Anita. Bobby Stanton. Matthew, the restaurant host. The Elvis wannabe. I even spot Amy, hand over her mouth, cowering behind the two biker dudes.

I am on display. And there's nowhere to run.

A gust of cold air hits me. Someone has opened the door and somewhere in the distance I hear an announcement that the plows have come through and the road has reopened. People are bustling around the front entrance. Shivering from the freezing temperatures and sniffing back the snot that threatens to stream toward my upper lip, I watch as the crowd makes its way out the door. And then, shoving his way through the crowd in the opposite direction, I see my brother. I smile through my tears.

Wait a minute. I must really be losing it.

What on earth would Zach be doing at Reggie's Classy Diner—just arriving, no less—on a night like this? It's clear I'm hallucinating. Next I'll probably envision Mom coming toward me with sincere concern and sympathy.

I don't have time to dwell on my pending insanity and crazy hallucinations. Sylvie's firm but welcome hand is suddenly on my back, shoving me almost to the point of causing me to trip and fall. As if I need another embarrassment to add to my long and growing list.

I've never been more thankful for my best friend than at this moment. She whisks me away to safety.

Sylvie. My hero.

But we're not alone. Fawn is behind us. I know this because even if I couldn't hear her raspy voice telling me to wait up, her familiar, sickening perfume closes in around me like a cloud of smog.

Sylvie stops abruptly in the hallway leading to the restroom and turns around. Fawn smacks into us, lurching all three of us forward a step.

"Fawn, please. Just leave. Haven't you done enough damage? Look at her. She's a wreck already!"

Sylvie whirls me around so Fawn can see—in case she doesn't already know—what a mess I am. I'm well aware of the fact that my mouth is turned down, Lucy Ricardo style, and my mascara—not waterproof—has left black trails down my cheeks. A snot-bubble pops, making me cry even louder. I've never been more humiliated, and I feel helpless to do anything about it.

"Madi." Fawn ignores Sylvie's outburst and grabs me by the shoulders. "You've got it all wrong. I thought you could tell from the picture. Lexi is not Richard's daughter. She's Ray's."

The clock stops ticking. For several seconds, it's just me, myself, and I. Oh—and the Holy Spirit. He's there, too. Gently and loudly convicting me of how stupid I've been. Except He doesn't use the word *stupid.* He uses the more biblical word *fool.*

Yep. The Holy Spirit definitely has a way of telling it like it is.

Slowly, the facts line up like a tick list in my mind: Lexi is not Richard's daughter. Lexi is Ray's daughter. Lexi is my niece. Richard and Fawn are not having an affair. Richard was telling the truth.

I am an imbecile.

Fawn and Sylvie are waiting for me to say something. I consider playing up my mental instability by pulling a Fawn and laughing like a lunatic. I mean, everybody already thinks I belong at the funny farm—might as well give them a good show. But I'm not so far gone that I don't consider the after-effects of my actions. Amy and Blake witnessed my mental breakdown and in all likelihood will relay the information to my kids. The last thing I want to do is give them more gossip to exaggerate.

"So you and Ray…"

"Ray doesn't know about Lexi, Madison. That's why I've been in contact with Richard. I thought maybe he could help me figure out a way to tell Ray that he has a daughter. I asked Richard not to tell anyone about it until I had a chance to tell Ray."

I snap out of my semi-comatose, hallucinatory state. "I'm not just anyone—I'm Richard's wife!" I snap.

Fawn frowns. Yes, she asked Richard not to tell anyone, but it's not her fault that my husband decided to comply and keep her secret. The relief that Richard didn't cheat on me is offset by anger that he didn't tell me about this. It could have prevented a lot of heartache. The separation could have been totally avoided. Emily wouldn't be wetting the bed. I wouldn't have pigged out on three cartons of Dibs in two weeks. Okay, maybe I would have. But I definitely wouldn't be snowed in at Reggie's Classy Diner, accusing Fawn Witchburn of breaking up my family. Or losing my mind in front of a million strangers and high school has-beens, with lipstick smeared on my jeans and beverage stains on my sweater and snot bubbles popping left and right.

I feel a scream coming on. Everything in me wants to let loose the loudest, most piercing scream the world's ever heard. Piercing enough to shatter glass and make hearing aids go haywire. But I need to put an end to my madness. Clamping my hand over my mouth, I take three big breaths through my nose.

Sylvie hands me a tissue. "Come on, Mads. The roads are open now. Let's go home." I hold the wad of tissue to my nose as Sylvie guides me like a child around Fawn and back to the party room to retrieve our jackets.

The party room is much less crowded than an hour ago; many of our former classmates have gone, although a few still linger around the tables. Those who do remain are trying a little too hard not to look at me. They pretend to be engrossed in conversations with each other, but I know their peripheral vision is working overtime. They all witnessed—or at least heard about—the show and are probably dying to know the juicy details of my altercation with Fawn Witchburn. Details I would never relay to high school has-beens.

Too bad, so sad, for them.

I am relieved to find Anita nowhere in sight. Maybe I will be able to flee this place before she catches sight of me and bombards me with a million questions. Or, worse yet, perky comments. I'm totally not in the mood for those at the moment. I no sooner think it than Anita's screechy tone pierces the air behind me. I cringe.

"Oh...there she is—the poor thing. I hope she's okay." Even her voice registers as false. I've got Anita's number, and it spells 555-FAKE.

I don't have to wonder who she is talking about, but I'm curious to whom her comment is directed. I slowly turn, bracing myself to see Eddie at her side.

But it's not Eddie. I should be relieved to find it's not the eight-armed octopus. But surprise and confusion give relief a hard shove.

Ten feet away, with Anita's arm hooked through his, stands my brother, Zach. So it wasn't a hallucination.

Zach grins the goofy crooked smile I always poke fun of. On most people, a crooked smile looks cocky, but it only makes Zach resemble a great, big doofus.

"What are you doing here?" I sniff. "And why are you just arriving when we're getting ready to leave?" And why are you linking arms with Anita Chiquita? So ew.

Zach slides his eyes to my left. I glance at Sylvie, who stands motionless at my side, staring at Zach. She doesn't even say hello, which is strange. But I don't have time to wonder about this, as Anita apparently decides the attention has been detracted from her long enough and starts babbling.

"I spotted Zach at the front entrance. He was telling me he's been stranded for the past two hours. He was on his way here and couldn't get through because they closed the road. Poor thing." She strokes his arm. "He's been sitting at McDonalds, a couple miles away, guzzling coffee while waiting for the plows to clear the roads. Isn't that right, Zach?" Anita beams. She probably thinks he battled the blizzard just to get to her. As if.

I cock my head. Why *is* Zach here?

"Are you okay, Sis?" he asks. "I hear you've had a pretty rough night." His comment tells me he witnessed—or more likely, Anita has filled him in on—the events of this evening. The crease in his brow also tells me he's genuinely concerned. Zach and I might not be Donny and Marie, but we watch out for each other.

My eyes are now dry. The snot bubbles have been popped and wiped away by the soaked tissue wadded up in my hand. My adrenaline has slowed to a reasonable pace. The dam behind which I hide my emotions has almost been rebuilt. But Zach asking me about my night is about enough for the water to come crashing through again.

"Aw, how sweet." Anita coos. She looks at me. "You're lucky to have such a caring brother." She turns her head and gazes at Zach adoringly.

For the first time tonight, I am thankful for Anita. Her comment helps me redirect my thoughts. "I'm fine, Zach. But you didn't answer my question. What are you doing here?"

Sylvie coughs.

"Oh. I—uh—thought I'd come and hang out with you guys."

I frown. "I don't remember telling you we'd be here."

Cough. Cough. Cough. All three of us stare at Sylvie, whose face is turning red. *Cough. Cough. Cough.*

"Are you okay? Do you need some water or something?" I pat her on the back a couple times.

She nods and continues hacking away, covering her mouth with one hand, fanning her flushed face with the other.

I flag down a nearby waitress who takes one look at Sylvie and hurries off to get a glass of water.

By the time I turn, Zach is at Sylvie's side. He drapes an arm around her. "Maybe you just need some fresh air, babe." Before I know it, he whisks her away, leaving me standing with Anita, who doesn't seem to know whether to tag along or start crying because her imaginary boyfriend has abandoned her without batting an eye.

Something's niggling my brain. What is it? Ah—now I remember.

Babe. Zach just called Sylvie "babe."

Anita catches me looking at her and smiles slightly, avoiding my gaze. Her perkiness and outgoingness has disappeared, replaced by what appears to be a sad, lonely woman hiding behind a plastic mask of cosmetic surgery. She's trying to cover her flaws and retain some sort of ill-conceived perfection. In a strange way, I feel sorry for her. I truly hope she learns how to be real.

Then I do something out of character for me. Especially when I've just experienced an informational bomb like the one I received from Fawn and I'm having a "poor me" moment and have spent a whole week giving God the silent treatment. But I can't stop myself.

"Do you go to church, Anita?"

"What? Oh. Not for years." She fidgets with the pendant on her necklace, ironically a large silver cross. "I figured out a long time ago that God doesn't have time for someone like me. If there is a God at all. Sometimes I wonder."

"I'll be honest and tell you that God and I have been experiencing a bit of turbulence in our relationship lately. But I do know that if it weren't for God, I'd be in the loony bin. Seriously. You have no idea."

For once, Anita doesn't say a word. She seems a little uncomfortable, but I'm almost sure I see a flash of hope in her eyes. I seize the moment.

"I go to Faith Christian Church. You should come. Great contemporary music. Even one or two single guys." I smile. That alone should warrant some interest on her part.

Anita reaches into her Coach purse and pulls out a card. She hands it to me. "Speaking of guys…can you do me a favor and give this to Zach? Tell him I'd love to get together sometime."

Well, Lord, you can't say I didn't try.

I glance at the Pampered Chef business card. It will touch the inside of a trash can much sooner than my brother's hand.

"I'd better get going, Anita. Thanks for inviting me."

She lets out a breathy laugh. "That's okay, Madi. No need to pretend you had fun. But I'm glad you came. Really." She touches my hand. "Don't forget to give my card to Zach, okay? Tell him to call me soon, or I may already be taken." She winks and bounces off toward the corner of the party room where Bobby Stanton happens to be sitting at a table by himself.

I pocket Anita's card and head to the door.

I just want to go home.

22

Of all the things I've lost,
I miss my mind the most.
MARK TWAIN

As I finally exit the doors of Reggie's Classy Diner, cold air slaps me in the face. Normally, I'd recoil, but compared to the stale, suffocating air I was trapped in only seconds ago, the fresh, bitter chill feels wonderful.

The wind has died down, although a few flurries still swirl around me. The small flakes pelt against my cheeks and weigh down the hair I spent so long styling. Oh well, no one to impress now. Not that there ever really was.

Dim lights illuminate the newly plowed parking lot and I scan the thirty or so cars scattered throughout. The Land Rover pops out at me like a black sesame seed stuck between two pearly white teeth. It is still covered in snow.

The feel-good cold lasts only seconds, and I give myself a hug, trying to warm up. Now where did Sylvie and Zach disappear to?

I spot Zach's brown SUV. Exhaust streams from the tail pipe, and I sigh in relief, my breath materializing in front of me like a cirrus cloud. I head toward the car in a half jog. Nearing the vehicle, I squint. The windows are completely steamed up, preventing me from seeing inside. A brief recollection of last week's lookalike van incident causes me to check the license plate to make sure it's Zach's before I go pounding on the door.

STD MFN.

Yep, it's his all right. The vanity plate was a gift from his last girlfriend. Zach has vowed to replace it in May, when he renews his plates. I don't blame him. Besides, "Stud Muffin" being a little cheesy, I've commented to Zach many times that STD isn't exactly an abbreviation I'd want plastered on the back of my vehicle for the world to see.

I yank open the back door. "I hope all that steam on the windows means it's warm in here. I'm freez—"

Sylvie and Zach jerk their heads in my direction so hard they may be complaining of whiplash in the morning. Their expressions are rather amusing. Their jaws are slack, cheeks turning pink, and eyes darting here, there, and everywhere, like they just got busted for parking or something.

Wait a second.

Nah.

But the fact their shoulders are touching is not lost on me.

"Hey, Sis. Hop in," Zach says, trying too hard to be nonchalant.

"So did you get that drink of water?" I ask as I pull the door shut. I stare at my friend, who is, once again, avoiding my eyes like a dog who got caught ransacking the garbage can.

She casually slides to her side of the car, holds up a Styrofoam cup, then drinks from it for good measure.

Zach struggles to maneuver his almost six-foot body completely around so he is facing me. He leans back a little too hard against the steering wheel, and we all jump when the horn blasts.

That lopsided, goofy grin appears again. "Sylvie and I have something we want to talk to you about." He glances at Sylvie. His face softens, his blue-gray eyes bursting with adoration or, dare I say, love? I've seen that gaze before. It's exactly how he used to look at Valley Girl Vicki.

Like, totally disgusting.

Sylvie attempts to look at me. "We've wanted to tell you for a few weeks now, but there hasn't been a good time. And lately, with everything you've been going through…" She gazes at Zach.

He reaches over and caresses a newly colored russet lock of Sylvie's hair, then looks back at me. "Okay. We're going to come right out and tell you. It's time you knew."

Here's the thing…I already know.

But I play dumb and give Sylvie my best blank stare. She flutters a nervous smile in my direction, noticeably uncomfortable with Zach's display of affection. I still can't get used to seeing Sylvie insecure and nervous. So not her style.

I roll my eyes. "Look, guys. I'm not stupid, okay?"

They exchange a look.

"Stop looking at each other like that. I've had my share of stupid moments, but this isn't one of them. As you said, Sylv, I've been a little distracted lately. The last thing I've been thinking about is my brother's love life. Or my best friend's romantic endeavors, for that matter. We all know I have enough trouble with my own. But tonight when you slipped and called

Sylvie 'babe,' well, that kind of gave it away." I reach over the seat and sock Zach in the arm. I am tempted to do the same to Sylvie, but I refrain, being the good friend I am. Unlike her, who seems to think keeping secrets from friends is acceptable behavior.

I shrug. "I'll admit, a romantic relationship between my brother and my best friend isn't exactly on the list of things I want to see before I die." I gaze out the window. "So, tonight, spare me the details, okay? I don't want to know how you kept it a secret. Or how you discovered your undying love for each other. Or the wedding date. Tonight I'm tired. I want to go home and sleep. And sleep. And sleep."

Zach smiles, smacks the seat, and blows a chunk of hair out of his eye. "Deal."

Sylvie props her arms on the seat and meets my eyes, probably for the first time tonight. "Mads, I'm sorry for the secrets. But I really do adore your brother. And I'm glad it's out in the open. At least now you know."

Hmmm. At least now I know.

Oy.

The telephone is ringing in my ear. Oh, why didn't I turn off that blasted ringer before drifting off to la-la-land?

I open one eye and look at the clock. Is it really noon?

My head is killing me. If I didn't know better, I'd think I had a massive hangover. Only I didn't drink anything. Well, besides gallons of Diet Coke, that is.

Charlie bats at my hair, wanting to play. I give him an irritated shove with one hand while clunking around for the handset with the other. I lift it off the base as the answering machine picks up. I wait for my voice to stop commanding the caller to leave a message.

"Mommy?"

Emily. My spirit soars to new heights, and my head aches a tad less.

"Hi sweetie." Struggling to sit up, I switch the phone to my left ear.

"Grandma made pancakes for breakfast. They were sooooo good."

Right on cue, my stomach rumbles. "Better than mine?"

She pauses, probably weighing the decision of telling the truth and possibly making me feel bad or doing something she knows is wrong—that would be lying—in order to preserve my feelings. Before she has a chance to answer, I continue. "I'm just teasing, honey. Everyone knows Grandma Nancy makes the best pancakes on the planet."

Emily's relief wisps through the phone line. "I helped make the batter."

"Oh, good. That means you now have inside knowledge. You'll have to let me in on her secret blue ribbon recipe."

Em giggles. "It's not her secret, Mom. It's Aunt Jemima's!"

I laugh.

"We got snow. Daddy says we didn't get as much as you got over there, but there's, like, three inches on the ground. I'm going outside to make snow angels in a minute. Daddy bought Grandma a snow blower, but her neighbor—this guy, Pete—is the one who usually clears off her driveway. But his snow blower broke, so I guess it's really for him. Daddy says there was a blizzard at our house. Was there? Do you think we'll have school on Monday? Because if the roads are really bad and school gets cancelled, Daddy says we might stay an extra night and take our time getting home. Did you go to that reunion thingy last night? Was it fun? "

She stops to take a breath. I caught most of what she said, but I have to admit the part about the snow blower was a little confusing.

"Wow, so many questions...let's see. Yes, there was a blizzard. The roads were pretty bad. Sylvie and I actually got snowed in at Reggie's."

She inhales deeply. "You did? What happened?"

"They closed the roads, so nobody could leave for a few hours. Then, finally, the plows came through and cleared the snow so we could go home."

"Did you have fun?"

"Mmmm...I wouldn't say fun, exactly. *Interesting* might be a better word. I would have rather stayed home with a good book."

"So what do you think about school? Do you think we'll have a snow day on Monday?"

That nine-year-old attention span—gotta love it.

"I hope not. I know how you would hate missing school."

"Yeah, right." Emily giggles. "Here's Dad."

What? Oh, that sneaky little daughter of mine—handing off the phone before I can protest. I listen as the phone is shuffled around. There's no time to prepare anything to say. So not fair.

"Hello? Madi?" Richard's voice is rich and smooth.

I need coffee.

"Hi." That was easy enough. I swing my legs over the side of the bed and head for the kitchen.

"How are you?"

"Fine." Wow. Such a word-master I am.

"I hear you got dumped on last night."

It takes me a moment to realize he's talking about the snow and not the information dump I received the night before.

"Yeah...a blizzard. I got snowed in at Reggie's Classy Diner. Not fun."

Rich chuckles. "Emily mentioned you were going to meet some old friends or something." He pauses, and I imagine him running a hand through his hair—a habit I used to find annoying but now brings a smile to my lips. "But at least you made it home okay."

His concern touches me. But the romantic feelings stirring in my soul are offset by aggravation. The events of the night before slosh through the forefront of my mind. I can't forget about the fact that Richard didn't tell me about Fawn contacting him or that she and Raymond have a daughter together. I'm Rich's wife; he should have told me. Period.

"So...," he says when I don't respond to his last comment.

"What? Oh. Yes, I made it home. Obviously, or we wouldn't be talking, right?"

"We do need to talk, Madi. There are some things I need to tell you."

So soon?

"You're right, Rich. We need to clear the air. Maybe when you drop off the kids tomorrow night, we can—"

"Hey, Madi, I'm really sorry, but I have to go. It's Mom. I'll call you later."

Click.

"Talk over coffee or something..." I finish the sentence that was so rudely cut off.

I slam the phone down on the counter.

Need coffee. Now.

I bang around in the cupboards, spilling coffee grounds and splashing water onto the countertop. Jamming my finger against the brew button, the Cuisinart growls and moans as it wakes up from its nightly reprieve.

Charlie is at my feet, playing with my fuzzy pink socks. Since the coffee is taking forever to brew, I fill the cat's food and water dishes, then press my back against the kitchen wall and let myself slide down to the floor. Beside me, Charlie gracefully nibbles on his cat food, regarding me every so often. Such a protective and sensitive cat he is.

Biding my time until the coffee pot fills, I think. When—or if—Richard calls back, what should I say? We definitely need to talk—that much is obvious. He has some explaining to do and I have...well, I don't know what I have to do. I might say butt-kissing, but I really didn't do anything wrong, other than assume the worst of my husband—for valid reasons, I might add.

So Rich didn't cheat on me. It is a huge relief to know my husband has remained faithful. And I sincerely believe that now, even if my mother will do her best to try to convince me otherwise.

But he did lie. Okay, maybe not directly, but isn't keeping a secret the same as lying?

A shrill ring sounds from a couple feet away and I jump. Because I don't want Rich to think I've been waiting by the phone like a lovesick teenager, I slowly get up and wait until the fourth ring to pick up.

But it's not Richard. It's my mother. Just the person to add some joy to my day. "What took you so long to answer?" she demands.

"Hello to you, too, Mom." I cup the phone between my ear and shoulder and pour myself a cup of coffee. Grabbing the phone with my left hand, I close my eyes and hold the mug to my nose, letting the steam and the hazelnut scent fill my senses. For one brief moment in time, all is right with the world.

But Mom is quick to bring me back to reality.

"Your brother called."

"And?"

"And he says you need me."

The temptation to laugh is right there. Zach will pay dearly for this one. He obviously assumed my never-ending nightmare isn't quite nightmarish enough so he had to throw a dose of Mom in for good measure.

But maybe I should cut Mom some slack. The fact she even called is a wonder. So she didn't come right out and ask me how I was doing. She didn't offer a sympathetic shoulder or a listening ear. But she took the time to call. In her own small way, she's trying. I should be thankful, right?

"So what kind of trouble do you have now?" Her tone is cranky and brash, as always, and she makes it seem as if I'm wasting her time. After all, my problems couldn't hold a candle to hers.

Forgive me, but I'm not feeling all that thankful.

"It's nothing, Mom. But I appreciate you calling." Liar, liar, pants on fire—on both counts.

"I knew it. You haven't needed me a day in your life. I don't know why I thought you'd start now."

Uninvited, tears sting my eyes and spill over my eyelashes and onto my cheeks.

If only she knew how wrong she was.

23

Being a princess isn't always
what it's cracked up to be.
PRINCESS DIANA

It isn't until I head to the bedroom to replace the phone that I notice the answering machine light in the kitchen is blinking. Due to my preoccupation with talking to Richard and my desperate need to get the coffee started, I must have missed it. The machine informs me I have three messages—probably all from the night before.

Sure enough.

"Madi, this is Candice. Just checking in, hon. I know the kids are gone for the weekend and thought you might be lonely. How does dinner on Sunday sound? After church? Around one?" She pauses as if waiting for an RSVP. "So, anyway, I'll wait for you to call back to confirm. But I'll tentatively plan on it, okay? Your dad and I would love to see you." Another pause. "Hope you're all right, honey. We worry, you know. Okay. Well, good-bye. Call us back."

Click.

I confess it's nice to be fussed over. What Mom lacks in the nurturing department, Candice makes up for it a hundred times over. That my dad married two such different women is amazing, although he's also a different person these days and his choices are a little…wiser. Candice must have her faults (other than singing out of tune, that is), but she hides them well.

But even though I love Candice to death and truly appreciate her concern and care, it's not the same as if it were coming from my mother. There's a reason for the word *stepmother*—she's a step away from the real one. Candice may try harder than my mother. She may communicate her love to me better than my mother. She may actually love me more than my mother loves me. Maybe it's not this way for everyone who has a stepparent, but for me, Candice's love and concern will never take the place of that which I covet from my mom.

The thing I have to come to terms with, however, is that Mom may never be capable of giving me the kind of love my heart longs for. In fact, every time I speak to her or spend time with her, it seems less and less likely. Can I deal with the possibility that she might never express her love for me in terms I can understand?

Do I have a choice?

A soft, gentle Southern drawl cuts into the air. "Hi, Max, it's me. I was going to text you, but I left my phone at my dad's. I would have called your cell, but your number is in my cell and, yeah. Well, you said you might be going to your grandmother's this weekend, so...um...that's probably where you are. Anyway, call me when you get home. Maybe we won't have school on Monday. That'd be cool. I'll talk to y'all later. Oh—this is Sam."

Ah...young love. It's rather amusing how Sam bumbled over her words and felt the need to clarify who was calling. As if Max wouldn't know. I can't wait to tell my son that his new girlfriend called.

Girlfriend. My son has a girlfriend. Never thought I'd see the day.

A week ago, I hoped Amy would fill the girlfriend bill. But now Amy is most assuredly out of the picture. I frown, remembering how my perfect daughter-in-law dreams were dashed last night in a dark hallway of Reggie's Classy Diner.

"Hello, I'm calling for Madison McCall. This is Celeste Hardaway."

As the third message begins to play, a butterfly takes flight in my gut. My hand instinctively makes its way to my stomach. *Flutter. Flutter.*

"I'd like to schedule a meeting to discuss the recent altercation between our daughters. My Paige will be sitting in on the discussion, as will Walter, my husband. It would be in your best interest if Christina and your husband were present, as well. I'd like for the six of us to meet as soon as possible. Frankly, we'd like to avoid the hassle of a lawsuit, if at all possible. Convince us not to press charges. Monday at 4:00 will work nicely for us. Ms. Jameson has agreed to let us use her office. I'll be gone most of the day, but please call 555-4279 later this evening to confirm this appointment. I'd really like this to be taken care of. If I don't hear back from you in the next twenty-four hours, I'll be calling again. Good day."

I roll my eyes. "Well, by all means, if Monday at 4:00 works for you, we wouldn't dare refuse."

Charlie takes a break from his kitty chow to peer at me.

"I wasn't talking to you, Charlie. Go back to your breakfast."

He obliges and turns away.

A glance at the calendar tells me that besides Emily's 6:30 dance class, the day is free.

Rats.

Emily's earlier question about the possibility of a snow day on Monday ignites a spark of hope. Through the big picture window I can see it's snowing again, but that doesn't mean much. Blizzard one day, sunny skies and temperatures in the fifties the next. The story of Michigan.

On the other hand, getting this meeting over with and putting the whole incident behind me sounds pretty good. So, because I am a woman and it's my prerogative, I change my mind and hope the snow lets up so school will indeed be in session on Monday. Sorry, Em.

I mentally file away a reminder to return Celeste Hardaway's phone call later this evening. I'll tell her that I may have to juggle things around a bit, but will be in Ms. Jameson's office Monday, promptly at 4:00. Okay, so maybe "juggle things around" is a bit of an exaggeration. But, hey, I do have a life that involves more than being at the beck and call of snooty school-board members. She doesn't need to know that by "juggle things around" I may be talking about a quick stop at Fred's Market. I've gotten pretty good with those grocery bags.

Next, I head to the computer and sign onto the Internet. After wading through a dozen junk mails, I come to one from Claudia Boeve. Over the past several months, I've received a handful of e-mails from Claudia, mostly inviting me to attend her "Losing Means Winning" workshop at church. But I have no interest in trading cow's milk for soy or spending extra money on organic foods. Not to mention the incomprehensible Losing Means Winning requirement of giving up Dibs forever. The nice thing about giving up my chocolate addiction now is that I know it's only temporary—until I lose those stubborn ten pounds. Then Dibs can be reintroduced into my diet, albeit in moderation.

But this time, the e-mail is not about health at all. At least, not the physical kind. The subject line reads, *Help for your marriage.*

I frown and sit back in the chair. How did Claudia Boeve, of all people, find out about my marriage problems? Of course, Claudia's best friend is Caroline Summerville, the church gossip who contacts naive church members and tricks them into disclosing all of their secrets by sweetly asking if there is anything specific they need her to pray about. She then tells other random "prayer partners" exactly what to pray for—John Stevens' struggle with pornography, Ann Mavrick's anger problem, Suzie Nelson's kleptomaniac daughter...

The thing is, Caroline constantly tries to recruit prayer partners and, before long, there's a whole slew of church members who know your business.

How she found out about my marital situation is beyond me. I certainly didn't tell her. And I can almost guarantee Rich didn't offer up any information. It troubles me that one of my kids may have disclosed our personal family matters to either Caroline or one of her six children.

As I click on the e-mail and begin to read, I breathe a sigh of relief. It isn't addressed specifically to me. It's merely an announcement about a new class that Claudia is leading on spicing up your marriage. No offense, but somehow the thought of Claudia telling me how to add romance to my marriage is a little like asking for marital sex tips from Mother Teresa.

Besides, my marriage needs a little more than romance at the moment. The truth is, romance is the farthest thing from my mind. Rich and I need to get things right between us outside of the bedroom first.

Speaking of getting things right, I type a quick e-mail to Sarah Price, asking if she has time for coffee. As a friend, not a counselor, although her counseling skills will likely come into play. I feel a little guilty taking advantage of her offer to chat outside of the office, but it's not like I'm canceling my counseling appointments to do it.

Almost immediately, my little mailbox flag pops up, indicating a response.

Madi,
     I've been thinking about you. I'm off to the Y, if you'd care to join me. We can talk while we burn calories on the treadmill. I have a visitor's pass if you're not a member. I plan on leaving in about twenty minutes. Hope to see you there!
     Sarah

I've been talking long enough about getting in shape, might as well do it.

It takes me several minutes to find something to wear. How bad is that? I make a mental note to hit the mall for some workout clothes. Finally, I find an old pair of Rich's sweats and a U of M T-shirt. Not exactly fashionable, but at least baggy enough to cover my flaws and keep me comfy. As comfy as can be while huffing and puffing on the treadmill. I wonder how much talking I'll be able to do before I'm wheezing away like I've smoked ten packs of cigarettes.

The roads are still pretty snow-covered and on the way to the gym I see a couple of cars in the ditch. I keep the speedometer at about thirty. Don't want to risk getting stranded. Especially in this outfit.

I'm grateful to find the lot only speckled with cars. Guess most exercisers decided chiseled abs aren't worth the risk of the icy roads.

As soon as I push through the doors, memories of my fitness days gone by slap me in the face. The scent of sweat mixed with shower gel...the energy...the overall feeling of well-being. Has it really been over sixteen years since I set foot in a gym? The last time I remember was before I got pregnant with the twins. I'll definitely be looking into a membership.

I spot Sarah right away. She looks fabulous, as always, in black spandex shorts and a fuchsia tank top. Her blond hair is pulled back in a ponytail and her face is void of makeup, but that does nothing to minimize her beauty, which makes me hate her.

Okay, not really. More like I hate the fact that I've let myself go.

She waves me over. "I told Stacia at the front desk that a friend might be joining me. She said we can turn in the visitor's pass on our way out." She proceeds to stretch her long, toned limbs. I follow suit. It's been so long since I've stretched like this, I wait for creaking sounds.

Ten minutes later, we're on side-by-side treadmills.

"So fill me in," she says, cranking her treadmill up to a fast walk.

I leave mine on stroll. "Well, you were right. Richard didn't cheat."

Sarah smiles and pats my hand, which is gripping the handle for dear life, even though it's still on the slowest speed. "I'm so glad, Madi. How did you find out?"

I proceed to fill her in on last night's events. She nods and comments in the appropriate places. It feels good to rehash the whole thing, if for no other reason than to more deeply process what happened.

"So now what?" Sarah asks. She reaches for her towel and dabs at her face. And no wonder—her treadmill's been cranked up to a steady jogging pace for the past fifteen minutes.

I would answer, but I can't. I'm huffing and puffing too hard. The sad part is, I never increased the speed. I've been walking steadily the entire time. I hold up a finger and shut down my machine.

I wait another ten minutes while Sarah slows it down to a fast walk again to cool down. I do some more stretching and try to look like I know what I'm doing. She finally joins me on the mat. Her breathing is normal, even after an intense workout. Amazing.

"I'm looking forward to talking to Rich when he gets back from his mother's. He still has some explaining to do."

Sarah raises her eyebrows.

"About why he didn't tell me about Fawn."

Sarah leans back on her hands. "Would you mind if I made a suggestion?"

"Of course not. You're the doctor. Suggest away."

"Let that part go for now."

In response to the dirty look I shoot her, Sarah continues. "You do deserve answers, Madi. But leave them for later. If you start in with accusations and demand answers, you'll put Rich right on the defensive again. Focus on the fact that he didn't cheat. That he loves you. That you're the only woman for him. That's what you need to be concentrating on right now."

"But if he had told me in the first place—"

"Now you're blaming him for your actions. For your insecurities. Maybe he should have told you about Fawn. But to be fair, he tried to explain at least twice, and you never gave him a chance."

I hug my knees to my chest and stay silent. She's right, of course. But there's a part of me that feels safer—more in control—holding on to it. Rubbing it in his face, even. Letting go would be allowing Richard to get away with hurting me. My pride's having a problem with that. I don't want to let it go.

I guess what it comes down to is I don't want to forgive.

Wow. I guess I'm more like my mom than I thought. Scary.

Sarah stands up and offers me a hand. I take it, and she pulls me to my feet. "Listen," she says, "I know this isn't an official counseling session, but I want to give you some homework, okay?"

I nod.

"When Rich comes home, tell him you love him. Tell him you're sorry you doubted him. And tell him you know he loves you—even if you aren't really convinced of it."

"Isn't that lying?"

"Nope. That's speaking in faith. The more you tell yourself—and Richard—that you know he loves you, the more you'll start to believe it. And incidentally, the more you meditate on Bible verses that tell you how much God loves you, the more you'll start to believe that, too. You *are* a princess, Madi, and Richard is your prince. And even though *perfect* princes belong only in fairy tales, I sense your husband's love for you is as genuine as ever."

I have to admit, the thought makes my heart pitter-patter. Maybe it's time for the Disney princesses to move over and make room for Princess Madi.

24

Part of being a winner is knowing
when enough is enough.
DONALD TRUMP

Once home and showered, I spend the rest of the day wrapped in my robe with a good book. It's great to finally be able to chill out while staying cozy indoors. Every so often, I look up from my novel and meditate on one of the eight Bible verses Sarah gave me. Other times, I absentmindedly watch the snow fall. The beauty astounds me and makes it almost impossible to tear my eyes away. The house across the street has several pine trees in the front yard and the snow clings to them like powdered sugar to a doughnut. Simply gorgeous! Despite the issues I've had with God recently, as I take in the beauty of His creation, I can't help wondering how anyone could doubt He exists.

Charlie keeps me company by stretching out on the top of the couch by my head. He's as lazy as I am, evidenced by our continuous yawns.

Before I know it, I'm waking up in the dark with drool on my chin. As the fuzz clears from my brain, it strikes me that Richard never called back. Hmmm. So not like him.

I look over at the old grandfather clock I inherited from my grandmother. Solid oak, it's by far one of the most beautiful pieces of furniture I own. Even though it's still dark, the moon reflecting off the snow lets in just enough light to see the hands. Four fifty-nine. The clock starts chiming. Make that five o'clock, exactly.

That it's morning already surprises me. Within the next couple hours I need to decide whether or not I'll be going to church and taking Candice up on her invitation for dinner.

I struggle out of the couch. Every inch of my body protests, from my sore leg muscles not used to thirty minutes on the treadmill to my neck. Sleeping all night in a half-upright position has taken its toll. I roll and rub my neck while heading to the kitchen for a couple of pain relievers.

After starting the coffee, I take a quick shower and try not to moan as the water pounds against my aching muscles, but by the time I dry off, the pain is subsiding. Fuzzy bathrobe wrapped tightly around me, I head to the computer and fire it up before making my way back to the kitchen to pump myself full of my morning addiction. Why someone hasn't yet invented a coffee IV is beyond me. I'd be first in line to get hooked up. But only if it came complete with the aroma and the taste—all part of the coffee lover's experience. Coffee breath, however, I could do without.

Finally, steaming mug of mocha java in hand, I sit down at the computer to check messages.

There is one from Rich that I notice arrived at 1:00 a.m. One thing Rich is not is a night owl. The last time I remember him up at one o'clock in the morning was when I woke him because I was in labor with Emily.

I click on the e-mail.

> Madi,
>
> Sorry I didnt call you back yesterdat. My mom was trying to snowblow the driveway by herself and sliped and fell on the ice. It took us an hour just to get to the hospital. It took another three hours before she was seen and we prety much spent the night in er. She has a spraned wrist, some bruses and a sore behind. Other than that shes ok. Im heading off to bed now. Ill call you tomorow. Snows still coming down pretty good and if schools closed tomorow I may hang out here and keep an eye on mom for another night. Hope thats ok.
>
> Love Rich

Okay, so I'm feeling like a bit of a heel for my annoyance with Rich for not getting back to me. Poor Nancy! What was she thinking trying to clear her driveway? She's seventy-five years old, for Pete's sake.

As I rescan the message, I'm shocked that Rich even spelled his own name correctly. As always, his typing is atrocious. He obviously doesn't look at his fingers or the screen when he composes his messages. I wonder if he closes his eyes.

I consider typing a reply, but I hold off. I'll wait for his call. Besides, if I start typing, I may never stop. All the stuff about Fawn and Raymond might come pouring out, along with my questions about why he never told me, and I really don't want that to happen. Gotta be a good girl and do the homework

Sarah gave me: focus on the fact that Rich didn't cheat. He loves me. Don't quite feel it, but I'm telling myself it's true, anyway.

I sit back in my computer chair and wonder if Candice will be up yet. I know she's an early riser, but 6:30 might be pushing it. I decide I will take her up on her offer for dinner. No use sitting home all day, dwelling on the events of Friday night, replaying it over and over in my mind like my old Abba record with the three-inch scratch. "Take a chance on me...take a chance...take a chance...take a chance...take a chance..."

I drain my coffee cup and reach for the mouse to click off the Internet when my little You've Got Mail flag pops up. Well, someone I know is up at the crack of dawn.

The address is unfamiliar, and at first I assume the e-mail is spam, wrongly delivered to my inbox. But something niggles my brain, prompting me to take another look: *Fandlexi@scb.com.* Hmmm. Fawn and Lexi Witchburn? Could it be? Only one way to find out.

> Dear Madison,
>
> I got your e-mail address at Reggie's from the girl in the yellow sweater with the big boobs. She said she didn't think you'd mind.
>
> I know we didn't exactly end on a positive note Friday night, but I want to let you know that I am telling Raymond about Lexi today. I'd like to chat with you first. I hope you can give me some inside scoop about your brother-in-law and how you think he'll react. I don't want to disappoint Lexi. It's time she had a father in her life, and I want this to go as smoothly as possible.
>
> I've included my phone number below. If you happen to get this message, and you're free today, maybe we can get together for a cup of coffee.
>
> Fawn
> 555-2857

My first instinct is to hit the *Delete* button and pretend I never opened Fawn's e-mail. Who would know?

But I've been making progress on confronting my problems instead of running to the door, the fridge, or mysolitaire.com. Ignoring Fawn's message would set me back a bit. *Don't want that.*

I tap my chin with my index finger and reread the e-mail, but unfortunately, the words are the same as they were thirty seconds ago. What choice do I have?

Before I make the call, I pour myself an extra boost of confidence. Fresh coffee in hand, I somehow feel more able to attempt this feat. I sink into the sofa and pull my legs up. Charlie makes himself comfortable in the crick of my knees.

My hand trembles as I begin to dial and I tell myself it's from the coffee, but I would need three times more caffeine to give me the shakes. Fawn answers on the second ring.

"Hello, it's Madi." I pause. "McCall." In case she happens to know three other Madis who might be calling at 6:45 a.m.

"Wow. That was fast." I would assume her thick voice was due to the early hour if I didn't know that it was normally deep and raspy.

I take a deep breath. "I got your message." Duh. Don't think I'd be calling at this hour, otherwise. Or at all.

"Mom?" A child's voice pipes up in the background. I hear the familiar hand-over-the-mouthpiece rustling and then Fawn's muffled voice telling her she'd be just a minute. I hope my calling didn't wake her.

"Sorry about that. Lexi's an early riser, too."

"My kids would sleep 'til noon if I let them."

Fawn chuckles. "She's gotten up at the crack of dawn since I can remember. She must take after Raymond, because I love to sleep in myself. But when Lexi was younger, I didn't want her roaming the house without supervision. I'm used to it now, and it's kind of become our special time together."

Somehow this impresses me.

Silence lingers between the phone lines, then Fawn says, "Lexi and I are going to church this morning. We could meet up afterwards. Will you be there?"

She catches me off guard. I stammer. "Oh. Well. Um. Ah. I, uh…I don't think I'm going to make it today."

There. Now why was that so difficult? For a brief second, I give it a second thought. Rich won't be there, no kids to get to Sunday school…but still. I don't think I'm up for it.

"Oh."

"But you could swing by my house afterwards. Why don't you and Lexi come over for lunch?"

I resist the urge to clamp my hand over my mouth and scream, "Did I just say that?" Maybe I dozed off at the computer and dreamed up the whole phone call—especially that last remark. I pinch myself to check.

Ouch! Guess that answers that question.

Maybe I extended the invitation to Fawn out of guilt for assuming the worst of her. Or maybe sleeping while sitting up on the couch all night sapped the sense out of me. Or maybe I'm a moron.

I vote for number three.

"I'll have to run it by Lexi. I promised her a Frosty from Wendy's after church." She hesitates and I find myself hoping she'll decline. Wouldn't want to deprive the girl of a Frosty, for goodness' sake. "But I guess I could pick one up for her on the way over." Another pause. "Oh, why not? I would like to talk. We'll be there."

I give her directions to my house and hang up the phone, still slightly dazed at how unpredictable I've become. Inviting Anita Langerak to the church I'm avoiding; confronting Fawn Witchburn and then inviting her and my newly acquired niece for dinner; meeting my shrink at the gym to actually talk about my problems. So not my typical behavior of locking myself up in my bedroom with a carton of Edy's Dibs.

Speaking of food, it's time to call Candice and tell her not to expect me. I've got other plans. Like trying to come up with an edible dish to serve my brother-in-law's daughter and ex-girlfriend-slash-formerly-suspected-husband's-lover who, at best, has questionable motives.

But backing out is no longer an option. Fawn Witchburn and her daughter are coming for lunch.

And that's that.

I feel like Mother Hubbard. My cupboards are almost completely bare. But wait—an unopened box of mostaccioli pasta and a jar of sauce sit side-by-side on my cupboard shelf. My mostaccioli rocks, if I do say so myself. I got the recipe a long time ago from a magazine and I tweaked it a bit, perfecting it over the years. It's the one homemade dish I make that I'm proud of. Okay, to be honest, it's pretty much the *only* homemade dish I ever make. My family loves it. Then again, from the way Max shot down my offer to make a mostaccioli dinner for Sam sometime, I'm thinking perhaps it's not quite as scrumptious as I've convinced myself.

Oh, how I wish I could be more like my stepmother, who's not only a wonderful cook but has the *desire* to be a wonderful cook. But it's just not there. I can't conjure it up no matter how hard I try. Eating out—doesn't matter where—is my first choice every time.

I dial my dad's phone number. Candice answers and can't disguise the disappointment in her voice when I tell her I won't be coming. She tries not to let on, but I can hear it in her voice. She doesn't need to know I declined because I'm having last-minute company of my own. I keep it as generic as possible and basically inform her I'm not up to going to church today—or anywhere, for that matter. Candice sounds curious but doesn't press, for which I am thankful.

Clicking off, I reach for the trusty yellow pages and *thunk* it down on the counter. It flops open to the restaurant section.

The roly-poly cartoon pizza chef (whoml I assume is Vino) stares up at me from the quarter-page ad, an exaggerated gleam emitting from his toothy grin.

I know the number by heart, but for some reason I still look it up every time. I dial and wait. It rings three times before Tori answers. She knows me well and thinks this gives her permission to tell me all about the blind date she had last night. She relays all the details of how she and this guy, Wayne, got stuck in a snow bank and had to wait an hour for help. Then the dude got food poisoning and ended up puking all over her. Needless to say, Tori is disgusted and will never—ever—go on another blind date again no matter how cute her sister claims he is. Can't say I blame her.

After I make all the appropriate sympathetic sounds and replies, Tori eventually remembers why I called and takes my order: a couple of pizzas and breadsticks. Later, I'll toss together a salad, for health's sake. I ask for delivery around 11:30. This should allow a few extra minutes to get things set up before Fawn and Lexi arrive. If I arrange it right, maybe they'll even believe I made the pizza myself.

Tori says that because many of the outlying areas still haven't been plowed, so there may be a slight delay. I tell her to shoot for eleven then. I can always pop the pizzas in the oven to warm them up, if necessary. I charge the total to my credit card, including the tip for the driver. Today it'll be one of the regulars—Dan, the Delivery Man, as the kids and I affectionately call him.

The next half hour is spent snow-blowing the driveway and shoveling the walk to the front door. One potential lawsuit is bad enough; I don't need another. Plus, it would be tragic if Fawn's stilettos ended up getting lost in a snow drift as she makes her way up the walk to my door.

Once inside, after guzzling yet another mug of coffee, I dress comfortably, yet casually classy, in a plain aqua top, black cardigan sweater and stretchy "skinny jeans" that I am sure take off at least ten pounds.

Let's see…is that it? The driveway is shoveled. House is still clean. Pizza is ordered. I am presentable. Yep, everything's pretty much in order.

Well, almost everything. My mental state is not exactly prepared for what lies ahead. First, meeting with Fawn, and then later with Richard. Plus, I still have to deal with Sylvie's and Zach's recent news bulletin and there's also the matter of my ornery, unloving mother. Oh, let's not forget the situation with the Hardaways.

Which reminds me. I never called Celeste Hardaway back last night. Oh, well. One thing at a time.

It's a little after ten, which means church is starting. Hesitating for only a second, I sign on to the Internet and surf on over to my church's website. I click on "Live Services" and *voilà!* Craig and Amanda, praise and worship leaders, appear on the screen. Craig jams out on the guitar and Amanda's fingers fly over the keyboard with familiarity and ease.

About a year ago, our church services were made available online for invalids, shut-ins, ill members, curious seekers, and stubborn people who are avoiding church or God—or both—for one reason or another.

When the music slows down and the words to "Shout to the Lord" appear on the monitor, my emotions get the better of me and a tear squeezes past my eyelid. That song always chokes me up. Sadly, though, I'm not sure whether my tears have more to do with the meaning of the words being sung or with the guilt I feel for distancing myself so far from God that I seriously believe it would take much more than giving Him a shout to get back in His good graces. Either way, it seems God is definitely trying to get my attention.

I knew He'd show up this weekend.

As the camera pans to the congregation, I catch a glimpse of Dad and Candice. They're hard to miss, with Candice's bright yellow floral dress. Candice's eyes are closed. Her arms are raised high, tears streaming down her cheeks—obviously lost in praising and worshiping the Lord.

Dad is peering sideways at Candice, a grimace turning down the corners of his eyes and mouth. I clamp a hand over my mouth and suppress a laugh. Candice's singing obviously has not improved. I'll have to admonish my dad for losing his focus during praise and worship. Then I'll warn him against making faces like that during a taped church service being watched by who-knows-how-many people around the world.

Suddenly, it feels a little like I'm witnessing an intimate bedroom scene between a husband and wife. Do these people realize just how many millions may be witnessing their personal and intimate worship time with the Lord? I close my eyes and let the music consume me. Before long, I am having an intimate moment of my own and find myself bawling like a baby, on my knees, sniffing carpet.

I have been such a dork! Not only have I been missing out on precious time with my Savior, but I've made a complete mess of my family. And why? Because I chose to listen to my mother's ridiculous claims that all men cheat and should therefore be wiped clean off the planet. Or at least thrown to the curb. Except, of course, for Zach. Although when Mom discovers he is dating Sylvie, she might include him, too. Mom has never liked Sylvie, probably because Sylvie is young and cute, has a twenty-five-inch waist and, in Mom's mind, is a stereotypical boyfriend-stealer. What Mom doesn't understand—because she never allowed herself to really get to know Sylvie—is that Sylvie wouldn't steal the extra roll of toilet paper from a hotel room, let alone another woman's husband.

I roll onto my back and lie there, looking up at the ceiling. "Please, God, forgive me for being such a fool. Have you ever seen a bigger fool than me, Lord? Wait. Don't answer that. I am the queen of the morons." I pause as another tear oozes from my eye. "Okay, so you're the ultimate miracle worker. And right now, I need a miracle, Lord. Two, actually. No, make it three.

"One, I need my husband and kids to forgive me. Restoring my marriage and my family would be really great. And seeing how I've been treating them lately, I wouldn't blame you if you're iffy on helping me out with this one. Most people probably think Richard and the kids would be better off without me. But you're not everyone, Lord. You love me, even though I am a moron. Can't quite wrap my brain around that, but I'm trying to convince myself that it's true. So anyway, if you feel like emitting some of that miracle power, getting my husband and kids to forgive me would be a great place to start."

I sniff and wipe my nose with the back of my hand.

"Two, I need to come up with the strength to apologize to Fawn. I've judged her, and that's wrong. Even if she does wear clothes way too tight and makeup way too dark and lipstick way, way too brown. Even if she walks around with more thigh showing than a bare-naked chicken and smells like a perfume factory. Even if her daughter knows words like *ho*. Even if...okay, Lord, there I go again. I need help with this one."

I can almost hear Him say, "Ya think?"

"Okay, third. I would really love to get past this insecurity issue. You know what I'm talking about, Lord. I know that blaming the parents is so cliché, but with Dad cheating and Mom relaying all of the gory details, I can't say I'm surprised at how I turned out. I'm not really blaming them. Okay, yes, I am. I realize I'm a big girl now, and I should know better. But come on! There are some things a girl should not know about her father. He may be a changed man today, but when it's drilled into you from a young age that all men cheat, including your own father, what else is a girl to believe?"

I sit in silence, waiting for God's answer. But all I hear is Pastor Sherman talking. He's well into the message by now, and his words prick my ears.

He's preaching on the woman at the well. How appropriate. That woman could be Fawn. She could be me. Heck, she could even be Sylvie, as perfect as Sylvie seems sometimes. The point Pastor Sherman is drilling home is that we all have different "wells" we dip into, hoping they will quench our thirst. When one doesn't work to satisfy, we move on to another. But, of course, there is only one that will truly quench our thirst: the One True Well of Living Water.

The story has been told a million times. But it's resonating with me this morning. Now I'm thinking about the many wells I've lowered my bucket into. When I was single and unsaved, I tried the wells of alcohol, sex, and astrology. Since I've been married, I've tried the well of the Romance Novel, the well of Edy's Dibs, even the well of Children. But relying on these things to satisfy my needs has not fulfilled me. Not the way God intends me to be fulfilled. In fact, they've only helped to mess things up—the Dibs have made me overweight, and romance novels have teased me with unrealistic (and consequently unmet) expectations of my husband.

Yep. It's definitely time to head to the right well. The one always within reach but which I *so* have been avoiding.

I breathe another prayer of apology and ask God to bless the rest of my day. I'm confident He's heard my plea. I've felt God's peace in the past, but not like now. Now the peace does surpass my moronic state and has settled not only in my heart, but in my mind, as well.

That doesn't mean, however, that I'm not nervous about Fawn and Lexi sitting at my kitchen table in less than an hour. Or about humbling myself before my husband and kids. Being at peace does not mean my heart won't quicken or my palms won't sweat and I won't stumble over my words today. What it does mean is that I know God will be there with me, cheering me on.

Pastor Sherman begins the prayer leading into the altar call, which clues me in that the service is coming to a close and that I'd better get a move on.

I stand and brush myself off, then head to the bathroom to fix my face. I've shed enough tears to fill up my Jacuzzi tub. Normally at that thought, I would be tempted to fill up that tub and soak away my troubles. But not today. Today, I will face my problems head on. Without chocolate. Without irrational behavior. Without escaping at the first sign of stress.

I will face my problems like the Warrior Princess I am.

Only sans the tiara. I hate those things.

25

It's been said that when you pray for something like, say, patience, God suddenly fills your life with opportunities to exercise patience. I have found this to be true in my own life. I've often joked that I'm not going to pray for patience, because then I'll no doubt get stuck for a month straight in the longest line at Fred's Market.

I haven't recently prayed for patience, but half an hour ago I prayed for help in the judgmental department. Already I am being tested.

If I say Fawn is underdressed for having come from church, it could be interpreted two ways. One, she has jeans on while every other woman is wearing a fancy dress. But our church is typically casual. Dresses, skirts, pants, jeans, shorts...you'll find it all.

No, in Fawn's case, there is a much more literal meaning in the term *underdressed.*

As she takes off her coat—a fake animal fur of some kind—I avert my eyes and say, "You might want to keep that on. The heat's been acting up, and it can get pretty chilly in here." I touch my nose, expecting it to grow an inch under my fingers.

"Does the way I dress make you uncomfortable, Madi?" Fawn rasps. I detect a hint of annoyance.

"Um, yes." *You asked.*

"If it makes you feel any better, I kept it on during the church service."

"That's a relief," I mumble. I imagine she was already getting plenty of looks with the coat on.

Fawn laughs and slips her arms back into the sleeves.

I am thinking, though, that maybe it would be better to take her coat and sneak it into the laundry room to douse it with Febreze. The thing could stand to be aired out and deodorized, as it retains the scent of smoke like I retain water once a month. The cigarette smoke mingles with her musky perfume and taunts my nostrils.

I do one of those "ah…ah….ah…" things like I'm going to sneeze. But—psyche!—I stop just short.

I sniff and turn my attention to Lexi, who stands next to me, chocolate Frosty in hand. I see Fawn's dressing "down" is transferring to her daughter. Lexi wears skinny jeans and a too-tight top that reads, *What are you lookin' at?*

See, this is where the real judgmental thing rears its ugly head. It's bad enough that Fawn chooses to dress like a…like that. But her nine-year-old? That's plain wrong.

So here's the question. Am I truly being judgmental or simply Christian-ly aware of her wrong choices? Would it be wrong to say something?

The Holy Spirit speaks to my heart. *With love. Always say it with love.*

I open my mouth. The doorbell rings.

Maybe later.

"Excuse me a minute. It's probably the pizza. I hope you both are okay with ham and pepperoni."

Lexi wrinkles her nose. Great.

Fawn asks where the bathroom is and I direct her down the hall before answering the front door. My stomach rumbles at the thought of pizza. Too much coffee has left an icky feeling in the pit of my gut.

At least, I'm pretty sure it's the coffee.

But it's not Dan the Delivery Man. It's Zach and Sylvie.

Apparently, now that I know about their relationship, they have no qualms about displaying affection. Zach's arm snakes like a boa constrictor around Sylvie's shoulder and she leans against him, shivering. They both have goofy grins plastered on their faces, and I fight the urge to gag.

"Hey, Mads, can we come in?"

"Only if you stop smiling. You guys are creeping me out." I step aside, and they stomp onto the blue rug I set out by the front door.

Sylvie hops on one foot while removing her way-cute, tall, sheepskin, sand-colored Uggs. "We thought we'd stop by to talk about…things," she says between hops.

"I actually have company right now."

"Oh." Sylvie stops hopping and looks at me. She mouths, "Richard?"

I shake my head. "No. He still has the kids with him. His mother fell on some ice, and since there will likely be a snow day tomorrow, they may stay for another night."

"Poor Nancy. Is she okay?"

"I think so. I'm hoping the kids call with an update soon."

She tilts her head inquisitively, and at that moment, Fawn and Lexi appear.

Is that Liz Claiborne I smell? Fawn used my perfume. I wouldn't care, except the mixture of the sickeningly strong scent of musk, Liz, and stale smoke is bringing back my headache. My head begins to pound like I'm stuffed inside of Max's bass drum.

Sylvie's jaw drops an inch, shock taking its appropriate place on her face. Because Zach is a guy, he stares like a dork, warranting a sharp elbow jab from Sylvie.

"I'm Fawn." Even her arm looks seductive as she stretches it toward Zach, three silver bangle bracelets clinking. Zach shakes her hand and eyes me.

I am really thanking God right now that Fawn put her coat back on.

"This is my brother, Zach, and you met Sylvie last night. Zach, Sylvie, this is Fawn's daughter, Lexi."

Sylvie offers a weak smile.

"Cool boots," Lexi pipes up, mouth half-full of Frosty.

"Thanks."

The comfort level is dropping by the second. But, thankfully, it seems Sylvie has gotten over her initial astonishment and is moving into her normal calm-and-collected mode. She smiles again, this time more warmly. She looks at me. "We can talk another time, Madi. We'll let you get back to—whatever you were doing. We certainly don't want to intrude. Right, Zach?"

Zach shrugs.

Sylvie's lips say one thing, but her eyes practically beg me to invite her and Zach to stay. I know she is dying to find out why in the world Fawn Witchburn and her daughter are standing in my living room.

But I'm not going to do it. Sylvie's curiosity will have to wait. "I'll catch up with you later," I say.

Sylvie takes a second to glare at me before turning back to Fawn and Lexi. "So did you get some gas for your car?"

I should have known she wasn't planning to leave. I fight the urge to knock Sylvie to the floor and push her boots back onto her feet so I can shove her out the door. She is such a brat.

"Yeah. I feel rather stupid. That's never happened to me before."

"You've never felt stupid before?" Zach asks with raised eyebrows.

Wow. Zach's surfer-dude mentality is in full form today. It's times like

172

this when I'm embarrassed to say I have a brother.

"I think Fawn means she never ran out of gas before."

"Oh." Zach's face turns pink. He shifts his weight and sticks his hands in his pockets.

"Oh, believe me, my mom has never run out of gas before." Lexi starts snorting at her own joke and a glop of Frosty drops to the carpet.

"Lexi, look what you've done." Fawn's voice is harsh, but there is no reference to, or hint of embarrassment about, the reference to her gastrointestinal issues. Gotta admire that.

"It's okay. I'll get a rag." I take off for the kitchen just as the doorbell rings again. "Can someone grab the door? It's probably the pizza!" I call over my shoulder. My stomach rumbles again.

After rummaging around in the broom closet for a rag, I take a quick detour to the bathroom. Not so much because the mention of gas reminded me I have to go, but because I want to take a moment to catch my breath and say an extra prayer before the day really gets interesting. Because it will; I'm sure of it. When I finally push Sylvie and Zach out the door, that is.

Voices are coming from the living room and as I walk toward them, I wait for the scent of hot pepperoni pizza to waft in and tickle my nasal passages. But all I smell is the lingering staleness of Fawn's jacket.

And now I see why. It wasn't the pizza boy at the door. It was my mother.

I have a feeling that *interesting* doesn't even begin to describe the way things are about to get.

♕

26

Having a family is like
having a bowling alley installed in your brain.
MARTIN MULL, COMEDIAN

"**M**om! Hi!" My voice comes out a little too chipper for my personality. But no one seems to notice, as they are all too busy concentrating on the scene my mother is making.

At the moment, she is struggling out of her bulky red parka with the fur-trimmed hood. Her purse is tangled around the sleeve, and she can't get her arm out. She looks like the Raggedy Ann doll I kept in the center of my canopy bed as a child. Arms flapping, coat sleeve whipping frantically, she tries to free it from the deadly grasp of her purse strap.

Zach takes a step forward to help, but Mom bites his head off. "I can do it!"

Amused, he wisely steps back.

"Geesh, Madison. You need to put salt on the walk. I about killed myself out there."

"Sorry, Mom, we're all out of salt. What are you doing out, anyway? Why didn't you call to say you were coming?"

As soon as the words are out of my mouth, I realize the absurdity of my question. Mom? Call first? As if.

"Edna was heading out to her son's house and she offered to drop me off on the way. *Her* son invited her to dinner." She narrows her brown eyes accusingly.

Before I can stop myself, I turn to Zach and grin sardonically. "Yeah, Zach. Some son you are. Invite Mom to dinner once in a while, would you?"

Hey, somebody's got to soften the mood around here.

He lightly punches me in the arm.

"Did you see what he did, Mom? He hit me." I rub my arm.

"You deserved it."

"But I'm a girl!" I whine.

"Hmmph."

Don't even want to ask what she means by that.

"Who's she?" Wow. It took Mom longer than I expected to notice the half-naked woman standing in my living room. Of course, being so occupied with herself and all...

I clear my throat. "Mom, this is Fawn and her daughter, Lexi." I purposely leave out her last name for obvious reasons.

"Fawn? Like the deer? What kind of name is that? Sounds like a stripper."

Leave it to Mom to talk PG-13 in front of a nine-year-old. Sylvie and I both glance at Lexi, who is presently on all fours, trying to coax Charlie out from behind the grandfather clock. She seems oblivious to the conversation going on ten feet away.

"So." Sylvie pipes up. "Why don't we all go into the family room and sit down by the fireplace? Brrr..." She shivers for effect. "Madi, I'll help you get some coffee going."

I glance at Fawn, who has puffed out her chest, planted her hands on her hips, and is giving Mom a "Who do you think you are?" glare, obviously still stuck on the stripper comment.

I think Mom has finally met her match.

Fawn puckers her brown-stained lips. As she starts to comment, Sylvie steps between them. Good old Sylvie. I would have probably let the scene play out and let the verbal chips fall where they may.

But here's the thing. Sylvie is exactly five-foot-three. As in tiny. Fawn, on the other hand, is probably five-foot-ten, give or take an inch. My mother is a couple of inches shorter than Fawn, which still puts her several inches above Sylvie. My best friend looks like a Chihuahua standing in the middle of two Irish Setters. No, wait. Make that a Pit Bull and a Rottweiler.

"Fawn, can I take your coat?" Sylvie stretches out her arm.

No! I inhale a pocket of air.

Fawn glances in my direction before declining. I exhale loudly.

Sylvie shrugs and turns to my mother.

"Your hair looks nice today, Mrs. Sanders." She smiles sweetly.

Huh?

I gape at Sylvie. If Mom entered a Bad Hair Day contest, she would take the prize, hands down. The left side of her dated and overgrown perm is flattened to her head and the right side looks like she just woke up from a restless six-hour nap.

Mom is now touching her hair, fluffing it out and away from her scalp, making it worse. This is because she's fluffing out the already fluffed side. All this does is make the bedraggled side of her hair stick straight out like porcupine quills. The other is still flatter than me at twelve.

But, lo and behold, the compliment seems to have worked. If I had known the key to Mom's heart was as simple as complimenting her hair, I would have tried it a long time ago. Of course, a beauty accolade coming from an expert like Sylvie Williams holds a little more weight. Even cranky-ol'-Mom can set aside her groundless dislike of Sylvie for a compliment. As phony as it is.

I see what Sylvie is doing, though. No matter how it's killing her to lavish on false flattery, especially in regards to appearance, Sylive's one smart Chihuahua. She and Zach have some news to spring on Mom. And it certainly can't hurt to start heaping on the praises.

"So what do you say? Why don't we all move to the family room where it's more comfortable?" Sylvie proposes for the second time.

Guess she and Zach aren't planning on leaving anytime soon.

Everyone troops through the kitchen to the family room. Well, I should say, Fawn *click clacks,* Sylvie bounces, Mom trudges, and Zach and Lexi stroll behind discussing the new Wendy's vanilla Frosty and how it compares to chocolate, which it doesn't.

"Mom, why don't you have a seat on the sofa?" I suggest once we reach the family room.

Mom's full of surprises today. She accepts my suggestion without a word. Maybe the compliment still has her speechless. If that's the case, I'd be willing to pay Sylvie to continue showering her with praises.

On second thought, I settle Mom into the overstuffed loveseat rather than the sofa. The loveseat is missing a spring and sinks a little farther down, making it more difficult to get out of. Mom makes me nervous when she has free reign of my home, so I'm not taking any chances. One time, I found her in my bedroom going through my jewelry armoire. She swore that when I left home, I swiped a pair of her gaudy, gold-plated, clip-on earrings and claims she was trying to get them back. Mind you, I had left home fifteen years earlier. Even if I was partial to gypsy-style costume jewelry, which I most certainly am not, those earrings would have been sold eons ago in one of the gazillion garage sales I've held. Plus, my ears have been pierced since I was thirteen. Clip-ons give me headaches.

The week after I caught Mom raking through my jewelry, it didn't surprise me—or bother me in the least—when I saw her wearing a gold necklace I had purchased for a costume party Rich and I attended years ago. I had dressed up as Sonny and Rich drag-queened as Cher. We ended up winning first prize for that one. And, I have to say, Rich made a much more attractive woman than I made a man. The three-inch thick mustache and sideburns took away any pretty I had left.

I smile at the memory.

"Where's that goofy grin coming from?" Sylvie asks, wrapping an arm around my shoulder. She feigns shock. "Gasp—you actually look happy. Which is really something, considering your home has been invaded by a bunch of uninvited dysfunctionals."

A comment could be inserted here about how she and Zach could definitely be included in that bunch. Even if they don't classify as dysfunctional in the same way that Mom and Fawn do, my best friend and my little brother were definitely uninvited. But as annoyed as I was that Sylvie wouldn't leave even when I tried to boot her out the door, now I'm glad she's here. I could use the moral support.

Back to Sylvie's question.

"Just thinking." I don't elaborate, which makes Sylvie even more curious.

"About…"

I say nothing, which I know makes her crazy.

I ask Zach to start a fire in the fireplace and he quickly complies, enlisting Lexi's help. It seems a new friendship has been formed today. An unlikely one, but I find my heart expand for my little brother. He'll make a good dad someday.

Wow. What do you know? A touch from the Holy Spirit has turned me into a sentimental sap. And it's not so bad.

Fawn has taken a seat in the black leather La-Z-Boy next to the fireplace. She reaches into her black purse-slash-tote bag, pulls out her cell phone, and busies herself with checking her voice mail.

Sylvie shadows me into the kitchen to put the coffee on.

"So spill it. What is Fawn Witchburn doing in your house?" she whispers as soon as we're out of sight.

"Long story." I pull a coffee filter from the cupboard and pour a quarter cup of hazelnut beans in the grinder.

"Come on. Give me the condensed version."

I ignore her and pour the water in the reservoir and watch the level rise in the see-through window.

Sylvie presses. "You're not going to tell me? I can't believe—"

I press the grind button and the sudden grating noise makes Sylvie jump. I point to the coffee maker, cup my ear, and crinkle up my nose. "What? I can't hear you!" I mouth.

Sylvie throws up her hands.

The grinder halts and the doorbell rings.

"It's about time. Would you mind getting that? It has to be the pizza. I'm starving." I smile sweetly.

Sylvie pulls the tie to her brown cardigan tighter around her waist, tosses me a sour look, and heads to the living room.

I lean against the counter and breathe in the strong hazelnut aroma as the coffee starts to brew.

A man's voice carries over from the living room. Must be Dan the Delivery Man. Once again my stomach growls in anticipation. I remove the plates from the cupboard and start preparing the salad. Now where did I put my big wooden salad bowl?

"Hey, sweetheart."

I pause, head still hidden behind the cupboard door. Okay. That's not Dan, unless he has morphed into an impersonator who has Candice's voice down to a T.

Poking my head around the cupboard, I smile. "Candice! What are you doing here?"

The question of the day.

Whoa—that dress is even brighter in person. Sunglasses-bright. I'll be seeing yellow spots for days.

Sylvie and Dad appear behind Candice. Dad is holding a bucket of chicken, which he sets on the kitchen table. Sylvie is making wide eyes at me. She knows my mother is in the next room and hurries off to either prepare Mom or distract her until I can get rid of my dad and Candice—I'm not sure which.

"We were worried about you, honey. We picked up some chicken for lunch. I hope you don't mind that we stopped over." Candice's voice is soothing. Her face is an artist's canvas of concern, blue eyes saturated with sympathy, mouth set in a slight frown.

"Of course not." Mom, however, may have a little problem with it. But I don't mention that.

Candice rushes over and pulls me into a hug. Her cheap, floral perfume invades my nostrils and sends me into a sneezing spree. I pull away but not before spraying phlegm all over her lemony shoulder.

"I'm so—s—s—sor—A-CHOO!" More flying particles.

A tissue appears out of nowhere, and I honk into it gratefully.

"It's okay, honey." Candice is squinting peripherally at her shoulder. She doesn't want to act disgusted, but she can't help it. Not that I blame her. Hello—it's gross. Candice's upturned nose crinkles and she glances back at my father who, typical Dad-style, is grinning ear to ear.

"Oh, Candice, honey. You probably want to change out of that dress," he says, then shifts his gaze at me, eyes twinkling. "Madi, maybe you have something Candice can change into?"

"Uh, sure." Like a runner off the starting block, I sprint toward my room and consciously avoid looking at Dad. All it would take is one second of eye-contact and I'd be on the floor, holding my sides.

"That's not necessary," Candice is protesting behind me, but I ignore her. That dreadful dress has got to go. At least then I'll be able to gaze at her without fear of going blind.

Two minutes later, I hold out a pair of black running pants and a Detroit Red Wings sweatshirt.

"You really didn't have to do this. If you have a wet rag, I can just—"

"Candice. Quit being so nice. It's the least I can do after giving you a phlegm shower."

Dad laughs. "She's right, honey. Do you really want to walk around with dried-up snot on your shoulder? I don't think so."

She half-smiles, offers her thanks, and takes the change of clothing. As she exits the kitchen, it's like seeing the sun itself disappear.

Dad is at my side and he nudges me with his elbow. "Thanks for sneezing on her. I was trying to think of a way to get her out of that dress."

I raise my eyebrows. "I bet you were."

He chuckles. "Now get your mind out of the gutter, missy. That's not what I meant."

"It's not like I sneezed all over her on purpose," I insist.

"Whatever you say. I could see you squinting as soon as we rounded the corner."

Sylvie reappears from the family room. "Your mother wants to know when we're eating."

"Maxine is here?" The twinkle in his eye disappears.

"Wow. She wasn't even invited for dinner, and she's asking when we're eating?" I turn to my dad. "I was just going to tell you..."

"We should go."

I almost agree. Almost. But then I think, *Wait a minute.* It's been twenty-eight years, three months, and however many days. It's time to end the bitterness. It's time to end the tiptoeing around Mom due to the driftwood-sized chip she has on her shoulder. And since she has never once shown an ounce of desire to try and forgive my father for what he did to her and move on, I guess I'll take matters into my own hands.

So at the risk of my mother disowning me or being the brunt of her wrath for the rest of her life, which really wouldn't be much different than now, I demand—not suggest, but demand—that Dad and Candice stay.

Dad appears unsure and studies my face as if to see if I'm really his daughter. Because the daughter he knows would not only agree that he should leave but would be shoving him out the door by now.

"I mean it, Dad. Stay. Mom will have to get over it."

Candice comes back, yellow dress draped over her arm. See how the first thing I notice is that dress? She looks much more comfortable in my sweats and sweatshirt, which hang on her tiny frame. Okay, I'm thinking about the fact that those are the sweats I jammed into my bottom dresser drawer the other day after trying them on—only to find them too snug for my big bottom. Candice is sixty-four years old, but if you looked at her from the neck down, she could pass as one of Christina's classmates. So not fair.

"Did I hear you say something about your mother?" Her face takes on the same expression Max had the other day when I mentioned inviting Sam over for mostaccioli.

Pure, unadulterated dread.

"It's okay, Candice. You guys have as much right to be here as she does. More, actually, because we sort of had dinner plans to begin with. Besides, this is my home, and I'm inviting you to stay."

"Do you want us to sit in the front living room until she leaves?" She transfers her dress to the other arm, careful to avoid the right shoulder area.

"Of course not. Come on. We are all civilized adults."

This warrants a blank look from Dad, Candice, and Sylvie.

"Okay, most of us are civilized, anyway. But still, why are we letting my mother control our lives? It's ridiculous." I shake my head. "If she doesn't like it, she can leave."

"Well, I don't want to be the cause of any drama." Candice eyes my dad.

I offer an eye-roll that would make Christina proud. "My mother is the star of her own dramatic production. It's called *Misery Loves Company*. Unfortunately, whenever she's performing—which is every minute of every day—all of those within twenty feet of her are thrown into the cast of characters. The thing is, her drama never has a happy ending. There is no applause, only tears. And anger. And hurt feelings." I throw up my hands. "It's so sickening. Isn't it about time we practiced some tough love? Or maybe we should organize an intervention like they do for people who are on drugs or have some other type of destructive behavior."

Sylvie steps over and puts an arm around me. "Now that's what I'm talking about. I see you've found your backbone."

"I guess I'm at the end of my rope. I've had it up to here." My face is a little warmer than usual. I pat my cheeks. "Is it hot in here?"

"It sure is." Zach appears from the family room. He's looking at Sylvie as he says it. She smiles and bats her eyes.

Talk about sickening.

Sylvie moves next to Zach. He's two heads taller, and she cranks her neck toward the ceiling as he gazes down with a big goofy grin. I hope they both have chiropractic insurance.

Against my will, I acknowledge that they make a cute couple. Wash my mind out with soap.

Dad, a question in his quirked brow, catches my eye. I point to the happy—or should I say sappy—couple and trace an invisible heart in the air with my fingers. He smiles and nods approvingly, while Candice just stares with a curious-yet-knowing expression.

"So!" I snap everyone back to attention. "What's going on in there? Is anyone bleeding yet?"

Zach clearly struggles to break his gaze from Sylvie's face. "Oh. I think Fawn is getting ready to leave. Much to Mom's delight. Mom's been giving her the evil eye for the last ten minutes. Surprisingly, though, she's kept her mouth shut. First time for everything."

I sigh. "You guys, not to be rude, but none of you were invited. I asked Fawn over because we have a couple things to talk about."

Eyebrows shoot up all over the room.

"Things that don't concern you. Look, I'm not kicking you out, okay? But can you all please go sit in the family room and amuse yourselves while I invite Fawn into the living room so we can chat privately? Handle Mom however you want." I pick up the bucket of chicken from the table. "Feed her. That will keep her quiet for a minute."

"Yeah, until she sees that we're here." Dad says. "She'll be like a bull let out of the pen."

"Well," I say, "at least all of my good china is put away."

♛

27

If you judge people,
you have no time to love them.
MOTHER THERESA

"So is your mother always this charming?"

Fawn is sitting in the burgundy armchair next to the grandfather clock. Her twig-thin legs are crossed, and I take a moment to regard her French pedicure. Sylvie doesn't like to do French pedicures. She says the stark white tips draw attention to the length and make it seem like your toenails could be used as orange peelers. So gross. But I have to agree. Who wants to think of food when looking at feet? All one color is a much better choice.

"Aren't your feet cold? I have a pair of socks you can borrow."

Fawn shakes her head. "I prefer bare feet. I only own maybe two pair of socks."

"Suit yourself." I shrug. "To answer your question, yes. Mother is always this charming."

"What about your house? Is it always this...busy? I was under the impression it would be just the three of us for lunch. Not that I care—it's your house, after all. You can invite anyone you'd like."

I pick a piece of lint off my jeans. "For the record, I didn't invite them. My family pops in whenever they feel like it. Whether I want them to or not. And it seems they have a knack for the 'not.'"

Fawn peers out the window. "I've never had that." It's a simple statement, said more to herself than to me.

"So what are you planning to do about Ray?"

This gets her attention. She switches legs so her left dangles over her right. Her foot swings three times, as if she's annoyed, and stops. "Before we get into that, I'd like to lay everything on the table and say that I'm deeply offended at the way you treated me the other night."

My heart picks up speed. I wasn't expecting a personal confrontation. This was supposed to be about Ray being Lexi's dad. But Fawn doesn't avoid confrontation like I do, so I should have prepared myself.

"I thought we talked about this at Reggie's."

She frowns. "*You* talked about it. You talked about how my reputation would suggest I had an affair with your husband. About how I dress. About how I am only after Ray's money. About how I demolish families."

Fawn stares at me, her brown eyes hard and piercing. I look away because, like I said, I hate confrontation. And because I know she's right.

My conversation with God from this morning replays in my mind. As difficult as this is, God is doing exactly what I asked Him to: giving me an opportunity to apologize to Fawn.

Fawn exhales. "Look. I'm used to it—the stares, the comments, the judgments. I've tried to let them slide off my back, but the more I thought about the other night, the madder I got. I'm tired of it all."

I open my mouth to respond, but she points her finger at me, then at herself.

"Me and you...we come from two totally different worlds." She tilts her head to one side, as if sizing me up. "Here's you: perfect, tidy world, great family, nice home. Always had everything you needed. The closest you've ever come to poor is when you realized you only had enough cash in your wallet for a Grande and not a Verdi Starbucks Frappaccino on your way home from the mall. You've been sheltered. Probably have never lived outside of this small, God-forsaken town. Probably haven't even been out of South Haven for more than a week at a time."

"That's not true. I went on a two-week-long mission trip to Mexico twelve years ago."

Fawn holds up her hands. "Oooh, well then, give the woman a Worldly Award." She rolls her eyes. "Be real. Have you ever struggled? At all? Have you ever wondered how you would pay next month's rent? Or if you'd be able to buy your kid a Christmas present? Have you ever had to swallow your pride and accept help from the food pantry at church? Do you realize how humiliating that is?"

"Look, Fawn, I'm—"

"You have no right to judge me. You don't know what my life's been like. I haven't had an easy go of it. But I've tried to do the best I can for Lexi. I love that girl, and I want to give her a good life. A life that doesn't include people looking down their nose-jobs on her because of what she wears or the fact that she doesn't have a dad."

"Fawn, really—"

"Excuse me." She stands to her feet, crosses the room, slips into her stilettos, and struts out the front door.

All righty, then. Not apologizing was not my fault. She didn't even give me the chance.

I watch through the window as she stands on the front porch and lights a cigarette. She takes a long, puckery drag. Even from here, I can see the dark brown lip marks she leaves on the butt. She hugs herself, shivering. I'll never understand an addiction that not only probably costs more per month than her rent, but is worth risking frostbite by standing outside in sub-freezing temperatures to feed it. At least she's still wearing her coat.

"Where's your cat?"

I turn to Lexi, who is standing in the entranceway.

"Um, I haven't seen him. He can be pretty shy. You might want to check behind the clock."

Lexi moves past me and gets on her hands and knees in search of Charlie. I'm not too optimistic that the cat will show himself. He typically keeps out of sight until he feels really safe. And with these people around, that means he'll probably hide indefinitely. I must confess I wish Charlie and I could trade places right now. I'd love nothing more than to go into hiding—for several days. Even a few hours.

Oh, why couldn't I have decided to face my issues tomorrow instead of today?

"So, Lexi, do you have any pets?"

"Yeah, right." She gives up looking for Charlie and plops down on the chair, hard. "I want a dog so bad, but Mom won't let me. She says I don't even pick up my room, so there's no way I'll clean up dog poop." She pauses to roll her eyes, then gives me a sincere look. "But I totally would. I would pick up the poop every day. I'd take it for walks and play with it and—"

"Stop already." Fawn steps inside, bringing a burst of cold air with her. The temptation to plug my nose is right there. Instead, to make it less obvious that I am totally grossed out and trying not to gag, I cough and cover both my mouth and nose with my hands, taking in a couple of deep breaths. My own breath may not be the most heavenly scent, but it sure beats the alternative.

Fawn snorts. "She believes she'll suddenly become responsible if we get a pet."

Lexi pouts.

Such a familiar sight.

I can't help wondering what my kids are doing right now.

184

"Lex, go in the other room. Mrs. McCall and I have to finish talking. As soon as we're done, we can leave."

"But we didn't eat lunch yet."

"Didn't you have some of the chicken my dad brought?"

"It's original. I like extra crispy. The original is soggy and makes me want to throw up."

Why doesn't she just tell it like it is?

Where is the pizza anyway? I'm getting annoyed. It is now after twelve, and my stomach is screaming for fuel. Maybe that would give me the energy I need to finish this conversation. At that thought, I glance out the window in the hope I'll see Dan the Pizza Man's clunky Volkswagen Beetle with the Vino's Pizza sign atop the roof sitting in our driveway.

But all I see is a snowy driveway.

No, wait. I take that back. Here comes a car. My belly rumbles in anticipation.

Car recognition slowly ignites in my brain. There is no Vino's Pizza sign. It is not a Volkswagen Beetle. It's a red Mustang convertible.

Ray.

♛

Part of me wants to not only groan at the sight of yet another uninvited guest, but also scream at the fact that it is Raymond. Talk about timing!

Then again, talk about timing. The groaning and screaming part of me is being shoved aside for the other part that wants to dig out my old Kool & the Gang album and "Celebrate" by doing a happy dance across the living room carpet. This is the perfect distraction. God provided a way out!

Okay, that concept is a little delusional. God is all about facing our circumstances, not running from them. And He most certainly would not present a way for me to escape saying I'm sorry to Fawn. He is the one who spoke to my heart in the first place and told me to humble myself and apologize. Reconciliation, building a bridge, admitting when we're wrong, asking forgiveness—the Bible speaks clearly and firmly about all of that. God is certainly not wishy-washy, an avoider of conflict, or one to run away.

A throaty half moan, half gasp elicits my attention. I glance at Fawn.

She has followed my gaze and is watching Raymond climb out of his car. She turns toward Lexi, whose eyes are scanning the room, probably searching for Charlie again.

Uncertainty flickers in Fawn's eyes. This is the most unsure I've ever seen her. One minute ago, Confidence could have been Fawn's middle name. But now, her eyes dart back and forth between Raymond and Lexi. Whatever she chooses to do, it'd better be quick. Ray is almost to the door.

"Lex, why don't you go in the other room? The pizza should be here any minute and—"

The doorbell rings.

Lexi brightens. "Ooh. That's probably the pizza. Can I get it?" she asks, already in route.

Fawn and I exchange looks and then Fawn springs into action, truly reminding me of a deer, only wilder. Her panic antenna is clearly extended.

In a single bound, Fawn leaps in front of her daughter and flattens her back to the door, spreading her arms across the length of it. Now even Lexi thinks her mother is a madwoman, as evidenced by her bewildered face.

"What are you doing, Mom?" She turns her wide eyes toward me.

I shrug.

"Lexi, go to the kitchen. Now," Fawn commands.

The doorbell rings again.

"But I'm starving."

"Come on, Lex. Let's go see if we can find you something to eat. Do you like pizza rolls? I'm pretty sure I have some pizza rolls in the freezer."

I say a prayer that they're not covered in frost or have freezer burn.

Fawn's face still reflects panic. I give her my best sympathetic look as I usher Lexi out of the front living room and into the kitchen. Fawn stares back at me, unmoving. I can't determine what she's going to do. At this point, I wouldn't be surprised if she crawls behind the clock and curls up next to Charlie.

Dad and Candice are in the kitchen. The newspaper is spread out on the counter and they are reading the Sunday comics. Dad stands behind Candice with his arms snaked around her waist, peering over her shoulder. They're giggling over one of the comic strips.

"What are you guys doing in here? Don't tell me you haven't even gone into the family room yet."

They glance up and say nothing.

I shake my head. "What a couple of chickens."

The pizza rolls are shoved in the back of the freezer, and I brush off a couple of ice chunks as I pull them out. Lexi is ecstatic. She says pizza rolls are her very favorite thing to eat in the whole world. Well, besides Frostys. Finally…score one for me!

Zach's head appears around the corner. "Hey, Mads, Mom spilled chicken grease down the front of her. We need a rag or something."

I sigh. "I'll be right there. Candice, will you guys keep an eye on the pizza rolls?"

"Sure, honey," she says, although I doubt she even heard me. She's now busy tickling my father. Which would be cute if it weren't so…gaggy.

When I get to the family room with a wet rag, Sylvie is helping Mom out of the loveseat.

"I'm sorry, Mom. We forgot your bib, didn't we?" It's meant as a joke but, of course, Mom scowls.

"Did you know that your brother and Sylvie are…dating?" She practically chokes on the word.

"As a matter of fact, I do know. I think it's great." *Great* may be too strong a word, and Sylvie's and Zach's surprised faces confirm it.

That Mom doesn't use Zach's name is not lost on me. She uses my middle name whenever she's annoyed with me, and when she's upset with Zach— which isn't often, I might add—she doesn't use his name at all. It's what's-his-name, your brother, that kid—anything but Zach.

"Just think. You'll get all kinds of great beauty products for Christmas," I joke.

Mom's eyes narrow, as if she's mulling this over. Lord knows, some extra beauty products wouldn't hurt her. Maybe a little spa treatment is exactly what Mom needs. Wouldn't it be nice if she could soak and pamper away all that bitterness and anger for good?

"We surprised her so much with our news that she missed her mouth and the chicken ended up down the front of her shirt," Zach says with a grin.

Sylvie puts a hand up and suppresses a giggle.

I hold the rag out to my mother, who shoves it aside. "I'll go wash up in the bathroom." With that, she takes off toward the kitchen, through which she has to pass to get to the bathroom. Which means she'll run smack dab into Dad and Candice.

Sylvie, Zach and I look at each other.

"Wanna follow her, or shall we just eavesdrop from here?" Zach asks.

I smile. "You guys can eavesdrop, but I need to go check on the pizza rolls I put in the oven for Lexi."

"I thought you ordered pizza," Sylvie says.

"Yeah, well—"

The doorbell chimes again.

If that's not the pizza, I'm calling Vino's right now and telling them I'm switching to Marco's.

28

Nobody can go back and start a new beginning,
but anyone can start today and make a new ending.
MARIA ROBINSON

Change is good—so some have said. Personally, I hate it. Especially when it involves giving up something I love. Like Dibs, for instance.

Or pizza. I do not want to switch pizza places, but it looks like Marco's it will be from now on. Because it is not Dan the Pizza Man at the door. (Where in the world is that guy?)

Instead, it is my worst nightmare. Well, maybe not my worst. The worst real nightmare I've ever had included Caroline Summerall and Claudia Boeve. Claudia was admonishing me for eating twelve cartons of Dibs. For every one I ate—and at twelve cartons, that's hundreds of the little suckers—she punished me by smacking me in the gut with a Yoga Booty-Ballet video. Then Caroline Summerall got wind of it and stood up in front of church and implored the congregation to pray for me. She told them that not only had I been belly-whacked thousands of times by Claudia Boeve, but that I'd gained a hundred pounds from those Dibs. The loud gasps from all over the sanctuary woke me in a cold sweat.

I gave up Dibs for four entire days after that nightmare. But then I started PMS-ing.

I'm so weak.

Today, my worst imagined nightmare would be my husband and Fawn Witchburn telling me they were running off together to France so they could start their own chocolate lipstick factory. And that my mother moved in to "help" me cope.

A terrifying thought, I know.

Almost as terrifying is the woman standing right inside my front door.

Celeste Hardaway appears to have stepped out of a limo and onto the red carpet. She wears a tea-length midnight blue dress with a sequined bodice and low-heeled matching pumps with sequin trim. Her white faux-fur wrap looks like it should have a polar bear head and be on the floor in front of my fireplace. Celeste has enough bling on her wrists, fingers, and around her neck to fill an entire jewelry store window display. I gawk at them, trying to decide if they are real diamonds or cubic zirconias. I don't even know where to start to tell the difference, so I give up and concentrate on her face.

She could be Joan Rivers' twin. Minus the smile. Celeste's mouth slopes southward, as do her eyes, as she peers down her nose at me.

With her hair swept to one side, her long face, and those heavily made-up, deep-set brown eyes, you could put a pair of sunglasses on her and she'd pass for Joan in any impersonator comedy club. But the comedy part might be a problem. I wonder if the woman has ever cracked a smile. I study her milky-white skin. Not many laugh lines around the eyes. I conclude she either never smiles or gets regular Botox injections.

"Hello, Celeste." I offer a tight smile and extend my hand. She ignores it and I pull it back, wiping my palm on my jeans.

Fawn and Raymond have moved off to the side. Ray's arms are shoved in his pockets and Fawn's are folded across her chest. They stand a couple feet apart and everything about their body language screams "tension!" They've barely had a chance to get reacquainted before yet another uninvited guest arrived to crash the party.

Celeste glances at the two of them and lifts her head higher. "It looks like you're having a wild party."

"Not exactly. But you look like you're dressed for a party." I attempt a smile.

She hmmphs. "My husband and I are on our way home from church."

I clear my throat. "Celeste, I don't know why you stopped over when we have an appointment tomorrow at four. But I—"

"You never returned my call," she interrupts.

"I didn't, did I? Sorry about that. Things got a little…chaotic," I say, for lack of a better word. "But I'm glad you're here."

Skepticism is written all over her prunish face.

Raymond says something to Fawn. I didn't catch it, but they both move past us to the front door. Ray stares me down as he passes. Not sure how to read that. He nods to Celeste and she awkwardly shuffles backwards, probably afraid some cooties will jump from his leather bomber jacket to her polar bear fur.

Stale cigarette smoke hangs in Fawn's aftermath. She glances over her shoulder before following Ray out the door. "Tell Lexi I won't be long."

Sure, I'd be happy to babysit.

Celeste is wrinkling her nose. "Oh, that woman reeks! Doesn't she know how utterly despicable it is to smoke? Now I'm going to smell like I've been in a bar all morning. What will my guests think? I can't have the twelve church members I've invited over for a luncheon thinking I've taken up smoking, for heaven's sake. Not to mention she has now exposed me to secondhand smoke. I could die of lung cancer."

Oh, puh-lease. The eye roll is right there, but I resist.

Celeste continues, "I can't imagine allowing a woman like that into my home."

I narrow my eyes. I want to lay into her, but something—or more likely, Someone—holds me back. I take a deep breath. "Look, Celeste. I want to apologize."

"And well you should. Your daughter's actions were clearly—"

"Celeste, please." My voice is loud and sharp which, from the surprise on Celeste's face, is not something she's used to. But she clamps her mouth together, and her lips merge together into one thin line.

"Don't get me wrong. I am not apologizing for my daughter. Rest assured, she will be making her own apology. Christina made a poor choice and has to face the consequences. But I can't help but feel this is partly my fault. My husband and I have been experiencing some...problems...and I haven't exactly been there for Christina. Maybe if I had been more attentive, she would have come to me and wouldn't have taken out her frustrations on Paige."

Then again, maybe not. A teenage girl's irrational behavior is like a pimple—you never know where it will pop up or how bad it will be.

"Mrs. Hardaway, I'm sorry about this whole situation. No matter what might have happened between Paige and Christina, your daughter did not deserve to be punched in the nose. I truly hope that Paige is okay and that you and your daughter can find it in your hearts to forgive and move on. Is there anything we can do to make this up to you?"

For once, Celeste Hardaway seems to be at a loss for words. I suspect when she arrived, she expected a fight. Now that she's not getting one—quite the opposite—maybe she doesn't know what to do.

"Well, I...you are aware we are within our rights to sue."

"I know that. And I'm begging you to reconsider. The truth is a lawsuit would be a huge blow to us. Is there any other way? Maybe Christina can do some work for you. Clean your house, shovel the driveway..."

I realize my suggestions are ludicrous. I'm sure the woman has a team of maids and a regular snowplow service.

Celeste's eyes shift, and she peers over her shoulder and out the window. Her Lincoln MKX still idles, exhaust pouring from the back. I see Mr. Hardaway sitting behind the wheel, a newspaper concealing his face.

My attention transfers to Ray's Mustang, parked on the street in front of the house. Fawn sits in the passenger's seat and I can see her hands flailing around. Must be some heavy-duty discussion going on in that car. I'm glad they took it outside.

"I will discuss this with Walter, and with our attorney, Mr. Pontstein of Pontstein and Cowell. I suppose it might be in our best interests to handle this outside of a courtroom." Celeste pulls a business card out of thin air and holds it out. Her hand trembles slightly, which surprises me a bit. Maybe she isn't as fearless and ruthless as I thought.

"We'll be in touch." She pulls her polar bear tighter around her shoulders and turns sharply. As she does, her heel catches in the rug. As if in slow motion, her arms fly upward, Polar Bear drops to the floor, and Celeste lands with a thud—dress tangled around her upper thighs, jewelry clanking noisily on the hardwood entryway, and Joan Rivers' hair barely missing the wall.

Not sure whose shriek is louder—hers or mine.

What I *am* sure of is that any chance of Celeste Hardaway reconsidering a lawsuit has just been reduced to zero.

Celeste Hardaway is gone. Not *gone* gone, although that sure would make things easier for me.

But now my front living room is filled with my remaining guests—if I can call them guests, uninvited as they were. Upon hearing the yelps, everyone came running. And Celeste, embarrassed enough, made a hasty exit. But not before I saw the fire shooting from her eyes. I wouldn't be surprised to hear from her lawyer within the hour.

The only one not present is my mother, who has yet to emerge from the bathroom, where I am told she is still trying to remove the chicken grease from her blouse. If I listen closely, I can hear the water from the sink running full blast. I wonder if she's planning on paying our water bill next month.

According to my dad, Mother isn't yet aware that he and Candice are here. Apparently, they ducked into the broom closet when they heard her coming.

So that explains their flushed faces. And...oh, wow. So wasn't expecting to see this, but...

"Dad, XYZPDQ."

"Huh?" Dad gives me a blank look.

I glance down—quickly—to his pants, motioning with my eyes. His zipper is halfway down, white-and-green-striped boxers exposed for all to see. So inappropriate. Embarrassing. *Disgusting.* I mean, I realize they're married and everything, but still…this one registers a fifteen on the Disgust-o-meter.

Dad follows my gaze. He laughs. The man is incapable of feeling embarrassment.

I sort of envy that.

"Oops" is all he says, but his eyes slide to Candice, who doesn't share Dad's non-embarrassment ability. Her cheeks color the same shade as the Red Wings sweatshirt she is wearing.

My Red Wings sweatshirt.

Ew. Won't be wearing that for a while.

"Where's my mom?" Lexi pipes up. She holds her plate of pizza rolls that, thankfully, someone took out of the oven before they burned. She picks one up and pops it in her mouth.

"Oh…she, uh, had to step out for a couple minutes. She won't be long," I assure her with a smile.

"Is she with that guy?" she asks around a mouthful of pizza roll.

"What guy?" I ask innocently.

"The guy who drove up in that cool red car. The one she didn't want me to see."

You know, kids are largely underestimated. We think we can pull one over on them, but they catch everything. Of course, throwing yourself in front of a doorway isn't exactly subtle, but still…kids are much smarter than we give them credit for.

Sylvie is at the window, cupping her face and peering out.

"Can you be any more obvious, Sylv?"

"Is that Ray?" she asks, her breath fogging up the glass.

"Yep." I feel the need to explain to Lexi. "Ray is my brother-in-law. Mr. McCall's brother."

"Oh." She pops another pizza roll in her mouth and heads back to the kitchen.

That's another thing about kids. They lose interest quickly. Which is not good when you're lecturing them on important topics or trying to get them to do their chores, but in this case, I welcome the short attention span.

"So what is Ray doing here?" Sylvie asks, planting her tiny hands on her tiny hips.

Now that I think about it, I'm not sure why Ray showed up. I certainly didn't invite him over. And judging from her earlier reaction, it's obvious that Fawn wasn't expecting him.

"Good question," I mumble.

"Madi Lee!" my mother's voice rings out from the bathroom.

Worried glances are exchanged all over the room.

"Geesh, you guys," I say. "Relax. What's the worst that can happen? She'll rant and rave and then leave. Big deal. She's done that a thousand times."

"But she can't leave," Zach reminds me. "She doesn't have a car."

I put a hand to my chin. "True." I smile. "Then I guess she'll have to stay and hear what I have to say."

More worried glances.

I move toward the bathroom. I pass Lexi, who has planted herself on a barstool at the kitchen counter, thumbing through one of Christina's *Teen* magazines.

Five minutes later, after helping Mom scrub the last of the stain out of her blouse with Dial soap and evaporating the wet spot with the hair dryer, we exit the bathroom. I stop Mom in the kitchen.

"Mom, just so you know, Dad and Candice—"

Sylvie flies around the corner of the kitchen. "Ray and Fawn are now on the porch. They're talking, but it looks like they're getting ready to come back inside."

Lexi glances up from her magazine. "It's about time. Maybe now we can finally go home."

What? Hanging around with a bunch of wacky adults isn't fun?

I hold up a finger. "Be there in a sec."

Sylvie flashes yet another worried look and disappears back into the living room.

"What about your father and his bimbo?" Mom asks.

Turning to face her, I grasp her hands. She tries pulling her hands away and I grip them as tightly as I can. Still, she wrestles out of my grasp. Definitely need to get that gym membership. Mom's seventy years old, for Pete's sake, but the woman is stronger than Arnold Schwarzenegger in his prime.

"Mom," I say firmly, "don't freak out, but Dad and Candice are here. In the living room."

She stares at me and doesn't say a word. I prepared myself for an outburst, but the silence takes me by surprise.

"Mom? Did you hear me?"

"I heard you." Something flashes in her eyes. Anger? Sadness? Fear? Hurt? Doggedly, she turns and marches toward the living room.

Now it's my turn to be nervous.

I follow Mom into the room and it's like I'm an Israelite witnessing the parting of the Red Sea. Sylvie and Zach move to one side, my dad and Candice to the other.

My mother doesn't even glance in Dad's direction. She tells Zach, "Take me home." It's not a request, it's a demand. And Zach, probably fearing for his life or at least trying to maintain his spot as Mom's favorite, heads to the closet to retrieve her coat.

"Wait a minute." It comes out louder than I intended. Everyone twists in my direction. "I have something to say."

Other than Mom, who is purposely avoiding my gaze, all eyes are on me.

"Mom." I take a stride closer and she shuffles away a step. I soften my voice. "Please, Mom, listen to me for a moment."

And then it happens. No, not the angry outburst we've all been anticipating. Not the dramatic scene we've witnessed a million times. Not the sarcastic comment we've all braced ourselves for. Not any of those things.

I'm talking about the lip quiver.

At first, it's barely noticeable. But then it starts trembling so badly she bites her bottom lip and it starts to bleed. Then her chin gets moving. It's going up and down at the speed of light and if it doesn't stop, I fear the top half of her face will shoot off like a rocket.

Suddenly it hits me. Mom is human. Behind all that anger and bitterness and downright crankiness is a frail and fragile woman who's been burned. Not once, not twice, but a gazillion times over the course of her life. The crotchety old lady I see before me actually has feelings. All these years, she's been covering up her hurts and insecurities with coldness and resentment.

Okay, so maybe I've known that all along but didn't want to see it. Maybe it was easier for me to be annoyed with my mom for how she treats me than to take a deeper look into what makes her that way.

Possibly for the first time in my life, my heart swells for my mother. I've seen her cry, but not like this. Right now she is more vulnerable than I've ever seen her.

I close the gap between us and wrap my arms around her and squeeze. She resists at first but then collapses into my arms. We stand for several moments as Mom's body catches up with her chin and starts wracking, violently. I close my eyes and simply hold her as she weeps. My own sobs blend in with hers.

When her cries are finally reduced to sniffling, I release her. Charlie rubs up against our legs. I look around to find that, except for my speechless cat, we are alone.

Twenty minutes later, I'm waving good-bye to Dad and Candice. Zach and Sylvie offered to take Mom home and, despite my invitation to stay awhile, she said she wanted to get home. I can't say I blame her, as it's been a bit of an overwhelming day. She did promise to call so we could do lunch next week.

Imagine that. A nice weekday lunch with Mom. Although, I suppose I should hold off on calling it nice until after it's over.

Ray and Fawn eventually made their way back into the house to retrieve Lexi. Unfortunately, they left their smoky scent to linger in the front entryway.

Boy, I wish I could have bottled up the look on Ray's face when he and Fawn stood there, waiting for their daughter to put on her coat and boots. It was priceless. Shock was definitely the emotion of the moment. But so was—dare I say—giddiness? The downright tender way he gazed Lexi made me wonder if there really was hope for Raymond.

But then, two seconds later, he made a derogatory comment toward Candice, blowing that theory to smithereens.

I'm praying for Raymond and Fawn to find the right words to break the news to Lexi. And I'm praying really hard that Lexi will take it well. That God will use this situation to draw all three of them closer to Him.

So now I'm waving good-bye to Dad and Candice. Candice promised to return my jogging clothes as soon as possible. I told her not to worry about it. *Please* don't worry about it! It's not like I have plans to take up jogging. And of course, there's that closet incident.

So not letting my mind go there.

As Dad's car takes off down the road, Dan the Pizza Man turns into the driveway.

Wouldn't you know…

29

Grace: the freely given,
unmerited favor and love of God.
DICTIONARY.COM

After an afternoon of endless activity, it feels a little strange to be by myself, but I'm ready for some peace and quiet. Of course, the Holy Spirit is still here, massaging my heart. I spend some time in the Word and reflect on God's love for me. It amazes me that, despite all of my mistakes, weaknesses, and moronic moments, God truly does love me.

Wow. Doesn't get much better than this.

I call Nancy's house but get the machine, so I leave a message, then promptly dial the cell phone number, hoping to get through to one of the kids. It goes straight to voice mail.

What's up with that?

I leave a message for the kids and call Sylvie. Ryder answers and tells me that she just walked in. I listen as Sylvie commands Ryder to start on his homework.

"Hey, Mads."

"So you got Mom home okay?"

"You know, we had a nice chat. She even wrote down Zach's favorite recipe and slipped it to me when Zach was out of the room. She said to surprise him one night soon with a romantic dinner. Wasn't that sweet of her?"

"What's the dish?"

"Um…she says it's her famous goulash recipe. It sounds yummy."

I burst out laughing.

"What's so funny?"

"Sylvie, I know this probably hasn't come up in your starry-eyed conversation, but Zach has a little, uh, intolerance to Mom's goulash."

"What do you mean? He doesn't like tomatoes?" Sylvie's voice elevates an octave, evidence of her confusion.

"I'm not exactly sure which ingredient it is in the goulash, but something doesn't like him. I think he's tried it three times in his life, with the same results every time." I laugh again. "Let's just say that if you served him that goulash—and if he was dumb enough to eat it—he'd be spending the rest of your date in the bathroom. And he wouldn't be shaving, if you catch my drift."

"No way."

"Way."

"But why would your mother…" She pauses. "Oh."

"I guess Mom hasn't quite warmed up to the idea of you stealing her son away."

After hanging up with Sylvie, I settle down at the computer. I wait for a minute, but the urge to play Solitaire doesn't come. Will wonders never cease? Laying off the Dibs, Solitaire addiction waning, facing my problems instead of running from them…it seems change is a recurring theme for me lately.

I have certainly had a few lessons in life skills over the past couple weeks, but the biggest change coming on is not so much a life skill as it is a *wife* skill. Then again, is there much difference? When I married Rich, my life became being a wife. Too bad it's taken me eighteen years to master it.

Rich didn't cheat on me! That thought makes my heart leap. The love I feel for my husband right now exceeds any I've experienced throughout the course of our marriage. And I can't wait to tell him.

Around seven, I hear a car pull into the driveway. Before I can even peer through the curtain slat, the door bursts open and I'm being pounced on by Emily. She smells like Nancy's house—a little musty with a giant spritz of Avon perfume mixed in.

"Hey, sweetie! What a wonderful surprise! I haven't heard from you all day. I didn't know what was going on or when you'd be home. Did you get my message on the phone?" I hug my daughter tight.

Emily pulls away. "I forgot to turn the phone off at night and the battery died. Christina said you were supposed to pack the charger, but we couldn't find it anywhere."

"Oops. Christina's right. I totally forgot. It's probably still in the office drawer. Sorry, sweetheart. My bad."

"It's okay, Mommy." She moves in for another hug. Oh, how I've missed Em's hugs.

"Hey," I say into Emily's hair, "how's Grandma doing?"

The front door opens, and Richard helps Nancy up the step. Champ,

Nancy's cocker spaniel, bounds in on their heels.

And I thought the surprises were done for the day.

I quickly stand, make my way over to them, and pull my mother-in-law into an embrace. "Nancy, how are you feeling?"

She stands stiffly, the perfect picture of someone who has recently fallen on the ice, then spent hours in a cramped car. She smiles, but I see through it to the pain. She is a master pretender that everything is okay when it's not. Hmmm…we seem to have something in common.

Rich clears his throat. "The doctor says she'll be fine. A little bruised, but fine. But I didn't want to leave her alone."

Nancy pooh-poohs him. "I told him not to worry about me, but he insisted. What would I do without my Richie?" She pats his arm and gazes up at Rich, eyes dripping with adoration.

Rich half-grins at me, a pink flush spreading across his cheeks. He always gets embarrassed when Nancy calls him Richie.

Christina and Max barrel in, shoving their suitcases in the door. Big surprise, Christina's iPod is attached to her ears. She makes wide eyes at me, followed by an eye roll, her teenaged way of saying, "Can it get any worse than spending five hours squished in the backseat of a car with my brother and sister?"

Max brushes past Christina and comes over to give me a hug.

"Hi, honey." So glad Max never went through a phase of not wanting to hug his mom.

Christina, on the other hand…no hug, no "hello" or "missed you, Mom." She breezes off to the kitchen, probably to call Brittany, her best friend. Or Blake. Hmmm. I hope he keeps his end of the bargain and breaks it off with Christina for good. But what will my daughter say if it ever comes out about Blake and Amy? I'm sure it won't be pretty.

"Did Sam call?" Max regards me with youthful hope, like a three-year-old asking if it's okay to play with the doggie.

"She left a message on the machine."

And off he goes.

"Hey, Em, why don't you go unpack your things while I talk to Daddy and Grandma."

Emily tilts her head and gives each of us a lingering look. "Okay," she says and grabs her Strawberry Shortcake suitcase. "But Mom? I really want a new suitcase for Christmas next year."

"How about for your birthday? It's only a couple months away, you know."

198

She grins. "I'll be ten."

"Yes, you will. So I'm thinking maybe something a little more grown-up...maybe something like iCarly."

"Mom! iCarly is so yesterday."

I look at Richard.

Richard grins.

I give Em a playful shove. She disappears up the stairs, Champ on her heels.

Nancy takes an awkward step forward. "I really need to use the restroom. I don't think I've gone since this morning." She chuckles. "And then I think I'll sit and rest in the family room for a few minutes. Assuming it's okay with you, Madi."

"Of course."

Nancy probably thinks she's being diplomatic, but it's so obvious she just wants to give Richard and me an opportunity to talk. I make a mental note to thank her later.

She limps away, bracing herself against the wall for support.

"Do you need help, Mom?" Rich calls after her.

Nancy peers over her shoulder. "No, no. I'll be fine. I'll be in the family room resting my eyes. Let me know when you're ready to leave, Rich. Unless, of course, you'll be staying here." She winks.

Such subtlety.

I turn to Rich, who stands with his hands in his coat pockets. His hair looks like he recently ran a hand through it, and he hasn't shaved in a couple days. Totally unkempt. Totally rugged.

Totally sexy.

"Going for a new look?" I ask.

He appears confused for a second, then rubs his chin. "Oh, you mean this? I decided to leave the razor at home—well, at Ray's—this weekend."

"I like it."

"You do?"

"I do."

He shifts his feet. "I wonder how Ray will feel when I bring Mom home. Probably won't be thrilled."

"Yeah...about that. I'm thinking Ray might need his space for a while. Especially since he'll be spending some time getting to know his daughter."

Rich looks surprised. "He knows about Lexi? *You* know?"

"It's been quite a weekend, Rich."

"Apparently." He studies me, brown eyes boring into mine. "You want to talk about it?"

I consider the question. Last week—heck, this morning—I would have said no. But now I want nothing more than to talk about it and get everything out in the open. I want to give him a play-by-play of my life for the past two weeks. I want to relay every detail, from how I felt the moment he walked out the door to seeing him with Fawn in the parking lot, to my meetings with Sarah Price, to Zach and Sylvie's unexpected relationship. I want to talk about our son's new romantic interest and Christina's heartbreak. Then there's the cheesy reunion and my confrontation with Fawn and my epiphany during the live church service this morning. I can't wait to tell him about my early-morning, impulsive lunch invitation to Fawn and Lexi, my dad and Candice sneaking into the closet, my mother's breakdown, and Celeste Hardaway paying me a visit. I want to talk until my face turns Smurf-blue.

Of course, I also want answers. I want to know why Rich didn't tell me about Fawn coming to him in the first place or about Lexi being Ray's daughter. I want to know why he didn't try harder to convince me of the truth. And why he didn't wrap his arms around me in the kitchen that day, even though I probably would have punched him if he tried.

But I will follow the homework instructions given to me by Sarah Price and leave the questions for later.

For now, I will apologize to Richard for what a fool I've been. I'll tell him how I've grown up in the past couple weeks and how I'm learning to see myself as a princess. I'll also explain that I realize now how much my insecurities have affected our marriage and that I will continue to get help to overcome those fears. I will tell him how desperately I've missed him. How lost the kids and I have been without him. How much chocolate I've consumed over the past seven days.

Well, maybe not that.

And finally, I will let him know that from now on, the only time I'll put on my running shoes is when I hit the track—which really could happen now that I'm focusing more on my health.

"Madi? Do you want to talk about it?" He repeats the question.

I do want to talk about it.

But not now.

Now I close the gap between us and melt into his arms, wrapping my arms around his waist and pressing my head to his chest. He seems taken aback by this, but only for a moment. Then his hands transfer from his pockets to my back and he pulls me close.

There's no need to say a word. Not now, not yet.

And for the second time today (or maybe the third), as Rich holds me in his arms, I allow myself to cry.

God is here, too. Just as I expected, He showed up this weekend. This time, I'm confident that He's here to stay. As long as I let Him, anyway.

It's a group hug. My husband holds my body and the Holy Spirit holds my heart, while I cling to both of them with all my strength, with all my soul, and—finally—with all my mind.

I've finally found my hiding place. Not in the Jacuzzi tub or a carton of Dibs, but in the arms of my Savior and my amazing—and very hot—husband.

30

You are a princess.
SARAH PRICE

As I arrive at my appointment with Sarah Price, I can't help thinking that life is good. I can now say without hesitation or cynicism or sarcasm that I'm anxious to get on with my therapy and see what God will do. I'm putty in His hands.

Which is what I am in Rich's hands, too. I mega-grin, as I've been doing nonstop for the past three days since my husband moved back in. Every moment has been bliss. Well, except for not being able to find five minutes to spend alone together. Emily has attached herself to Rich like Velcro to ensure that he doesn't leave again. And Nancy, bless her heart, is always *there*. She tries to help with absolutely everything I do, despite my attempts to shoo her to the living room to put her feet up. And for someone like me, who relishes silence and my time alone, having someone around 24/7 is not exactly easy.

Then there's Champ. I keep hoping Charlie will warm up to him, but Charlie hasn't spent this much time behind the grandfather clock since we house-sat my neighbor's German Shepherd. I'll need to pick up an extra box of fishie treats to make up for the trauma we're putting him through.

My own mother stopped by a couple days ago, and we had a nice chat. I counted only four times that she verbally bashed my father, which is several less than last time, so she's making progress.

Sam's been coming around, too. Max even invited her over for dinner last night and didn't argue (too much) when I started preparing the mostaccioli. I pretended I didn't see the phone book lying on the counter next to the stove with the page opened to Vino's. Max looked a little worried as Sam took the first bite but visibly relaxed when she raved about it being the best Italian meal she's ever had. Okay, so that might be pushing it a bit, but hey, I'll take compliments where I can get them.

Christina is already over Blake. And it seems like she's been avoiding

Amy, as well. I don't know if my daughter somehow found out about what happened in the dark hallway of Reggie's Classy Diner or if she's developing her women's intuition, but I'm glad the drama over Blake seems to be winding down. I still get a twinge of heartache when I think that Amy most likely will not eventually become my daughter-in-law, but then again, you never know. As I've discovered, things can change in a matter of moments, especially when it comes to love.

Speaking of which, Paige Hardaway apparently met the love of her life at a party on Saturday night, as is plastered all over her Facebook page. Christina couldn't wait to show me the comment she received from Paige saying all was forgotten and they wouldn't be pressing charges. That life is too short to dwell on the past and Christina can have Blake if she wants him. Which, thank goodness, she doesn't. Of course, because of the whole rivalry thing, Paige added a brief warning for Christina to stay away from her new man. This shouldn't be a problem since the guy's last name is Spiderwick. Even the thought of dating someone whose last name might give her nightmares is enough to keep Christina from looking twice.

The waiting room of the Reflections Counseling Center is even busier than usual. Lots of people with oodles of problems. Not a nice thought, but at least we're making an effort to deal with them.

I can't help looking around for Charles Manson. And there he is, engrossed in a conversation with the lint-picking girl from my first visit. Wow. Didn't see that coming. The girl fidgets like a mime washing her hands with pretend soap and water. But at least there are no piles of lint anywhere to be seen. She smiles shyly and avoids making more than ten-second eye contact with Chuck, but there is no mistaking the blush in her cheeks. The two are obviously smitten with each other.

Charles doesn't even glance my way. I'm glad he's moved on, although it bums me out a little to think I've been replaced with a recovering lint-picker.

I squeeze into an empty seat next to a gum-smacking teenager wearing purple leggings, black sneakers, and more makeup than I applied on Rich when he dressed as Cher for that costume party. She stops chomping long enough to give me an evil look as if I am invading her space.

I smile sweetly in return.

Ten minutes and two magazines later, I'm being ushered into Sarah's office.

She stands up when I enter and gives me a hug. Sarah looks sharp, as always, dressed in a long denim skirt, black suede blazer, and the same black boots I commented on last week. Her hair is pulled back in a ponytail at the nape of her neck and silver earrings dangle to her shoulders. She smiles.

"I'd say you look like a woman in love."

My cheeks grow warm. "What makes you say that?"

"We psychologists are trained to detect these things."

"Really?"

She laughs. "No, not really. But your response makes me suspect I'm right."

I expel a long sigh. "I can't believe it's that obvious. But yes, things are going...well. Rich even offered to come with me today, but I think I need to work on some of my own issues first."

Sarah motions me to have a seat and pulls her chair around from behind the desk. "I'm so glad, Madi. I've been praying for you guys ever since you made your first appointment."

"Well, between you and Sylvie, the devil didn't stand a chance."

I fill her in on what's been going on.

"It must be tough rekindling your marriage with your mother-in-law living with you."

"You think?" I laugh. "I love Nancy to death, but sometimes I wish she and Ray got along so she could stay with him for a while." I sigh. "I think Rich and I need to go on a nice, long vacation and leave Nancy to babysit."

Sarah nods. "That's not a bad idea, you know."

"Yeah, the idea's great. But the timing isn't. And our bank account isn't exactly overflowing. We've got some money put away, but that's going toward a car for Max and Christina. Then it won't be long before they both start college and Emily will need braces. The list goes on."

"Think of it as an investment. An investment into your future. It could be the best one you ever made."

"Maybe..." I worry my bottom lip. "Sylvie also mentioned they have an opening for receptionist at her salon. That could help."

Sarah slaps her knee. "There you go." Her face brightens. "Hey, I think I read something about a class starting up at church that's designed to help couples put the romance back in their marriage. Have you heard anything about that?"

"It's being taught by Claudia Boeve." My chipper voice has turned dull.

"And..."

"Do you know Claudia Boeve? I mean, have you actually had a conversation with the woman?"

"Actually, yes. I went to the 'Losing Means Winning' workshop that she taught. She knows her stuff."

I hmmph.

Sarah narrows her eyes. "Okay...do you want to talk about the problem you have with Claudia?"

I twist my mouth and chew on my cheek some more. "You said it. It's *my* problem. She intimidates me."

"We'll have to work on that, won't we?"

"So, anyway," I say, trying to regain some of my chipperness, "I was thinking about the whole princess thing and I finally figured out which princess I relate to most."

Sarah smiles and leans back in her chair. "Which one?"

"Princess Aurora."

"Sleeping Beauty?"

I nod. "Okay, not so much the Beauty part. But I do feel like I've been sleeping for the past twenty-six years—ever since my parents' divorce. The curse that put me to 'sleep' was believing the lie that all men cheat. That just because my mother has been burned a million times, it wouldn't be any different for me. I didn't believe any man would ever love me—not my father, not my husband. But, more importantly, like you mentioned at one of our sessions, I related to God as I related to my dad. And I didn't truly believe that God could love me. But I'm beginning to realize that God does love me— which you're helping with, by the way—and I'm waking up from my sleep. I'm beginning to see the princess that God created me to be. Although you'll never catch me in a ball gown or wearing a tiara. I hate those things."

Sarah regards me with another smile. "You're well on your way, Madi. Now you simply need the maintenance tools."

I nod. "Hey, speaking of maintenance, I was wondering. Do you do any personal fitness training? You may have noticed the other day at the gym that I'm not in the best shape."

She chuckles. "We can talk about it. You know, changing the outside is the easy part. But I'm really proud of you for getting a handle on the inside." She taps her temple. "The mind is the hardest thing to change. That's why renewing your mind every day with the Word of God is so important."

"Yeah. I've got a long way to go, but it's good to be on speaking terms with God again."

"What about Raymond? How did he take the news about Lexi being his daughter?"

"Supposedly, he's taking it pretty well. We're all getting together for dinner tomorrow. Should be interesting, to say the least."

"I expect a full report. Maybe you can fill me in next week at the gym,"

Sarah suggests wryly.

"I don't know. Now that I think about it, I can't remember reading even one story where the princess goes to the gym. Working out is not very princess-ish."

"Ah, but you're thinking of the fairy tales. Real-life princesses definitely work out. It's one of the best ways to gain the prince's attention. It certainly can't hurt."

I raise my eyebrows. "Tell that to my butt."

♛
31

Breakdowns can create breakthroughs.
Things fall apart so things can fall together.
UNKNOWN

So far, so good.

I didn't burn the roast, the potatoes, or the rolls, much to the surprise of my kids and me. So it isn't the most delicious meal I've ever cooked—if my cooking could have ever been considered delicious—but it isn't half bad. I about fell over dead when Raymond complimented me on the green bean casserole. I waited for the sarcastic comment, but it didn't come. Will wonders never cease?

Fawn is appropriately dressed in slacks and a sweater, even if the sweater is a little clingy. Raymond has been unusually polite. Most importantly, no fights have broken out—yet. It's still early, after all.

The only slight snag so far has been Lexi informing me that she can't stand roast and potatoes. She requested pizza rolls and fries. Unfortunately, I haven't replenished the pizza rolls she finished off the other day, so we had to make a quick run to McDonalds for Chicken McNuggets and fries. Emily whined how it isn't fair that Lexi got fast food while Em had to suffer through eating a home-cooked meal. Ouch. I was tempted to give in, but Richard said no.

Sorry, Em.

Lexi seems to be taking the whole "dad" thing in stride, which she's demonstrating right at this minute.

"Hey, *Dad*, can you pass the ketchup?"

"Sure, *daughter*," Ray says back.

They smile at each other, obviously getting used to this new relationship. I can't help wondering if this new fatherhood status will help my brother-in-law grow up. If not, he's more hopeless than I thought. Then again, I know what God can do with the hopeless. Just look at me.

Meanwhile, Zach and Sylvie are still sickeningly in love, evidenced by the gaggy way they gaze at each other and discreetly (so they think) brush their fingertips together while reaching for the butter.

Zach is getting to know his niece, and their teasing banter cracks me up. There's no doubt about it: he'll definitely make a good dad someday—maybe to Sage and Ryder.

Then there's Nancy. She's trying a little too hard and I'm sensing some annoyance from Lexi and Fawn. They are obviously not used to overly sweet personalities. This would be a perfect opportunity for Ray to interject nastiness toward his mother, but, as I said before, so far so good.

My parents were not invited today. Even though there is hope on the horizon, I don't quite trust my mother to control herself in the presence of my dad and Candice. Common sense says not to rush it.

Although my dad's input might come in handy about now, as the kids are talking about *Survivor*. Dad's record of choosing a winner early on in the season is impressive, and the kids are wondering who their grandpa would pick this time.

I feel a hand settle onto my thigh. I put down my fork and grasp Richard's hand under the table. I turn toward him. We lock eyes and smile. My heart starts beating a little faster.

He leans over and whispers in my ear. "Meet me in the bathroom?"

Okay, not the most romantic meeting place, but I can't get out of my chair fast enough. A little air (and a few kisses) sounds heavenly.

Five minutes later, the bathroom door opens, and laughter from the kitchen follows Rich in. He locks the door and leans against it, breathing heavily, as if escaping from a pack of starving wolves.

I giggle. "Did you ever imagine we'd be here?"

"Alone in the bathroom together? I might have imagined it a few times." He does the Groucho Marx eyebrow thing.

I give him a playful swat. "You know what I mean."

Suddenly, his face is two inches from mine and he kisses me. "Dinner was great."

"I should have known that food was your motivation for getting me alone."

"Well, it wasn't *that* great."

"Hey!" I swat him again. Although if I think about it, he's actually paying me a compliment.

"The kids seem to be getting along with their new cousin," Rich says.

"And Ray seems to be getting along pretty well with his new daughter."

Rich shakes his head. "Never thought I'd see the day." He brushes a lock of hair from my eye. "Zach and Sylvie are getting along well, too."

I make a face. "That's an understatement. Talk about never thinking you'd see the day..." I snuggle up close and catch a whiff of the Lagerfeld cologne I love so much. "I know two other people who are getting along fabulously these days."

Rich steps back, mock puzzlement on his ruggedly handsome face. "Who?"

"You know who."

His face grows serious. "I love you, Madi Lee," he says.

"You love me madly?"

"That, too." Rich lifts my chin toward the ceiling and leans his six-foot frame down for another kiss.

And they lived happily ever after...
FAIRY TALE STORIES EVERYWHERE

THE END

Coming Soon...

LYNDA LEE SCHAB

All Madi Lee McCall wants
is to fall madly in love again...with her husband.

After a rough patch, Madi's determined to get her marriage back on track. She's even taking a romance class at church and getting great suggestions...that fail miserably. The distractions are plenty. She has just reentered the workplace as a health spa receptionist. Her 16-year-old daughter, Christina, is pushing the limits, and Christina's twin, Max has fallen hard for a girl who isn't Madi's picture of a perfect match for her son. Even younger daughter, Emily, is developing a teenager-ish attitude.

When her mother-in-law moves in—temporarily, of course—the stress starts to drive Madi a little crazier than normal. What she wants, more than anything, is some peace among the chaos.

THE MADI SERIES
Delightful. Witty. Entertaining. Real. Poignant.
Light-hearted Women's Fiction at Its Best

www.LyndaSchab.com
www.onthewrite-track.blogspot.com
www.oaktara.com

About the Author

LYNDA LEE SCHAB got her writing start in greeting cards (Blue Mountain Arts, Dayspring) and from there went on to write articles and short stories (*Mature Living, Christian Home & School*) and in many places online (including www.Examiner.com and www.wow-womenonwriting.com), but her passion has always been fiction.

Mind Over Madi, her debut novel, is near and dear to her heart. Lynda admits she has a lot in common with the character of Madi. Not only are they both addicted to ice cream, chocolate, and computer games, they struggle with the same types of insecurities and continually require a hefty dose of God's grace.

Lynda works behind the scenes at FaithWriters.com and is a member of ACFW. She is a regular book reviewer for FaithfulReader.com and is the Grand Rapids Christian Fiction Examiner and the National Writing Examiner for Examiner.com. *Mind Over Madi* received Runner-up in the 2007 FaithWriters Page Turner contest, was a finalist in the 2007 RWA Get your Stiletto in the Door contest, and won second place in the 2008 ACFW Genesis contest, Chick Lit category.

Lynda lives with her husband, Rob, and two teenagers in Michigan.

www.LyndaSchab.com
www.onthewrite-track.blogspot.com
www.oaktara.com

CPSIA information can be obtained at www.ICGtesting.com
Printed in the USA
LVOW091722281111

256812LV00006B/94/P